AVEN ELLIS

Connectivity

British Isles Billionaires Series – Book 1

For Samantha and Stephanie...Thank you for being my people.

Contents

Acknowledgement

Thank you to Joanne Lui for her masterful edit. You always have a way of seeing through my words and finding all the things that need polishing and helping me find solutions when needed-while keeping my voice mine. I love you!

Thank you to my proofreader, Alexandra Morris for re-reading this book again, bouncing ideas with me, and catching all the things that needed to be reworked. You are the best.

To my beta team-Jennifer DiCenzo and the SJFC girls-thank you for encouraging me, coming up with ideas, and being the most supportive friends a girl could ask for. You all are the best!

Holly Martin and Alexa Aston-thank you always critiquing my work and making it the best book it can be.

And finally, to all my readers. None of this happens without you wanting these stories and loving them so much. I'm blessed by each and every one of you.

Chapter One

My timing for the first big jump in my television career is a freaking fabulous fail of epic proportions.

Of course, having started out life being named after an Olsen twin, can I really expect anything less?

I sigh heavily as I scan the news on my iPhone on the train. The city of Chicago rolls by in a blur on this dreary, snowy January day. I find the article I am looking for and read during my commute:

WILLIAM CUMBERLAND PURCHASES COLLECTIVE MEDIA ENTERPRISES

First foray into US market for British Media Mogul

I bite my lip. The announcement came down yesterday at Collective Media, where I have worked as an assistant to the General Manager of Total Access Total Sports—also known as TATS—for almost a year now. Which is ironic because I hate sports. I am not the best executive assistant in the world, but I kept my eye on the prize: a transfer, after one year, to the Beautiful Homes Network, a sister station. BHN is my dream place of employment. I would do *anything* to work in creative program development there. Which includes taking any job at the company to make that dream happen.

But now is it all for nothing? Will this sale completely change the stations, the direction, and the staff?

I glance at the photo of Mr. Cumberland. He's young, thirty-two, and made his fortune developing Connectivity, a social media site that connects everything in one place: your career networking and portfolio, a place for updating family and friends, photo sharing, video calling, quick connect messages with your status. And you have the choice to "connect" these aspects with each other or keep them separate.

Lately, he's been buying up various media outlets to expand his empire, with Collective Media Enterprises being his most recent acquisition.

And he's the British mogul who could change the course of my future.

I take a deep breath. *Stay calm, MK*, I tell myself. *Let the dust settle from this move and see where opportunities may arise. You have worked and sacrificed a lot to get this chance.*

The L stops where I need to get off, so I zip up my parka and head to my office on Michigan Avenue. It is brutally cold today. The winds roar off the lake, and despite the fact that I have a scarf wound almost completely around my face, my chin is already frozen.

I head inside the tall skyscraper, peeling off layers as I go. I reach my cubicle and notice a big pile of crap from my boss on my chair.

"MK!" Paul Metzinger bellows from his office. "Is that you?"

"Yes, Paul, I'm here," I say, lifting the haphazard pile of papers to my desk. I put my tote bag on the floor, quickly pull off my boots, and change into my heels.

"I need twenty bound copies of those ASAP," he yells back.

"We have a meeting with the Bears about training camp coverage this summer, and I need those."

Oh no. Oh no, no, no. *Please, not bound. Please.*

"Um," I say, getting up and peeking my head into his doorway, "are you sure you don't want an electronic presentation?"

I cross my fingers behind my back and hope for the best.

Please don't say no. Please, oh please, oh please.

"No, I need them bound." Paul shifts his attention back to the newspaper spread out on his desk, which I can't help but notice has a huge picture of William Cumberland on it.

"That's all, MK," Paul says, looking up at me.

"Right," I reply, blinking. I turn to my desk, scoop up the papers, then head down the hall.

As I step into the workroom, I face my nemesis. *The binding machine.* I give it the evil eye as I begin running the original through the copy machine. This machine is an old piece of crap that sticks, jams, and tears. It takes forever to make a set of bound copies.

And in all my television classes at Northwestern University, this was somehow never covered in the curriculum.

With warm copies in my hand, I take a deep breath and unscrew the buttons. I meticulously line up the copies and begin punching them.

But as I go to punch one of the last sets, the lever jams. I jerk it back and forth and hear the paper tearing. Shit! Now the lever won't budge, and I'm pulling as hard as I can.

I reach across so both hands are on the lever, and suddenly it jerks open, and the teeth of the machine are grabbing the sleeve of my black cashmere cardigan, snatching it in a death grip.

"Are you freaking kidding me?" I blurt out, my arm stuck.

"Are you seriously freaking kidding me?"

"So, please do tell," a deep British voice says from behind me. "Does this particular piece of equipment always elicit such a response?"

I freeze. My heart drops into my stomach. Slowly, I turn my head and see none other than William Cumberland staring right at me.

Holy crap! What he is doing here? There was no memo about Cumberland coming, nothing in the papers.

And now he's staring at me. With my arm stuck in a binder machine.

My face begins flaming, and I know the color matches my copper-red hair.

"Um," I say, completely stunned. "It's that ... it's really old ..." I'm fumbling, just fumbling, as I look at him. He walks closer. His light blue eyes dart instantly to my arm.

"Quite a quandary you are in this morning," he says, shifting his eyes back to my face.

I pause for a moment. He is unique looking, with strong cheekbones and a firm jaw. Tall and thin, he has dark, wavy hair that looks like it takes a fight to keep under control.

But his eyes are his most interesting feature. They are very intense. Observant. And right now, they are zeroed in on me.

Frustration fills me. "I don't even see why I need to be making bound copies," I blurt out as I try to free my cardigan from the pinchers of death. "We should be digital. We should be sending presentations electronically. It's greener anyway."

Cumberland approaches and slowly removes his black leather gloves. Now he is next to me, and I notice he is wearing a glorious gray cashmere trench coat. And that his cologne smells like pine needles.

4

He wordlessly reaches over, and with a flick of his fingers, removes my now torn sweater. "That is all very fascinating information that I shall keep in mind," he quips, his blue eyes appraising me. "And what is your name?"

"MK Grant," I say. "I am the assistant to Paul Metzinger at TATS. And it is an honor to meet you, sir. I have read so much about you—"

"MK," he interrupts, his stare unwavering. I feel sweat forming at the base of my neck. "What does that stand for, Ms. Grant?"

I consider quitting on the spot so I don't have to answer.

"Mary-Kate," I say simply, taking the torn copies out of the machine as a distraction.

"Not Mary-Katherine?"

Oh God, don't make me explain my name. Why does he care? Why?

"Um, no." I glance up and know instantly he is not going to let this go. "I'm named after Mary-Kate Olsen. One of the Olsen twins."

He says nothing as he loosens the black scarf around his neck. Now I panic and feel like I need to fill the dead air with a more detailed explanation.

"You know, the Olsen twins played Michelle on *Full House*, that old sitcom," As soon as I say it, I want to reel the words right back into my mouth. Like he cares? Or even knows what the heck I am talking about?

But I keep going, like a car that has driven through the "Bridge Out" caution sign and is barreling toward a cliff. "My mom loved that sitcom, but it wasn't that funny, so it really shouldn't be called that, but I digress. She liked the name Mary-Kate. So that is who I'm named after. Mary-Kate, who

5

played Michelle. Oh, but she shared the role with her twin Ashley. They both played Michelle."

Cumberland is staring at me like I'm a total loon. Any chance I had at moving out of an assistant role has been blown to hell. He is probably wondering how I got hired for any position in the first place.

"Interesting, Ms. Grant," he finally says in that deep voice.

Suddenly, I hear heels against the tiles, and his attention is diverted, thank God.

"Mr. Cumberland, there you are," another British voice calls out. I see a very pretty blonde headed over to us. "I have the conference room secured for you. As you can imagine, the office is buzzing now that your presence is known. Your security detail is making a sweep through the remaining floors now."

"Very good. Ms. Dalton, this is Ms. Mary-Kate Grant, an assistant at TATS. Ms. Grant, please meet my assistant, Ms. Arabella Dalton."

"Fabulous, you're an assistant," Arabella says quickly. "We are going to need some proper tea in the conference room for Mr. Cumberland. He likes it with lemon."

"Pleasure meeting you, Ms. Grant," Cumberland says, nodding at me. "Until then."

Then Arabella leads him to the conference room.

Oh, crap. He's British and is not going to find the generic black tea bags in the conference room a proper tea. I hurry back toward Paul's office to get approval to at least go to Starbucks and get something halfway decent to give to him.

I go into Paul's office, and some of the directors are huddled around his desk, discussing Cumberland's surprise arrival. The tension in the room is thick, and I'd rather go anywhere but in there, but I have to resolve this tea issue.

"Paul, I'm so sorry to interrupt, but Mr. Cumberland has requested a proper tea, and we have none, so I was thinking—"

"MK. Tea is tea," Paul snaps. "That is the least of my problems this morning. Now go fetch him a cup from the break room before he's pissed we haven't given him anything to drink."

Riiiiight. Tea is tea. I try to swallow down the nerves attacking my stomach as I go to the break room. I rummage through the cabinets, praying that by divine intervention, a box of Earl Grey had dropped down from the heavens, but no such luck. I cringe and grab the black and white box of "Tea Bags." I check if we have a nice ceramic cup to put it in, but everything has a Chicago sports logo on it and is chipped.

Shit. I'm going to serve William Cumberland tea bag tea. In a Styrofoam cup. With a squeeze packet of lemon juice. Awesome times.

I put the tea bag into the cup, add hot water, grab the lemon juice packet, and head to the conference room. His British entourage is surrounding him, and they stop talking when I enter.

"Your tea, Mr. Cumberland," I say with the calmest, most confident voice I can fake.

Cumberland stares down at the cup for a moment, and then back at me. Then he pushes the leather chair back from the table a bit and puts his fingers together in a steeple position up against his lips.

Oh, good God. I wish he would throw the tea across the room in disgust and fire me already.

Then again, Cumberland is probably just contemplating some super articulate way of kicking my ass to the curb right now.

"Right," he says simply, his eyes focused on me. "That is all, Ms. Grant. Thank you."

I can't get out of that room fast enough. I go back to my cubicle, sick to my stomach, certain that my year of hard work is for absolutely nothing. I have yelled at a machine, torn my cardigan, babbled about *Full freaking House,* and served him tea bag tea with a lemon juice packet.

All within the span of fifteen minutes.

Yes, that has *impressive* written all over it, doesn't it?

So the rest of the day crawls by, with Paul running in and out to meetings and totally stressed. The office gossips are whispering that Cumberland is going to roll heads and possibly blow up the networks for his own version of programming.

I hide in my cube, praying I don't cross paths with William Cumberland or any member of the British entourage for the rest of the day. It is too humiliating to deal with.

Finally, it is six o'clock. I breathe a sigh of relief and shut down my computer. I am about to change into my boots when I feel a presence behind me. I turn around in my chair and find Cumberland standing at the edge of my cubicle.

Damn it.

I watch as his blue eyes dart over my cube, and I can tell he is assessing everything he can see. Which is really annoying. I mean, if he is going to fire me, can't he just do it already?

His laser eyes shift to me.

"Assorted items," he says briskly. "First, that binder machine is going into the bin. It is a relic, and we don't need it. Not after I issue iPads that will be used as presentation tools. Second, I have arranged for a proper tea service and tea to be shipped over from London tomorrow morning. Will you please see to it when it arrives? I like my tea served at eight-thirty."

"Yes, Mr. Cumberland," I say. Okay, he's not going to fire me. I have a chance here to make a second impression.

He slips into his expensive trench coat and turns to leave. But then he stops and comes back to my cubicle.

"One more thing," he says. He reaches into his suit jacket and pulls out an American Express card. "Give this back to Ms. Dalton when you are done, but please order me a 'Full House' DVD from Amazon." His blue eyes pierce through me. "Yes, I know I could watch it on demand, but what can I say? I'm feeling nostalgic. And I'm rather fascinated by the anecdote you told me earlier today."

Then he turns and walks away.

Chapter Two

"It was absolutely the worst day ever," I moan.

"*What?*" Renee and Emily shout back at the same time. I roll my eyes. I am in a crowded bar in Lincoln Park. You know, the trendy type with lots of twenty-somethings milling around. The music is vibrating off the walls, people are shoulder-to-shoulder, and you can barely hear yourself think, let alone speak. I am here with my best friends and roommates, ready to commiserate about my awful day.

Yet that is practically impossible to do without screaming.

I look around at the people getting drunk, the girls giggling at some total tool in a suit. Really, this is my own version of some dimension of hell.

I take a sip of my wine. Which is awful. And somehow suited to my rather craptastic introduction to William Cumberland.

"Won't the big British mogul be going back to England?" Emily screams at me. "Don't worry about it!"

Her boyfriend, Dan, slides up with a fresh beer in his hand. He's wearing a V-neck sweater and a backward Chicago Cubs baseball cap and still looks like a college boy even though he's been out of school two years now. "What are we talking about?" he shouts.

"MK's evil new boss," Renee replies, tucking a lock of her long dark hair behind one ear.

"So what did he do?" Dan asks, taking a sip of his beer.

"He came from England and—" Emily starts, but Dan cuts her off.

"A foreigner. There's your problem, MK," he says, nodding knowingly at me. "British people are arrogant snobs. And what does a British guy know about US television?"

Okay, now I'm annoyed. So obviously, William is a total snob because he is from the UK? How gracious to slap that assessment on him. And he can't possibly know anything about US television because he lives in a different country? What a dumb thing to say.

I inwardly sigh. Seriously, why am I here? I feel like my friends and fellow peers love this kind of social scene, but I hate it. I can't decide if there is something wrong with me or if I'm mature.

Mature. I'll roll with mature.

"I'm going home," I say. I open my little purse, pull out some cash to cover my drink, and hand the bills to Renee. "I've got to go figure out how to save my career."

"No, stay," Renee begs. "You need to forget about today."

"And we just got here fifteen minutes ago," Emily adds.

"No, I need to refocus," I insist, sliding out of the booth.

"Remember, MK, he's a British jerk," Dan says firmly.

"Right," I reply, questioning why Emily would be with this guy. He's so stupid. Ick.

For the five-thousandth time, I embrace my single status. I bundle up and step outside. Luckily, we went to a bar that is down the street from our apartment. It is not snowing, but the air is frigid cold. I keep my chin down in an effort to stay warm.

Okay, thinking time. I need to redeem myself tomorrow. I'll wear a very professional, fashion-forward outfit. Let's face it: Impression is about looks, too.

I must serve the perfect tea. So I will get there early to get the tea service as it is delivered. Luckily, I took a class last summer on serving tea, as I thought it would be a cool topic for my blog, so I know how to do that. But, what else, what else? Scones! That's it. I'll make scones to serve, too. I have the perfect lemon thyme scone I created last summer. I will show Cumberland I can go the extra mile and think outside the box by adding that personal touch.

Ooh, I can blog about the scones. Perfect!

I get home and am in the zone. I turn on some music, get all my kitchen prep stuff out, and begin to cook. I make the scones, and they turn out perfectly. I grab my camera, arrange them on a plate with some fresh thyme sprigs, and take a few pictures. Inspired, I get my iPad and go to my blog.

I don't know why I even bother. It is my collection of recipes and decorating ideas, and nobody knows I do it. But it is my little way of being creative, of using my skills. Of having a way to show the world who I am, other than an executive assistant at TATS.

I upload a photo of the scones and add my thoughts before typing in the recipe:

Today, my new boss arrived in town. He is a Brit, and I shall call him Mr. X. And Mr. X likes nothing more than proper English tea. I will be giving him that tomorrow per his request, but I will also be adding these lemon thyme scones to the tea service. After all, what is tea without a scone? And furthermore, Mr. X is too thin and could use a scone. Or five.

I smile at my post and add the recipe. Then I close my iPad and exhale. *Bring it on, Cumberland. I'm more than ready to impress the hell out of you tomorrow.*

* * *

I arrive at work extra early the next day. The tea service is set on a tray, complete with lemon slices and scones. I put some thyme sprigs around the scones to make it look nice. I have the electric teakettle heating in the break room, so indeed, I'm ready.

I leave that on my desk and go to the restroom to make sure I look sharp, stopping in front of the full-length mirror. I'm wearing a crisp white shirt, white camisole, and sleek-fitting gray trousers. I took a bunch of pearl necklaces and pinned them together with a brooch for my necklace, and a bright pink and orange vintage Pucci scarf is tied up as a hairband in my straight red hair.

I adjust the gold cuff bracelet on my left arm and take a breath. My neutral eye shadow is flawless and brings out the brown in my brown-gold eyes. I'm wearing a hint of peach blush and a swipe of neutral lipstick with an apricot gloss on top. Neutral, but nice. I smile confidently and go back down the hall. It is now eight-fifteen.

I walk past the temporary office where Cumberland is working while he is here and see the door is open and the light is on. Perfect. I can show him I'm early in addition to being highly efficient. I get the teapot, take it to the break room, and fill it with hot water. Then I go back to my cubicle and pick up the loaded tea tray. Okay, this is heavy. But I can manage. I shift it a bit until I have a perfect grasp on the edges and head toward his office.

I come around the corner and stand in his doorway. He's scrolling through his iPad when I clear my throat.

Cumberland's head lifts up, and his intense blue eyes laser in on me.

"Mr. Cumberland, I have your tea—" I say, but as I step forward, I bump right into the leg of a guest chair. I lose my balance and go flying forward, sending the tea tray sailing through the air. I land face first on his carpet.

Crash!

The smashing of china and clattering of silverware practically bounces off the walls of his office. Then the collateral damage from my fall rains down on me and the floor.

"Ms. Grant! Ms. Grant, are you all right?"

Crap, crap, crap! I frantically shove myself to a kneeling position and don't even look at him. My face is absolutely on fire with mortification, and I glance down and see my shirt has tea splattered all over it. And, oh, mother of God, I feel scone stuck on my chin.

"I'm so sorry!" I gasp, rubbing my chin. I quickly pick up broken pieces of china and put them onto the tray. "I am very, very sorry, Mr. Cumberland. I caught the chair leg and lost my balance and—"

Suddenly, I'm aware that he is on the floor with me.

He is crouched down across from me, calmly picking up china pieces.

Oh my God. I want the floor to open up and swallow me whole. The British mogul is on the floor picking up scone bits with me it can't be any more humiliating than this.

"Perhaps," Cumberland says slowly in that deep British voice, "I should get you a tea trolley for service, Ms. Grant."

I snap my head up. Okay, now he's pissing me off. And since odds are he's going to fire me anyway, I tell him exactly what I think.

"With all due respect, Mr. Cumberland, I am not going to serve as a flight attendant pushing a drink cart. Or air hostess or whatever is the proper British term for that."

Good Lord, am I talking to the most powerful man in communications like this?

But I'm so worked up, I can't stop.

"Furthermore," I continue, "I will be happy to bring you a cup of tea, but I'm the assistant to Mr. Metzinger. So while I'm more than glad to assist you while you are here, I will not let you treat me as a server."

Cumberland trains that intense, observant gaze right on me. "Who is treating you like one?" he asks. "And I do believe you were the one who brought scones in an effort to impress me, Ms. Grant."

Ooh I'm furious. Because I know he is right.

"I was not trying to impress you," I lie. "I was trying to be nice."

Cumberland stands up. He puts his fingertips together in front of his lips and stares down at me on the floor.

"Oh, Ms. Grant. Please do not lie. It does not become you."

Argh! Now I'm in an embarrassed rage. I angrily pick up the mess on the floor and decide I am not going to speak to him unless he asks me a question.

Which, of course, he does in a nanosecond.

"So what kind of scones were they, Ms. Grant?"

"Lemon thyme," I say through gritted teeth.

"What a pity. They sound like they would have been delightful."

I pick up the tray with the mess and stand up. Cumberland is still assessing me with his damn laser eyes, and I want to toss this tray straight at him.

"If that is all," I say, still gritting my teeth, "I would like to dispose of this and call the janitorial staff to come up and vacuum, please."

"Oh my God. You *destroyed* his tea service?"

I look over my shoulder and see Arabella in the doorway. She eyes me with a combination of repugnance and horror.

"Do you have any idea how expensive that was?" she cries. "What a bloody mess!"

I am about to apologize when Cumberland interjects. "It is not a travesty, Ms. Dalton. Please go out and purchase a new set for me today," he says.

Arabella, looking like a total kiss-ass, nods gravely at the situation. "Oh, absolutely, Mr. Cumberland. Please do trust that I will take every precaution to ensure this doesn't happen again."

Then she shoots me a look of disgust and leaves the office.

I swallow hard. Just put another check in the awesome column for me as this morning is going oh so fabulously.

I swing back to Cumberland. "May I leave now?"

"Yes, of course," he says, sinking down into his chair.

I'm about out the door when he speaks again.

"Ms. Grant?"

I turn around, and he is staring at me, his fingers once again in that steeple position he seems to favor. "I hope you put a rush delivery on that *Full House* DVD," he says as he puts his fingers to his lips. "I am rather anxious to see your namesake."

I stare at him. Holy crap, are his eyes actually sparkling? They are! Those intense blue eyes have a light in them I haven't seen before. Is this *fun* for him?

I hate you. I really hate you, Cumberland.

And if he isn't going to fire me, then he cannot go back to England fast enough.

Chapter Three

"Why haven't you responded to my Pinterest pins? Or Connectivity posts?" my sister demands. "I have a wedding to plan, and you are *not* helping like a maid of honor should."

I roll my eyes as I listen to my sister rant into the phone. Freaking fabulous. Bridezilla, AKA Michelle, is not getting married for another year yet is convinced we have to plan her wedding *every day*. I think my sister is more prepared for this wedding than FEMA is for a natural disaster.

"Michelle, this week has been challenging at work. I have had to deal with William Cumberland and—"

"The Connectivity guy. You have used that excuse like a million times, MK," she says.

I twist my neck to relieve stress and decide to ignore that comment. "Well, he is leaving on Friday. I promise I'll come up to Milwaukee on Saturday," I say. Thank God he is leaving. I cannot wait for things to get back to normal at the office, which is impossible when Cumberland is around.

"Fine," Michelle says, sighing heavily. "But if you could spare a single second from your precious career to reply to my posts, it would be really nice of you."

Hmm. I'm willing to bet that royal weddings are planned

with less fanfare than Michelle's.

I indulge her while working on my iPad. It is almost seven o'clock in the evening, and out of habit, I check my work email. Then I see I have received one from William Cumberland.

What? Cumberland sent me a personal email?

"Hey, Michelle, I need to run. I'll see you on Saturday," I say. Before she can protest, I disconnect the call. Then I click open the email:

From: William Cumberland

To: Mary-Kate Grant

Subject: Full House

Ms. Grant, I completed my review of Episode 1 of the Full House DVD you so kindly ordered on my behalf. My assessment is that your name situation is quite favorable, considering the fact that your mother could have named you after the character DJ. Or Joey.

WC

I read it over and over. What the hell? William Cumberland seriously took time out of his day to watch *Full House* and send me an email about it?

He is doing this to annoy me.

And it worked.

I type back because I will be damned if I let him have the last word:

From: Mary-Kate Grant

To: William Cumberland

Subject: RE: Full House

I find it hard to believe that a man who is running a world-wide media empire has the time to watch an episode of Full House. My guess is you just read the back of the DVD cover. At least I hope that is the case.

19

MKG

Then I hit "send."

And he replies right back.

From: William Cumberland

To: Mary-Kate Grant

Subject: RE: Full House

Running a media empire has given me vast multi-tasking skills, Ms. Grant. I am also certain the scene where Joey and Jesse try to change the nappy must have been an instant classic for American television in 1987.

WC

I stare at the screen in shock. Holy crap, he did indeed watch it. Is William Cumberland emailing me about *Full House* to irritate me? What is the point of this exchange? I don't know what to think about him. And I am so exasperated that I don't even know how to respond. I click out of my email and put my iPad aside in annoyance.

The door opens, and Emily interrupts my thoughts. She drops her purse on the floor and dissolves into sobs.

"D-D-Dan broke up with me," she manages to say. "H-He said we-we-we're over b-b-b-because he doesn't love me anymore."

I jump off the couch, and Emily throws herself into my arms.

"Oh, Em," I say, holding her tight. "I am so sorry. So sorry."

She bawls into my shoulder.

I lead her back to the sofa and sit with her as she cries. It is so painful to hear her cry like this, because I know her heart feels irrevocably broken.

As I try to comfort her by stroking her hair, I can't help but think this will be better for her in the long run. Dan was a total idiot, and she can do so much better. And once again, I feel blessed that I am focused on my career and not love.

I have definitely made the right decision, I think as sobs rack Emily's body. *I'm thankful that I have my priorities straight.*

And I always will.

* * *

Thank God it's Friday.

Not only has this week been painfully long, but Friday also means that within hours, Cumberland will be on a plane back to the United Kingdom. Thank God, thank God, thank God, he's going home.

I head downstairs to the big sports studio with the rest of the employees for the TATS Network. Cumberland is giving his big employee address, and because it is being shot in our studio, we are invited to go watch it live.

"Hey, MK, do you think it's true he's going to totally redesign the networks and replace us with his own people?" Amber Logan, a public relations coordinator, asks me.

"I haven't heard a word," I say. Which is a lie. I have heard about 3,873 different rumors, but I have not heard, or seen in writing, anything directly from Cumberland himself, so I keep my mouth shut.

But the thought does worry me, since I have been nothing short of a clumsy, foul-mouthed, and short-tempered disaster in his presence. I'm sure I will be the first one he fires when he has a spare moment to have Arabella draft up my termination letter.

I make my way down the winding hallways to the studio, which is kept ice cold because of the equipment. I wrap my arms around myself to stay warm and keep a careful eye on all

21

the cables crossing the floor as I walk. I find a spot next to my boss, Paul, to watch the big speech.

Cumberland is already front and center, leaning on the anchor desk. His team is fluttering around him: someone is going over papers, presumably a script; a makeup artist is powdering his face; lighting is being checked; and Arabella is running around with a headset and has a bottle of water, which she hands him. His security detail, which I've learned tend to blend into the woodwork, keep their eyes on the room after they already assessed it for any threats.

I tilt my head to the side and stare at him for a moment. Today, he is wearing a fitted, long-sleeved shirt, one that seems tailor made for his lean frame. It is a light blue color, which really looks nice against his pale skin and dark hair.

I ponder him for a moment. Cumberland doesn't look like anyone I have ever met, but that makes him intriguing in a way. You know, in addition to being mysterious, brilliant, and aloof.

Suddenly, those blue eyes are staring right back at me with laser precision. I feel my breath catch in my throat. God, that gaze. I feel like he can see every thought in my head. I narrow my eyes at him and forcefully project the "I am *so* happy you are leaving" thought right back into his brain.

People are moving into position, and the stage manager begins a countdown. Cumberland remains in front of the desk, leaning against the side, and projecting a casual, relaxed image for the camera.

Soon, his deep British voice fills the studio, and his voice, and presence, command the room. He reveals his plans to integrate the networks with Connectivity; how he is not afraid to make changes to make us stronger; how he wants exciting programming and we should not fear change but the status quo instead.

Then Cumberland pauses for effect before continuing.

"Obviously, we have a monumental task ahead of us," he says, his eyes very, very intense now. "Yet, I know each and every one of you are up for the challenge. And to make sure my vision becomes reality, I am temporarily relocating to Chicago to oversee this process."

What? I can't breathe. *Oh no. Oh no, oh no, oh no. He's staying?*

"My assistant, Arabella Dalton, will go back to the United Kingdom to assist my team there," Cumberland says smoothly.

I glance at Arabella, whose mouth is wide open. *Holy crap, she didn't know this was coming*, I compute.

"And while there are many qualified candidates between all the networks here, I have chosen Mary-Kate Grant from the TATS Network to be my personal assistant here in the United States."

What????

I feel dizzy. Sweat forms on the back of my neck. My heart is pounding, and I feel everyone in the studio looking at me.

He chose me? Me?

I stare at Paul in shock. He stares back at me, and I can tell he is as floored as I am.

"So please contact Ms. Grant directly if you need to reach me," Cumberland continues. He speaks for a few more minutes, but I can't hear a word he is saying over the pounding in my head, and then he signs off.

A crowd of people instantly forms around him. I stare at him in stunned silence. I stand still, waiting for everyone to empty from the studio. Finally, his eyes meet mine, and I watch as he excuses himself and comes directly over to me.

"Let's go over here," he says, gesturing to a remote corner of the almost vacant studio.

As soon as the last person leaves, I launch into my questions.

"I don't understand," I say, shaking my head.

"I need an assistant. You are one. What is not to understand?"

"What is not to understand?" I repeat. "Between all the networks and departments in this building, you have thirty different assistants to choose from."

"I am well aware of that number and that fact, Ms. Grant," Cumberland says, his blue eyes never leaving mine.

"But—"

"No buts. I *loathe* that word."

I feel my face turn red in embarrassment. "I can't even bind."

"Irrelevant, as you yourself pointed out."

"I dropped your tea set."

"Replaceable."

"Why are we playing verbal tennis?" I spit out in frustration.

"I wasn't aware that we were," Cumberland says, lifting an eyebrow up. "Are we, Ms. Grant? Playing a game here?"

Argh! I want to scream, but I can't.

"No," I say through gritted teeth. "We are not."

"Good. Now details. I will be moving up to an office on the 15th floor, the same floor as the Beautiful Homes Network. You will relocate up there with me. They are installing the bullet proof doors and windows to my office over the weekend so by Monday it will be ready."

Okay, I see a silver lining in hell with that bit of information. Wait a minute—did he say *bullet proof*?

"Why does your office have to be bullet proofed?" I ask,

alarmed.

Cumberland lifts an eyebrow. "Comes with the owning of an empire."

It hits me that he is a billionaire. And with owning a social media company, a target of threats. Hence his security detail that seems to reside in the lobby ever since he arrived.

While I'm stuck on that thought, William proceeds with business information. Because for him, having bullet proof doors and windows is ... normal.

"Please be there Monday at eight-thirty sharp. We have a lot to do next week."

"All right," I concede, shifting my thoughts back to him. "I will be there."

"Brilliant. I shall see you Monday, Ms. Grant." Cumberland turns to walk away, but I decide I want the last word.

"Mr. Cumberland?"

He pauses and turns back around.

"Do not expect service from a tea trolley on Monday."

And before he can respond, I turn and walk away.

Chapter Four

"I want gold champagne fabric," Michelle declares, going through mounds of swatches on the kitchen table. "Not *beige* champagne. But *gold* champagne. That is very important. MK, do you *understand* the difference?"

I sigh. I'm trapped in hell. Which today is apparently located at my mother's Pottery Barn kitchen table in suburban Milwaukee.

"Yes, Michelle, I get it," I say, absently flipping through a fabric book.

"It must look like a glass of champagne," she says with the seriousness of a CIA agent planning a covert mission. "Because that is my favorite drink, and all the bridesmaids are going to be dressed in champagne fabric."

"Right," I reply.

"And it is so perfect for a New Year's Eve wedding," my mother gushes, happily flipping through yet another pile of potential fabrics.

I get up to refill my coffee as they both squeal in delight. Yes, leave it to Michelle to hijack a holiday for her wedding. It is just so ... Michelle.

As I put the pod into the coffee machine, I watch my mom

and Michelle eagerly touch the fabric, *oohing* and *aahing* and seriously weighing the merits of each.

I wrinkle my brow. How am I from this family? My brain doesn't operate like this. I mean, there's no talk of Jason, her fiancé, or the romance. It's all about the *production* of this wedding. Like this is a royal wedding or something.

I pull out the bottle of amaretto creamer from the fridge and pour it into my mug. As I stir it, I gaze out the big window in the kitchen and watch the snow come down in big, fat, puffy flakes on this Saturday morning.

I bet Cumberland is at the office, I muse, taking a sip of my coffee. He's a total workaholic, at least from the recon mission I have self-conducted since I learned I was going to be reporting to him yesterday.

What fascinates me most is the story behind Connectivity. Cumberland studied economics at Oxford and went straight to work in the corporate finance world upon graduation. He was brilliant at investing, but completely bored in his job. So he decided he wanted to develop his own business.

Cumberland, also very media savvy, noticed how people used different social media applications, and he didn't understand the inefficiency of storing your pictures one place, giving brief character updates in another, using another site to keep your friends updated on your life, going somewhere else for video calling, and yet another for career connections and online portfolios of work.

Never one for inefficiency and seeing a gap in the vast social media world, Cumberland created Connectivity—the one place you could manage everything in your social media life. Connectivity "Connects" are coded how the user sees fit—business, personal, etc.—and you can "Connect" things and people together—or not.

Now this is where it gets interesting. Loads have been written about Cumberland's brilliance, his innovation, his ability to surround himself with people who could help his vision come to life, yet—and this is very intriguing to me—I have read *nothing* about Cumberland that is personal.

People interviewed in the articles referred to him as a "business associate" or "acquaintance" but not "friend." In fact, the man who created one of the front-runners in the world of social media is not social at all. In fact, the exact opposite. Cumberland is business-only and keeps personal matters— even small ones—to himself.

Then, of course, there are rumors that he is asexual due to his lack of any romantic interests.

I take another sip of coffee. I don't think that is it at all. I think he is focused on business, and sex doesn't even land on his radar screen.

Which, oddly enough, I can completely relate to.

"MK!" Michelle bellows, interrupting my thoughts. "You are not paying attention, and you are not helping like you promised."

My mother lets out an exasperated sigh. "MK, really, if you could think about your sister this morning and focus, it would be nice."

I come back to the table. Michelle is pouting, and I'm fuming. Have either one of them, since I got here this morning, taken five seconds to ask how my job is going? To ask what the Cumberland takeover has done to my company? If I am worried about losing my job?

Of course not. Because for my mom and Michelle, my worries are stupid. In fact, in their minds, I should be flipping out because I haven't had a date in two years. This is what is considered to be a DEFCON 1 crisis. Not a silly little corporate takeover where I work.

"I'm sorry," I say, picking up a pile of swatches. "Gold champagne. I'm on it."

But I'm not. Not at all.

I act like I care, but my head is already thinking of Monday, my first day as Cumberland's assistant. I have decided to approach this as my reboot, if you will. I am actually going to be with people at the Beautiful Homes Network. I will work hard, be visible, and impress my new colleagues.

And this time, I will not be derailed.

* * *

I get to work insanely early on Monday morning, lug my box of belongings up to the 15th floor, and open the doors to the Beautiful Homes Network offices. A shiver of excitement rips down my spine as I step through the gorgeous lobby. *Wow. Wow! I am here. I am going to be walking through these doors every day, at my dream place of employment.*

I happily find the empty cubicle outside of Cumberland's new office—complete with bullet proof doors and windows so new it still smells like construction over here— and set the box down. I slide out of my winter wear and go about decorating my cubicle. After all, I need to show everyone here my unique style and taste, and what do they see first when they come over to Cumberland's office? My cube.

I put up my silver desk lamp, add a small tartan pillow to my chair, artfully arrange silver-framed pictures of me with Emily and Renee, display my old-fashioned Roman numeral desk clock, and put out my white orchid plant.

There. Now everyone can see I have a decorator's eye.

Next, I walk to the restroom to do an appearance check. I'm carrying over the theme of looking fashionable, but of my own making. Today, I put on a vintage tweed, black-and-white cropped jacket; multi-layered stone necklace; black trousers; and black high-heeled boots.

Satisfied, I go back to my cubicle and snap a few pictures with my iPhone. I can use this for a new blog article about creating a stylish workplace.

I boot up my computer and log in. Since it is just eight o'clock, I decide to visit my blog for a second so I can download these pictures. The last post comes up—the scones—and I take a moment to transfer the pictures over. Then I go to the break room to begin tea prep. I fill the electric teakettle and turn it on, so the water will be hot and ready for the teapot the second Cumberland arrives.

After I get the kettle going, I go back to my desk.

And find Cumberland standing there, staring at my computer screen.

Oh my God. I panic as I realize he is looking at my blog, which I must have left up when I went to do the tea.

"Mr. Cumberland," I say in a rush, "I—"

"Was looking at the Internet on company time?" he supplies helpfully, lifting an eyebrow at me.

Crap. I fly into my chair and immediately click out of the screen. Damn it. *Damn it, damn it, damn it!*

"I'm so sorry," I say sincerely, looking up at him. "I pulled it up for a second while I went to start the water for your tea. It will not happen again, I assure you of that."

Cumberland's laser eyes stay on me. "I see," he says in that deep British voice as he pulls off his leather gloves.

Which is not exactly the "it's okay" or "no big deal" response I was hoping he would give.

Then he turns and goes into his office without saying another word.

While he is in his office, I fight the urge to throw up on my desk. I take the teapot and go fill it, then come back and arrange the tea service items on the tray. Ugh, I feel so sick. I do not want to face him. But since I have no choice, I pick up the tray and walk into his office. Luckily, I manage not to face plant this time.

Cumberland is already on the phone and typing on his computer as I arrange his tea on his desk. He turns around at the sound and nods at me without even breaking his conversation.

I retreat to my cubicle and find an IM waiting for me. From William Cumberland.

Please read the attached corporate policy on Internet use. Let me know if you have any questions upon review. WC.

Oh no! My face is on fire with humiliation as I read the message and then the attachment, which specifically states that the Internet is for company use only. I swallow every ounce of pride I have, because Cumberland is right on this one, even if the entire company surfs the net during the day. It is still a rule. I respond:

I don't have any questions, Mr. Cumberland, and I will comply fully. Please accept my sincerest apologies. MKG.

The rest of the day, I lay as low as possible. Luckily, Cumberland has meeting after meeting with all the network people in Chicago, so he's busy. Arabella has sent me a slew of bossy emails from London dictating what kind of supplies I need to order for him, how he likes things organized, blah,

blah, blah.

I'm working through the massive supply order list when my cell phone beeps with a notification. I have it parked next to my keyboard, so I pick it up.

And to my surprise, I see it is a response to my blog.

Yes! A real reply to my blog. My first real response!

I excitedly open the message on my phone.

William Cumberland is now following your blog.

I gasp out loud. Oh no. No, no, no, no, no! My heart begins to pound. My stomach completely bottoms out.

Beep!

William Cumberland has commented on one of your posts.

Panic engulfs me. I access my blog from my iPhone. Oh mother of God, he is reading my posts. *In which I talk about him!*

He has written a comment on the scone one, in which I oh-so-brilliantly commented that he was too thin and needed to eat more scones.

I read his comment in horror:

I prefer the word "lithe" instead of "too thin" myself. WC

Beep! My phone goes off again.

William Cumberland has commented on one of your posts.

I put my forehead into my hands and groan. Apparently, Cumberland is going to read every single thing I have ever written.

Beep!

And comment on it as well.

Beep!

I shut off my phone. This is nothing short of a disaster. And

I have no clue how I'm going to face him after this.

Chapter Five

I sit at my desk for a good hour, fighting the urge to throw up, before I finally decide to take the bull by the horns and step into his doorway. Cumberland is on his cell phone, walking around his office. He is in front of the large window, which has a fantastic view of the Magnificent Mile, sprawled out below in all its glory.

He sees me and holds out his hand, signaling for me to wait. I watch him as he stops in front of the window. The snow is cascading down from the gray sky, and I can't help but observe how his crisp white shirt stands out against the backdrop.

I notice a lock of his dark, wavy hair has fallen out of place and is resting against his forehead, and as I combine the image with the brilliant and in control way he is speaking right now, there is something very magnetic about him. You are drawn in, and you can't help but stare at him.

He finishes the call, and as soon as he does, I clear my throat.

"Mr. Cumberland, I want to thank you for following my blog," I say simply. Then I see it. A slight expression of surprise flickers across his face. *Ah-ha!* He didn't expect this, and that is good. My confidence grows, and I smile at him. "And you are absolutely correct that lithe is a better way to describe you."

Cumberland folds his arms across his sleek white shirt. That is all he wears: modern-cut designer shirts.

"You have a talent for writing, Ms. Grant," he says, interrupting my thoughts.

I feel my face burn hot. *No, don't blush.* I will myself. *Don't.*

"Thank you," I say quietly.

"Why am I the only follower?" he asks, his eyes riveted to mine.

I swallow hard. And then I give him the honest truth. "I don't want pity follows."

Cumberland's brow creases. "Pity follows?"

I nod. "Yes. Like my family and friends following me because I ask them to, not because they really want to. Does that make sense?"

"Very similar to people telling me 'yes,' no matter what the question is, because my name is William Cumberland," he says slowly.

I realize that we might be more alike than I ever could have imagined. We are both career-oriented, and we are both prideful. It's an interesting thought.

We simply stare at each other for a moment, surprised by this revelation. Then Cumberland gets the intense look in his eyes that I have come to recognize on sight.

"With that said, Ms. Grant, why on earth are you an executive assistant? Your considerable skills and a master's degree from Northwestern are not well-matched with your current position."

My pulse leaps. He sees me. Unlike Paul, my old boss, Cumberland has known me for about a week, yet he completely gets it.

"I took the job to get my foot in the door," I explain. "I know you have to work from the bottom up. I had no delusions about that. And I'm willing to work hard, learn different things, and eventually move over to the Beautiful Homes Network."

"Do you even like sports?" he asks.

I feel my face grow hotter. "Um … no," I confess. "I do not."

I can tell by his face that he is assessing my words.

Cumberland raises an eyebrow. "So you must really want to work for the Beautiful Homes Network if you are willing to make that sacrifice."

He pauses for a moment, then says, "I have a proposal. I like what you have done with your blog and your cubicle. Why don't you decorate my office, write an article about it, and I will personally have it posted to the Beautiful Homes Network website? They could use some fresh voices over there. Then I ask that you stay with me for six months, while the transition is the heaviest, and then I will release you for any job you want. In the meantime, though, let's see if we can get you writing over there, in addition to the duties you have for me, of course."

Elation pours through me as his offer sinks in. Cumberland is going to help me. He's going to let me write and use my brain and get my foot in the door at my dream company.

"Mr. Cumberland, I cannot even begin to tell you what this means to me," I say. "Thank you so, so much for the opportunity. I promise it won't interfere in any way with the work I have to do for you. That is always going to be my top priority, I assure you of that."

"Very well then." He moves back around to his desk, and I'm about to walk out the door when he stops me.

"And Ms. Grant?"

I turn around. "Yes?"

"If I see any décor items that say 'Keep Calm and Carry On,' I will scream," he says, sinking down into his chair.

I can't help it. I burst out laughing and laugh so hard, I snort.

And much to my utter shock, Cumberland joins me with a deep, throaty laugh that catches me completely off guard. It is so rich sounding that it completely fills the room.

I'm in shock, because I didn't think he could laugh, and when he did ... oh, it was very attractive.

What am I thinking? This is Cumberland. Media mogul billionaire William Cumberland. My boss. Have I lost my freaking mind?

"Did you just snort?" he asks, his intense blue eyes now dancing at me.

"Um ... yes," I say, feeling my face grow warm for the sixtieth time.

He chuckles and shakes his head. "Thank you for the verification, Ms. Grant."

And just like that, Cumberland's expression goes back to serious. Almost as if he realized he has shared too much of himself with me.

"All right," he says, clearing his throat as he picks up a silver pen and begins reviewing a contract on his desk.

I go back to my cubicle and bite my lip. Something just happened in there. For a moment, a brief moment, Cumberland became *William*. William, who revealed he knew people liked to "yes, sir," "whatever, sir" him. William, who had a deep, contagious laugh ...

And for some reason I cannot explain, the realization unnerves me. More than I care to admit.

* * *

During the next few weeks, I begin to understand how insane Cumberland's world is. Everyone wants a piece of him—his cell is always blowing up; his email is overflowing; my line is ringing constantly with a person who has a crisis only he can solve.

He travels a lot, too. In just the month, he has been back to England once, to Tokyo, and to South Africa. I have no idea how he keeps his time zones straight. I really don't.

Yet, no matter where he is in the world, he always comments on my blog. And I always text him back my thoughts, which leads to a little conversation via text.

Beep!

I smile to myself. Like now. I'm sitting on the couch watching the reality TV dating show *Is it Love?* with Renee, and Cumberland is in Los Angeles, a quick one-day trip to be the keynote speaker at a conference. And he has already replied to a post I loaded an hour ago about rosemary-scented cleaning supplies.

I pick up my phone and see that he has texted me:

Did you post this on company time, Ms. Grant? WC

I smile again. I know he is teasing me. I text him back.

With all due respect, Mr. Cumberland, you have your time zones messed up. I am sitting on my couch in Lincoln Park. I posted that an hour ago. MKG

I take a sip of my wine and keep my phone in my hand. I want to see how he responds to that.

Beep!

I read his response:

With all due respect, Ms. Grant, I was giving you the

benefit of the doubt that you might be working late to show your due diligence during my absence. WC

Before I can respond, another text comes across:

I am so bored. Please blog something else for me to comment on. WC

"Who are you texting?" Renee asks, lifting her gaze from the TV to me.

We always watch *Is it Love?* together. Emily used to join us, but since the big breakup with Dan, she can't handle romantic stories without crying, so she went to a yoga class instead.

"Cumberland," I say as I text him back.

Mr. Cumberland, I would love to entertain you with another witty blog, but I'm very busy keeping my roommate company and watching the less-than-realistic dates on Is it Love? You do have your finger on the pulse of that American pop culture touchstone, yes? MKG

"Do you realize you have a ridiculous smile on your face right now?" Renee asks in an accusatory tone.

I throw down my phone as if I am holding something toxic. "*What?* Oh, no, he sent me a very entertaining text, that's all."

"Right," Renee says, taking a sip of her wine.

"Oh, no, no, no," I say, shaking my head. "It's not like *that*."

Beep!

My phone goes off, but I ignore it. Although I really want to see what Cumberland has to say. *Does he think I am a loon for mentioning Is it Love? Or does my quirkiness intrigue him?* Hmmm.

"Oh, I think it is exactly like that," Renee declares. "I think you are getting a little crush on your boss."

"What?" I cry. "That's insane. I'm not even attracted to him."

"Oh, really?" Renee picks up the remote and hits pause, because heaven forbid we miss the one-on-one date that is going on right now on our flat screen. "Then how come I know he wears modern dress shirts, has ridiculous dark, wavy hair, intense blue eyes, sculpted cheekbones, and a deep British accent?"

I begin to fidget. I do not like where this conversation is going.

And I really wonder what Cumberland just texted me.

"Those are character details," I say quickly. "I'm a communications person. I like providing details."

"I don't know anything about your other boss, and you worked for him for a year."

My face grows hot, and I feel all flustered inside. "But ... Cumberland is different. He is brainy sexy," I blurt out.

Oh crap. I do think it. I do think he's attractive and sexy.

But he is so damn smart that it makes him hot. And you add in those cheekbones, the way he puts his fingertips to his lips when he's thinking, the way a curl of his dark hair escapes and falls down on his forehead ... I grab my merlot and take a big gulp. Gah, how did I not even realize this was happening?

"I knew it!" Renee yells gleefully.

"Okay, so I think he's hot," I admit. "But he's my boss. Off limits. *Very* off limits. And he doesn't date. Period."

Besides, when would he have *time* to date? *No wonder he has no personal life,* I muse.

"True," Renee says. "Well, at least he's fun to look at."

She un-pauses the show, and the oh-so-important episode of *Is it Love?* continues.

And while Renee is sucked back into the world of elaborate, over-the-top dates, I am left shaken by my thoughts.

I swallow hard. I didn't even realize I was talking about him. I didn't know I had relayed every detail, or that I liked the fact that he texted me, and not about work. That I liked that Cumberland reads my blog, that he shares his thoughts on it. That his dress shirts look so damn good on his lithe frame, that his intensity is so intriguing, that his sexy deep British voice reverberates in my head.

Yes, I'm attracted to William Cumberland.

I didn't realize it because I have never felt this way before, had this kind of attraction to a man like this.

But as I told Renee, he's off-limits. Like he'd even look at me anyway. I'm simply the quirky American assistant he's helping along the career trail. He's like a mentor.

And he doesn't date anyway.

But if he did, Cumberland would date someone as equally sophisticated as him.

Like a British society woman.

I bite my lip. Even though I know all that is true, how come I don't like that answer very much?

Chapter Six

By the second week of February, my decorating project is complete.

I stand in Cumberland's office and take one final assessment. He is due back any minute now. His driver has picked him up at O'Hare after a trip to London and New York. And I want everything to be perfect for the reveal.

I purchased some silver lamps and vintage office accessories to spruce up his office. I pick up the pair of antique binoculars that I have strategically placed on his desk. I added plants, hunter green and plum plaid pillows for the tweed guest couch, a plum rug for a pop of color.

I smile with satisfaction. Cumberland told me to run with the décor and surprise him like one of the shows on the Beautiful Homes Network. And I can't wait to see his reaction to his new office.

Suddenly, I hear him. That deep British voice talking into his cell from down the hall. A shiver instantly shoots down my spine in response.

"Ms. Dalton, I sincerely hope after all this time you are able to render a decision like that on your own," he says firmly. "… Yes … No. Absolutely not. Do not even discuss her with me—"

Cumberland stops speaking as soon as he sees me in his office.

I bite my lower lip, wishing he'd finish that sentence. Who was he talking about? What woman would he not want Arabella to talk about?

My heart leaps for a brief second. *Me? Could he be talking about me?*

Wait. Am I on drugs? Why would he be talking about me? Cumberland could be talking about *anyone*.

"I need to terminate this call," he says, his light blue eyes burning into mine with such intensity that my stomach does a flip. He punches his phone and stands in his doorway, staring at me.

I swallow hard. Good Lord. The man can wear a scarf and trench coat like nobody's business.

"Good to see you, Ms. Grant," he says, his voice a completely different tone than it was a second ago.

"Welcome back to Chicago, Mr. Cumberland," I say.

He steps into the office and stops. I watch as his eyes widen and dart around, and I can tell he is assessing every detail, every change, every addition I have made.

"Ms. Grant," he says, pulling off his gloves and tossing them onto his desk in a smooth, fluid motion, "I have to say this is rather impressive. I think it is brilliant. Just brilliant."

Okay, why do I feel like doing cartwheels across his office?

"Thank you. I'm glad to hear that," I reply.

Cumberland takes off his scarf and trench and moves behind me to hang them up. As he goes past, I smell him, the scent of pine needles and soap on his pale skin. Sexy smelling. Very sexy indeed.

He moves around the office, picking up objects and inspect-

43

ing them closely. Finally, he picks up the binoculars, and I can't contain my excitement about them.

"Aren't those cool? I found them in a little antique shop out in Long Grove," I say excitedly, referring to the suburban Chicago town. "They are my second-most favorite thing in the room."

Cumberland turns and raises a brow. "And the first?"

"Wait a second," I reply, smiling. I go out to my desk and pick up the object. I hide it behind my back and walk over to him.

"It just wouldn't be British without this," I say. Then I show him a bright red "Keep Calm and Carry On" coffee mug.

Cumberland stares at it, then at me, and a huge grin passes over his face.

My heart jumps in response, as it is a genuine, beautiful smile that he is giving me right now.

"Bloody hell, Ms. Grant," he says, laughing deeply.

I laugh with him, and he's still smiling at me.

"You Americans and your love of this slogan. I don't understand it. Nor do I get the fact that you put mince turkey into everything either."

I furrow my brow. "What?"

"Ground turkey, as you Americans call it," he says, putting the mug on his desk. He walks around and sinks into his chair. "The woman next to me on the flight this morning was raving about how she uses it instead of beef. You put it into everything, and it is horrible. I don't understand that."

I put my hands on my hips. "This coming from the country that gave the world steak and kidney pie?"

Cumberland grins at me. "*Touché*, Ms. Grant. *Touché*."

Suddenly, his phone rings, and we are jolted out of our

conversation. I circle behind him and pick it up, answering professionally. "William Cumberland's office, this is MK speaking ... yes ... please hold, and I shall see if he's available."

I put the caller on hold and turn to him. "It's Louis Steele," I say, referring to a lead attorney with Connectivity. "He said he has a very urgent matter to discuss with you."

"Right," Cumberland says. He instantly shifts gears, seamlessly going into "the man who runs an empire" mode.

I go to leave, but before I do, he stops me.

"Ms. Grant?"

I pause in the doorway.

"Thank you for the mug," he says, his eyes intense. "I shall find a way to repay you in kind for it."

I laugh and walk back to my cubicle. *I'm sure you will, William Cumberland. And I look forward to it.*

* * *

On Valentine's Day, I find myself in another dreaded Lincoln Park bar for the evening. You know, to cheer up Emily in the face of the worst holiday of the year for the brokenhearted. Or, if you asked my sister and mother, a tragic holiday for—*gasp*—single people like me.

Of course, being out with Renee and Emily gives my roommates ample opportunity to tell me my crush on Cumberland is a recipe for disaster.

"MK, seriously, there are like a million guys in the city of Chicago for you to pick from," Renee yells from across the table. "There is no need to get hung up on your unobtainable boss."

I glance around the bar at all the complete fools surrounding me. Drunk, young, and upwardly mobile. *Yes, I have choices, all right. Many, many craptastic ones. Ugh.*

My phone vibrates in my lap. The whole time I have been here with Renee and Emily, I have been texting with Cumberland. I have told him I am miserable and stuck in this stupid bar for the sake of solidarity in the face of the Valentine's Day holiday. I told him I'm sending back drinks and giving out the 'leave me alone' vibe, etc., but nobody can read it.

Of course, the texting didn't start out that way. He was giving me feedback on the article I drafted about his office makeover and, as it always did, it became a conversation about everything but the article.

"Quit texting him, MK," Emily begs, putting her hand on my arm. "This is so dangerous, what you are doing. He is your *boss.*"

"He could be texting about business," I say, knowing that is a complete lie. "So I have to check when he texts me, okay?"

But to prove a point, I ignore my phone for the next hour.

Which gives me a twitchy feeling inside. I ponder what Cumberland might be saying or if he is wondering why I haven't responded to his last witty text ...

Thankfully, I manage to divert the conversation away from my quote unquote unobtainable boss. And after an hour of discussion on how men are jerks, of turning down drinks being sent over to the table, and other assorted drunken tomfoolery by guys in the bar, I am done. I'm ready to go home. I want my yoga pants and hoodie, and I want to be reading witty text messages from Cumberland.

I'm about to announce that I am leaving when a server comes over to our table and puts down a cocktail napkin and a glass of red wine in front of me.

"A gentleman at the bar would like for you to have this," she says.

I shake my head firmly. "No, no, thank you. Please tell the person who sent this over that I buy my own drinks."

"He said you would say that," she explains. "He asked that I tell you 'To Keep Calm and Carry On.'"

My heart stops. "W-what?"

"The gentleman at the bar. British guy in a very nice coat," she says before walking away.

Renee and Emily's eyes widen. "Cumberland!" they gasp at the same time.

I begin to shake. I turn and peer through the crowd of people to the bar. And there is William Cumberland, staring right at me. Oh my God. He's *here*. Cumberland is *here*.

"Excuse me," I say, grabbing my purse and phone and sliding out of the booth. I fight my way through the crowd, and I can see him doing the same. We meet halfway.

"What are you doing here?" I scream over the noise.

He shakes his head as if he can't hear me. Then, to my complete shock, he takes my hand. A shiver shoots down my spine as I feel the warmth of his hand wrapped around mine.

Before we can go anywhere, a man moves in front of us and one behind us. *His detail,* I realize. We follow the first guard through the crowd and out of the bar. They discreetly move off to the side and William leads me down the sidewalk out to the street, where he releases my hand. I wrap my arms around myself since it is snowing, and I have no coat. Of course, wearing a black wool sheath dress with tall black boots and no coat isn't exactly smart, but since we were cabbing it, I didn't see the need for one.

"Good Lord, Ms. Grant," Cumberland says, immediately

taking off his trench coat and gently draping it over me. "Are you aware it is snowing outside?"

I shiver violently, but it has nothing to do with the freezing temperature.

"William, why are you here?" I blurt out. Then I slap my hand over my mouth, realizing what I just called him. My face burns in horror, and I try to apologize. "Mr. Cumberland, I am so sorry, I—"

"William," he interrupts softly, "is fine, *Mary-Kate*."

The current of our relationship just changed in this very moment. Which is exciting and scary, and I have never felt more confused about anything in my entire life.

"But to answer your question, Mary-Kate, I am here because I could detect the SOS in your texts," he says, the corners of his full lips hinting at a smile.

"That's very MI5 of you, William," I say, teasing him.

Or is it flirting? Good God, I am so confused.

"Yes, isn't it?" he replies, staring back at me.

He's wearing a gray suit and has a beautiful light blue shirt on, one that is the exact shade of his intense eyes. Snowflakes whirl around us in the air. They are falling in his dark waves, which are illuminated by the streetlight, and, oh, he looks so beautiful I can hardly function.

I swallow and try to refocus on what he is saying.

"But using the powers of deduction one would learn at MI5, I can see why you sent me the urgent SOS," William continues. "Those people in the bar are utterly annoying."

I can't help it. I burst out laughing and snort, which makes him burst out laughing, too.

"You sound like Peppa Pig," he laughs.

"Who?"

"A British cartoon character," William tells me, his eyes sparkling. "Peppa is a pig who *snorts*."

"I do not sound like a pig," I cry, laughing.

"I think I need to call you Peppa," he says, lifting an eyebrow. "So Peppa—"

"Stop that!" I giggle. Good God, I'm giggling now?

Why am I acting like I am sixteen? What is this man *doing* to me?

"... I was thinking you needed an excuse to leave," William continues. Then he pauses for a moment. "... and I was wondering if you would like to pop over to the Peninsula Hotel for a drink. Mary-Kate, will you have a drink with me?"

Chapter Seven

I stare back at William, stunned by what he just asked. My pulse begins twitching. My heart is racing. He asked me to go have a drink with him. A drink. Is this dangerous? This is my *boss*. Is this inappropriate for me to accept, no matter how much I want to?

Or do I even *care* if it's inappropriate?

And what does this mean? Could he actually be interested in me?

I'm so shocked by the invitation that I don't answer.

William stares at me, his light blue eyes questioning mine, waiting for a response I don't know how to give.

"Mary-Kate," he says softly, "I don't want you to interpret this as anything other than what it is: just a drink."

My cheeks burn. I'm an idiot. Of course it would be just a drink. He's my *boss*. I'm his assistant. William is being nice and rescuing me, period.

So why does that thought—of him not seeing this as more than a drink with someone who works for him—sting my heart so much?

But as I gaze into those magnetic eyes, I know what my answer is going to be.

"Yes," I say. "Yes, I'll have a drink with you."

William nods and leads me over to his car, where his driver is waiting. He opens the door for me to climb in, and he takes a moment to talk to his security detail. Then William gets in next to me. I send a text to Renee and Emily, telling them I'm going with him, I'm fine, and I'll talk to them later.

Then I shut off my phone and drop it into my purse before the texts of lectures and warnings come flooding right back to me.

While I am doing this, William is texting someone on his iPhone. I don't interrupt him, as I know he gets like three-thousand messages a day and is constantly texting people back.

We arrive at the hotel, one of the most expensive and sleek in Chicago. After his detail goes in ahead of us, William escorts me to the bar, which is gorgeous and sophisticated and perfect for a glass of wine. We grab a spot near the open fireplace, and he helps me take off his coat that I'm wearing. I sink down into a cozy chair and breathe an appreciative sigh.

"This is so much better," I say gratefully. "Thank you for the rescue, William."

He studies me for a moment as he sits in the chair across from me. "You're an old soul, aren't you?" he asks slowly.

I watch as the light from the fireplace flickers across his amazing cheekbones. "Just like you."

He stares back at me, but I already know what he is thinking. That I get him like nobody else does. I can't explain it, but it is a feeling I have, one that is so strong and so powerful that I know I'm right.

And he understands me better than anyone ever has, too.

"Welcome back, Mr. Cumberland," the server says, dropping two cocktail napkins on the coffee table in-between us and interrupting my thoughts. "The usual?"

"No." William looks at me. "What would you like to drink, Mary-Kate?"

"A glass of pinot noir sounds nice," I say.

"Then I would like a bottle of your best pinot noir, please," he tells the server. She nods and then leaves.

"Hmmm. 'Welcome Back?'" I say slowly. "Do you regularly bring the ladies to this bar, William?"

Did I just ask him that?

He studies me. "Would you like to know, Mary-Kate?"

"Only if you care to answer, William," I say, matching him.

My pulse jumps again as I wait for his reply. Here we go. We say we are employee/boss. But we don't speak to each other like that. And now there is this damn undercurrent of attraction, of sexual tension that I like *way* too much, and I feel like my whole career, my dreams, and my future could go up in flames because I am playing with a match here.

But at this moment, in this bar, I don't care.

"No," he answers, his eyes never leaving mine. "I lived here when I first arrived in Chicago. I would have drinks here during that time." Before I can say anything else, he continues. "For the record, you are the first woman I've brought here for a drink."

My heart leaps at this information, but I keep that close to the vest and banter back with him. "Is that so?"

"I didn't meet anyone who I wanted to have for company. Until now," he says, his gaze meeting mine.

Ooh!

Before I can reply, the server arrives with what I can only assume is an outrageously-priced bottle of wine. She goes through the whole procedure: presenting the bottle, doing the cork bit, pouring a taste, etc. Finally, our glasses are filled and she retreats, leaving us alone again.

I take a sip and, oh my, this is the best wine I have ever had. Rich and lush and tastes like pure velvet going down my throat. I'm in heaven right now. "William, this is wonderful," I say. "Thank you so much for treating me to this."

"You're welcome," he replies, taking a sip from his glass.

We fall silent for a moment, drinking wine and staring at the flames dancing in the fireplace next to us. But it is a comfortable silence, and for once, I don't feel like I need to fill the space with my words. I'm content to simply be here with William.

Suddenly, his iPhone rings and breaks the moment. He reaches back and fishes for it in his suit jacket, which is draped across the back of his chair. I watch as he picks it up and shuts it right off.

"I think the empire can run without me for an hour," he declares, dropping the phone back into the jacket pocket.

I can't believe it. William shut off his *phone*. I have never, ever seen him without his phone, let alone his phone turned off.

And my heart jumps in response as I realize he is giving me his full attention. Something I think nothing, and I mean *nothing*, except his career ever gets.

"So what about you?" he asks, breaking the silence. "Is there a man in your life?"

I look him straight in the eyes. "No. I'm like you, William. I'm focused on my career. My sister is obsessed with planning her wedding, my friends are actively seeking boyfriends, but that's not me. My last boyfriend was back in graduate school. He was nice, but ..." My voice trails off, as I have never admitted this to anyone before. "... but I wasn't in love with him."

"That would pose a problem," William says, his eyes burning into mine.

"Quite problematic," I say smartly, and mentally high-five myself for that brilliant answer. I take another sip of my pinot. "So what about you? What about the women in your past?"

"You already know my history," he replies. "It is everywhere for you to read."

"Not true. There's no history in print. And I'm sorry, but your Connectivity account is written by your PR team. It doesn't sound like you at all."

William rubs his fingertips over his lips in that sexy thinking way. "Maybe I don't have much to share."

"Oh, you have things to share, but you just don't care to."

"Is that so?" he asks. He pauses to take a sip of wine. "And what would you like for me to share with you, Mary-Kate?"

Oh crap. He's testing me. I feel hot and flushed. And it is not from the fireplace I am sitting next to. "Do you want to play twenty questions with me, William?"

Did I say that to my boss?

"I'm game, Mary-Kate," he says. "Let's play."

And the game is on. I know not to get too personal, not tonight, so I fire general questions at him, from his favorite color to his favorite book and vacation spot. And with each question he answers, I get more and more surprised by how much he reveals to me. To my delight, he turns the tables on me and asks the very same questions.

As we drink our wine, I find out that William loves gourmet food, wine, books, and poetry. I'm floored by what I am learning, and with each question he answers, I find my heart fluttering in response. He is so breathtakingly smart and interesting and sophisticated, unlike any man I have ever encountered before in my life.

And he seems just as intrigued by my answers to his questions, too, as we banter back and forth and peel the layers off to see who the other person really is underneath.

It is by far the most perfect first date that I have ever had. *Except it's not a date*, I remind myself. Before I know it, we have drained the whole bottle of wine, and I feel flushed, floaty, and happy.

And since it is late and the wine is gone, I know it will be time for the evening to end soon, which makes me sad, because I don't want it to be over.

"Do you have a current passport?" William asks, interrupting my thoughts.

Now my heart is pounding. "I do."

"Good," he says, draining the last of the wine in his glass. "Because I need to go back to London in two weeks. And I want you to go with me."

Chapter Eight

William wants me to go to London.

He wants me to go to London. *London*! I don't know if it is the wine or the idea of going to London with William, but my head is spinning. I blurt out the first thing that is on the tip of my tongue.

"But … don't you have Arabella there?"

William rubs his fingertips over his full lips. "The obvious answer, Mary-Kate, would be that I would take you to London to see the headquarters and meet the people that you are working with on my behalf," he says slowly. "And Ms. Dalton has the rather unfortunate habit of annoying me."

I can't help it. I laugh at that comment.

William takes his index finger and slowly runs it around the rim of his empty wine glass. "But the truth is I want you there, Mary-Kate."

And then he stares at me with such intensity in his eyes that they practically smolder.

My pulse is rapidly climbing at a rate that one might seek medical treatment for. I swallow hard and try my best to be very calm, when in fact I feel this odd combination—this oddly exhilarating combination—of sexual tension and pure elation inside.

"Then I shall put that on my calendar, William," I say, my eyes focused directly on his.

"Brilliant," he says.

"Yes, brilliant," I reply softly.

We both fall silent for a moment. Then he clears his throat. "We should be going."

I nod and stand up. William quickly moves around to me, draping his coat over me. He slips back into his gray suit jacket and calls his driver, asking him to bring the car around as we stroll out of the bar. I notice his security detail has moved around us as well, and I realize I was so engrossed in William I forgot they were there.

"I'll grab a cab," I say as we walk outside.

"No, I shall see you home," he says.

"No, William, it's late." I glance down at my watch and to my shock, it's midnight. How did that happen?

"No," he says firmly.

And I know by that tone, which I have now heard many times before, not to even bother arguing with him about it. His driver brings the car around and opens the door for us. I step in, then William slides in next to me, and we head toward Lincoln Park. I gaze out the window, and Chicago is all lit up around us, the moon shining down on the city on this cold February night. Then I turn and glance at him, the light of the city illuminating his face, and he's so beautiful that it takes my breath away.

I force myself to look away, but everything about him is etched in my mind. And every moment of this evening is, too.

As we pull up to my brownstone, he gets out of the car with me.

"William, I'm good from here," I insist.

"Mary-Kate, I shall see you to your door," he says, smiling at me.

Okay, so although I am protesting, I'm glad he's not listening. I secretly love the fact that he's being such a gentleman and doing this for me.

We walk up the two flights of stairs to my apartment. I dig my key out of my purse and try to put it in the lock, but I miss. I feel my face flame in embarrassment. Shit, I'm tipsy.

William puts his hand over mine, and the second he does, electricity jolts through me. "Allow me," he says in that rich baritone voice.

He takes the key and turns it in the lock, and the door pops open.

"Thank you," I say in a whisper.

"You're welcome," he replies softly.

I begin to take off his coat, and he helps me slide out of it, draping it over his arm after I have it off. We both stand there in the silent hallway. I hope he doesn't hear my heart pounding the way I do right now.

"Have a good weekend," he says.

"You, too." I pause. "And thank you. I had a lovely time tonight."

William nods. "You're welcome."

I open the door and am about to step inside when his voice stops me.

"Mary-Kate?"

I turn around and see that he has stopped right as he is about to go down the stairs. "Yes?"

"Happy Valentine's Day."

Then he leaves, dashing down the stairs and disappearing out of sight before I can say anything in return. I walk inside the apartment and shut the door behind me. I lock it and lean against the hard wood. Despite my somewhat tipsy state, I know one thing for sure. Tonight, I took that match out of the book and struck it. And I'm going to have to be very, very, careful to keep it in check, or else I'll get burned.

* * *

I wake up the next morning in a somewhat tired state. My brain wouldn't shut off last night. All I could think about was William and London and London and William and how last night was the best night I had ever had with a man, but it wasn't a date. Because I don't want to date anyone. And neither does he.

So how come my chest tightened at that thought?

Could this be any more confusing or complicated? I'm beyond attracted to William, but I know he doesn't get involved. *Ever.* And he wouldn't date his assistant anyway, if he did date. Which he doesn't.

Not that I would want to date my boss.

My sexy, brilliant, sophisticated, British boss.

I mean, could I commit any bigger career suicide than by having a fling with William Cumberland? I don't want that. And neither does he.

But if I don't want that, then why can't I stop thinking about him? Coffee. I need coffee to clear my head.

I stumble out of bed and open my door. I walk into the living room, and Renee and Emily immediately quit talking. Which of course means they were talking about me. I feel my face grow warm as both of them stare at me with wide eyes.

"Good morning," I say, padding past them and entering our tiny kitchen. I open the cabinet door to grab my favorite coffee mug, one I got from Dean & Deluca on a trip to New York my freshman year of college.

"MK, what happened last night?" Emily asks.

I take my mug and select a coffee pod. "I had a drink with William. That's all."

"MK, you went out with your *boss*," Renee says, walking into the kitchen. "This wasn't like a company happy hour. This was a *date*."

I pause from making coffee. Anger begins bubbling up inside of me.

"No," I say firmly. "It was *not* a date. It was two people having a drink. It's what mature adults *do*, you know. They can have a drink and just have it be a drink."

I go back to making coffee, but Renee isn't finished yet.

"This is not like you," she says, her voice full of concern. "Not like you at all. You haven't had a date with a guy in years. And now you decide to have drinks with the biggest media mogul in the world? Who happens to be your *boss*?"

"Renee is right," Emily chimes in. "You can't do this, MK. Cumberland is not the guy to be flirting with and having drinks with. My God, what if this gets out? What will people in your office say about you?"

I whirl around. I know they are right. But for the first time in my life, I don't care. "You know what? I can have fun and keep this under control. I am sure of that. William and I are on the same page. We are career focused. We enjoy each other's company. Is there anything wrong with that?"

"Oh, come on, MK," Renee says. "You know this is a recipe for disaster."

"What if William does this to all his assistants?" Emily adds. "What if he flirts with them, or takes them out, sleeps with them? You don't know what he's like in his office in London or with other assistants. You don't know—"

"I do know him," I interrupt. "I know him, I get him, and if I want to have a little fun flirting with William, then I will." I grab my cup of coffee and storm off to my room, slamming the door shut behind me.

I eye my coffee cup. Shit. I forgot the creamer. But I'm so livid right now, I'll be damned if I go back out there and get some. I park the mug on my end table and grab my iPad. I am going to spend the morning working on my blog. That will help me do two things: decompress from the anger I have right now and hopefully distract me from thinking about William.

William. I realize I haven't checked my phone since last night. I get up, grab my purse, and fish it out. I turn it back on and find a zillion text messages: ones from Renee and Emily after I left the bar last night, several from Arabella asking why I won't answer my phone, some from Michelle about bridal party shoes and champagne-colored eye shadow, and ... William.

My heart skips a beat as I immediately open his message:

I do hope you have managed to locate the keyhole this morning. WC

I sit down on my bed and tuck my legs up underneath me. I immediately text him back:

I have not yet attempted but feel I shall be successful when the time arises. MKG

I wait, and he immediately responds:

I am comforted by that fact, Mary-Kate. WC

I laugh to myself. I love that he initials all of his texts. So I always add my initials back in return. But before I can reply, another message drops in:

What are you doing today? WC

I hold my breath. Then I type:

Working on the blog that only you read. You? MKG

Once again, an instant response.

I need to select furniture for the new place. Would you like to assist me with this task? WC

That weird tingling sensation rips through me as I type back:

I would love to but need to see your space first to assess your decorating needs. MKG

I take a sip of the black coffee—*blah*—and in a moment, William responds:

Meet me at my place at 1 p.m. WC.

And just like that, I have taken another match out of my book and struck it

Chapter Nine

I head over to William's apartment building with a feeling of excitement bubbling inside of me. Being on the edge of Millennium Park and near Lake Michigan, his place of residence is considered one of the hottest addresses in all of Chicago.

I get out of the cab and gaze up at the high rise. Of course, his apartment is PH 57, as in penthouse on the 57th floor. My heart flutters a bit as I stare up at the modern building. I seriously cannot wait to see where he lives. I have only seen pictures of places like this in magazines and in features on the Beautiful Homes Network. Never in a million years did I ever expect to be invited into a penthouse.

A multimillion-dollar penthouse.

But the more I get to know William, the more I find myself in positions I never thought I'd be in. Like this one.

I enter the posh building and check in with the concierge, who calls William, and then I am allowed access to the pent-house level. I feel the butterflies shift in my stomach as the elevator ascends. I still can't believe I'm going to his *home*. That he wants me to pick out furniture with him. That I am going to spend the day with my boss on a Saturday and no business is involved.

The butterflies shift again. *But he doesn't feel like my boss,* my heart whispers. *William is William to me.*

The doors open to the 57th floor. I get off and nervously go to his door. I take a moment, draw a deep breath to fight the anxiousness, and ring the doorbell.

A few seconds later, he answers and greets me with a fabulous smile. "Thank you for being agreeable to the in-house decorating call." He gestures for me to step inside. "Please, come in."

I can't speak for a moment. Nor can I move.

Because, oh mother of God, he's wearing a gorgeous black leather jacket and jeans. *Jeans.* He is wearing freaking jeans, and I have never seen him in jeans. William Cumberland is known for his exquisite custom suits. For the rich sweaters, the sophisticated cashmere trench coat.

But, William—William, who invited me over to his home this Saturday afternoon—is in *jeans.*

He's beyond hot in this outfit. I'm distracted by the charcoal gray sweater, the white T-shirt peeking out underneath, the gorgeous black leather jacket ... My eyes flick over him, and I swallow hard. I feel my cheeks burning, and now I'm mortified because I checked him out head to toe and *more* than like what I see standing in front of me.

"Mary-Kate?" William asks, a crease forming on his brow.

"Um ..." I instinctively jerk at the scarf wound around my neck as I move past him. "Uh, I'm hot. I'm hot in these layers."

So now I'm trying to undo my scarf and not stare at him, which is hard because he's so totally gorgeous. I am tugging and unwinding the scarf and still staring at him in his damn leather jacket when *bam!* I crash right into his entry hall table and bang the hell out of my hip. I hear the glass table rattle loudly, and a very expensive-looking vase with flowers wobbles violently. Oh God, not his vase!

"Crap!" I yell, throwing myself forward, grabbing the vase before it topples over and shatters into a million pieces.

Whew! I saved it. *Thank God.* I exhale loudly.

"Mary-Kate?" William asks quickly. "Are you all right?"

Ugh, I want to die. Can I be a bigger idiot in front of him?

Never mind. I don't want to tempt fate by asking for the answer to that one.

"I'm so sorry," I say, forgetting the scarf for a moment and rubbing my hip, which is stinging like hell right now. "I didn't mean to run over your table. I—"

But then I look up and stop dead in my tracks. I actually gasp as I take in his penthouse. I cross to the center of the living room in front of me, and there is nothing but a wall of floor-to-ceiling windows providing a breathtaking view of Lake Michigan and the surrounding skyscrapers.

I continue forward, utterly entranced. "William," I gasp, my eyes not believing what I am seeing, "this … this … this is …"

"Rather quaint?" he quips behind me.

I turn around and find a smile playing at his full lips. "'Quaint' isn't the word I was looking for," I say, moving across the hardwood floor to the amazing windows. "This is breathtaking. This view … I can't get over this view."

I finish taking off my scarf and gloves and put them down on his black leather couch. I go to take off my coat, and within a second, William is behind me, helping me. This time, he's so close, I smell rich Italian leather and pine needles and, good God, he smells glorious.

"Thank you," I manage to say.

"You're welcome," he says, taking my coat and heading over to the hall closet.

I watch as he hangs it up. Holy crap, he hangs up his clothes. I have never been with a man who hangs up his coats.

Wait, I'm not with William, I remind myself.

"Here, let me give you a tour," he says, interrupting my thoughts. "Right now, I want to focus on the living room and study. Everything else can wait."

I nod and take my cell out of my purse. We walk through his penthouse, and I snap pictures of the rooms from all angles, my creative brain kicking into gear as I visualize how this place could look.

Even the kitchen has fantastic views of the city. It's beyond words. And he has every appliance known to man, all stainless steel, all practically restaurant-quality. I'm drooling simply by looking at them.

"Let's go back to the living room," William says.

I follow behind him, and I can't help it. I check out the view in front of me and, damn, his butt looks freaking *hot* in his jeans.

"I'm most interested in replacing the furniture in here," he says, turning toward me and gesturing with his hand. "It came with the place, and I loathe it."

"Hmm... I thought you only loathed the word 'but,'" I tease, smiling at him as I remind him of our conversation in the studio the day he made me his assistant.

William stares at me for a second, and I see a lightness shining in his gorgeous blue eyes. "I'm very flattered you remember that," he says, his eyes never leaving mine.

I feel the match flickering between us as we banter. I'm hot again, but this time, I have no layers to blame.

66

We walk down the hall, and he gestures for me to enter his bedroom. Oh dear God, I have to act normal as I look at William's *bedroom*? Can I be tested any more right now? Jeans? Leather jacket? *His bed*?

But it would be awkward and weird if I said no. What would be the reason? *Gee, William, I am fighting this intense attraction to you, and my mind gets all sexual at the idea of your bed, so can we skip this part of the tour for my mental health, please?*

I clear my throat and follow him into the room. I avoid looking at his bed and focus on the view, which is of the skyscrapers surrounding his building. At night, it must be beautiful in here. I can picture the light streaming in from the buildings in the dark and how sensual that sight must be—

"Okay, let's move on," I say, turning back around. I need to get out before I pass out on the floor with a thud.

But one thing I notice in my quick scan of his room, besides the view, is that he has no personal pictures in here. None were in the living room, either. No family pictures or pictures of friends ... there are no personal pictures of anything.

We're moving on to the study, and I decide to ask him about it.

"William," I say, snapping a photo of his study, "do you have any personal pictures? Anything I can frame and display?"

To be honest, I am motivated by curiosity as much as décor when I ask him that.

"No," he replies, his eyes intense on mine. "None."

I feel my brow crease. It is so ironic that the man who developed a social networking empire, one based heavily on people wanting to share details and pictures, has none in his home. If that isn't the height of irony, I don't know what is.

"Let's go back for a moment," William says, changing the

subject. "You have to see the master bathroom. It is brilliant, if I do say so myself."

We go back through his room and to the master bathroom. And as soon as I enter, I gasp out loud. The bathroom is magnificent. There are dual-head steam showers, raised sink basins, and the crowning jewel of it all: a raised bathtub that overlooks Lake Michigan.

"Wow," I gasp. "This is breathtaking."

William laughs. "I take it this receives your approval, Mary-Kate."

I'm about to answer when my phone rings. I glance down and then look up at him. "It's Arabella."

William's brow instantly creases. "What? Why is she calling you on a Saturday?"

I shrug and answer the phone. "Hello?"

"Nice of you to answer, MK," Arabella snaps at me in a clipped tone. "Do you happen to have any idea where Mr. Cumberland is? There is an urgent matter that needs his attention, and I am unable to reach him by mobile."

I glance at William for a moment, and his brow is still furrowed. "I am sure I can locate him if absolutely needed," I say.

She lets out an exasperated sigh. "Oh, really? Like, do you have ESP and you can figure out where he is? First of all, you should know his schedule at all times. If you do not know, you do not know. Don't be a twit about it. Just say you do not know where he is."

Okay, now I'm pissed. "Arabella, there is no need to call me a twit," I snap back at her.

William's eyes instantly flash. He grabs the phone from my hand and puts it to his ear, and I can hear Arabella yelling at who she thinks is me on the other end of the line.

Oh, I want to laugh so hard, I bite my lip.

But then I notice William's blue eyes are flickering with anger.

Big-time anger.

"Ms. Dalton," he says in a cold, controlled voice, "you shall *never* speak to Ms. Grant that way again. Ever. Or I will sack you, do you understand?"

Wow! He is *livid.* And if I were Arabella, I'd be shaking in fear.

A tingle of excitement whips down my spine as I realize that William is furious on my behalf.

"Now what is so urgent that you need to disrupt my Saturday afternoon?" he snaps. "Yes ... no ... fine ... Tell him to call me Monday ... All right. And to be clear, you shall treat Ms. Grant with the utmost respect. Your job depends on it."

Then he disconnects the call and hands me back my phone. "Does she always talk to you like that, Mary- Kate?"

"William, I can handle her."

"So that's a yes. That pisses me off."

"No need for it to," I say calmly, not wanting him to be irritated for the rest of the afternoon. "Now, are we going to go shopping? Because that is the only sport I enjoy."

I see the anger evaporate from William's beautiful eyes. He rakes his hand through his hair, making a mess of the unruly waves, and my breath catches in my throat. His hair is stunning. I wonder what it feels like.

Focus, I will myself. *Do not be distracted by the hair. Do not.*

"So," I continue, redirecting my thoughts to the task at hand, "are we ready to 'Keep Calm and Carry On?'"

William throws his head back, and the rich sound of his laugh echoes off the tiles, wrapping wonderfully around me.

"Watch it, Peppa."

Now I laugh, snorts included. But as we bundle up and get ready to leave, I do think I need to watch it. I glance at William's profile as we step into the elevator, and my heart catches. Because I know I could easily go through all the matches in my book for him.

And I could get badly burned at the end if I am not very, very careful.

Chapter Ten

As I step into the offices of the Beautiful Homes Network on Monday, I am beyond excited.

This morning, I am going to submit my article on redecorating William's office to Jennifer Lewis, the web editor for the Beautiful Homes Network. I feel the butterflies shift in my stomach at the thought. I worked on revisions yesterday and had William look it over one more time, and now it is ready to go. If she likes it—God, *please* let her like it— this could be the beginning of big things for me.

I get to my cubicle and begin unwrapping all of my winter layers. More good things happened. I have, as of this morning, five blog readers. And the only one I know personally is William. The other four found me, like my writing, and actually subscribed to my blog.

I am finally on my way, I think as I lean over and boot up my computer. Things are starting to happen for me with my career.

And things are happening with William, too, my heart adds, joining the conversation.

I head down the hall to get the water going for tea. I spent all afternoon with William on Saturday. We went to Michigan

Avenue, and he requested that I direct him to my favorite stores, rather than custom furniture stores or interior design studios that I know people with his type of wealth frequent.

So based on what I like, we went shopping at Crate & Barrel, Restoration Hardware, and Pottery Barn. I made him sit on furniture and pick up pillows and test everything.

It was funny. I could tell he usually has "people" do these things and has never done furniture shopping by himself.

I took loads of pictures of potential pieces for his penthouse. And then I made him take silly pictures, like ones of him testing out chairs at Pottery Barn. Then he insisted on taking my picture, too, and we were laughing our heads off and being completely stupid.

We were just being William and Mary-Kate, I think while filling the electric teakettle with water.

After we shopped, I made him stop at Gino's East, the famous Chicago pizzeria, for a break. William had never had it before, so he put me in charge of ordering, and we shared a thin crust pizza. We talked and laughed, and I think I went through half the matches in my book on Saturday alone.

I take a deep breath of air as more butterflies flutter around in my stomach. But this time, they aren't for my career.

They are for William.

In a few weeks, I will be in London. *With William*. I still can't even believe that it is happening. My life is changing so fast on so many levels.

I go back to my cube after I have the electric teakettle started and see William has slid in while I was in the break room. My pulse leaps, and I stick my head inside his doorway, as I am excited to see him.

He is already at his desk, talking to someone on speakerphone. William is in a crisp white dress shirt and, oh mother of God, he looks stunning in it.

As I am standing there trying not to drool on myself, he looks up at me. His laser eyes lock with mine and I know, without him saying a word, he wants me to wait until he is off the phone.

"No, that is not what I requested, and I anticipate this situation will be rectified immediately," William says firmly. "You have twenty-four hours to correct this problem, and I trust I will not have to follow up on it again. Do I make myself clear?"

Damn. William is hot when he is in full-on mogul mode.

He punches the off button on his phone and turns around in his chair. Then he brushes his fingertips against his lips and stares at me.

"I'm sorry, but the idiocy of some of the people employed at this group of networks is astonishing," he complains. "How did they get to this level? How?"

I smile knowingly at him. "Agreed," I say. Often, I felt like I was aboard the ship of fools at TATS, so I'm glad that William sees things the same way as I do.

He lowers his hands from his face. "Good morning, Mary-Kate," he says softly. "It's good to see you."

My pulse races as I see the way he is looking at me.

"Good morning," I reply. "It's good to see you, too."

Nothing more is said for a moment, and we simply stare at each other. The relationship has changed between us, that I know, but I also know this is the office. So I clear my throat and address the business at hand.

"I will be back with your tea in a moment, but I wanted to confirm that Guy Kennedy is arriving within a few minutes,"

I say. "I arranged for a car service to pick him up at the Four Seasons and bring him over for your meeting. I also ordered some whole grain, low-fat muffins and fresh organic fruit from a healthy café, and I will leave to pick that up once I have your tea ready."

William gazes at me with his piercing eyes, digesting my words. He has the fingertips back in steeple position, a dead giveaway that he is in assessment mode. "You know about the heart attack Guy Kennedy had a few years ago, don't you?"

"Yes. I did my homework as soon as you scheduled the meeting. I read how he changed his life habits and is a big proponent of healthy living."

Guy is one of William's trusted advisors, one of many he surrounded himself with because he's running an empire at such a young age. And I did read that Guy had a heart attack two years ago at age fifty.

I watch as William's eyes flicker in approval. "Brilliant. But I'm learning I should expect no less from you, Mary-Kate."

My heart flutters from the compliment. "Thank you," I say quietly. I go on to remind him of the three conference calls he has today, and that I made a reservation for lunch at an upscale seafood restaurant.

"Thank you," William says. Then he takes his fingertips down and stares at me. "Did you submit the article to Jennifer?"

"I'm going to this morning," I say, drawing an anxious breath. "I hope she likes it."

"Likes it?" William repeats, creasing his brow. "She is going to love it. It's brilliant, Mary-Kate."

"Well, I had a really good editor," I say smartly, smiling at him. "Thank you for doing that for me last night."

He grins. "My pleasure. Much more entertaining to read than the dismal ratings I had to go over last night for some of these networks."

"So Guy has perfect timing for his visit," I say knowingly.

"Yes, he does."

I nod. "I'm going to get your tea. Does Guy take tea as well?"

"Yes."

"I'll be sure to bring in an extra cup. I'll be right back."

I retrieve the water and fill his teapot. Then, as I do every day he is in Chicago, I prepare his tea and bring it into his office, and this time, I leave an additional cup for Guy. William is already taking another phone call, so I discreetly put the items on his desk and slip out without saying anything.

I bundle back up and take a taxi to the café, pick up the food, go back to the office on Michigan Avenue, and carry everything back up to my cubicle. When I near William's office, I immediately hear another British-accented voice. Obviously, Guy has arrived. I go to my cubicle and arrange the food nicely, then pause outside William's door, rapping on the frame lightly.

Both heads turn toward me.

"Mr. Cumberland, I have your breakfast," I say. Which sounds so freaking weird coming out of my mouth. To call him that when he is now *William* to me.

"Ah, yes, thank you, Ms. Grant," he says, standing up. And as he says "Ms. Grant," I see his beautiful blue eyes shining at me, as if to tell me he thinks calling me that is weird, too.

"Guy, I'd like you to meet my assistant, Ms. Grant," William says. "Ms. Grant, this is Mr. Guy Kennedy."

I put the tray down and extend my hand to Guy. "It is a pleasure to meet you in person, Mr. Kennedy."

Guy smiles warmly at me and shakes my hand. "Pleasure, Ms. Grant."

I arrange everything on the corner of William's desk. "Will that be all, Mr. Cumberland?" I ask.

William and Guy sit back down, and William's eyes burn into mine. "Yes. Thank you, Ms. Grant."

I nod and head out of the office. I am about to go back to my cubicle when I realize I didn't ask Guy if he took milk with his tea. Shit, I should go offer that.

I'm about to reach the doorframe when I hear my name. "I have heard a lot about MK," Guy says.

I stop in my tracks, listening.

"Really," William says flatly, as if he has zero interest in this topic whatsoever. My chest tightens a bit from his tone.

"Lots of rumors are flying around London," Guy says slowly, "that she is more than your assistant."

My face flames in humiliation and anger. *That freaking bitch Arabella must be slandering my name over there,* I think. *Which is the last thing I need since I am going over there with William soon.*

"That is utter rubbish," William says, interrupting my thoughts, "because I have absolutely no interest in Ms. Grant other than her performing well as my assistant. She is a nice girl and has been tremendously helpful with my transition to Chicago. And she is smart as a whip. I can see her being a tremendous asset to this company in the future. But beyond that? No. Outside of her professional capacity, there is *nothing* I am interested in. I don't get involved. Ever. And I don't intend to start with Ms. Grant. Now, shall we get on with ..."

I don't even hear the rest of what William is saying. My throat has closed up. He ... he ... oh, why are my eyes stinging with tears? Why does it hurt to breathe? Isn't this what I want? To be known as the very professional Mary-Kate Grant? To be known as a career woman? To be recognized as a "tremendous asset" in the eyes of the most powerful man in media?

So if that is true, which I tell myself it is, then why do I feel like William just picked up a sharp knife and launched the tip into my heart?

I successfully manage to avoid extended contact with William for the rest of the day, as he and Guy visit all the networks, take meetings, have power lunches, and the like. But even small interactions make me feel sick to my stomach, because all I hear in my head are William's words about me, about how I am just an assistant, and I feel like such an idiot that I had any kind of romantic notions about him at all.

So other than sending Jennifer an email with my article, I have autopiloted through the day, simply grateful that I have managed somehow not to burst into tears.

Finally, at six I poke my head into William's office. Guy has gone back to the hotel, and I know they are having dinner at the hotel at seven-thirty.

"I'm heading out now," I say, my tone formal. "Good night."

William raises his head from his computer screen. His blue eyes focus sharply on me, and he completely turns around in his chair, putting his fingertips together and brushing them against his lips. Oh no, he is totally assessing me now.

"Mary-Kate, is something wrong?"

"Absolutely nothing," I lie, forcing a smile. "Good night."

"I didn't dismiss you," he says firmly.

Now I'm pissed. I march into his office and put my hands on my hips. "Excuse me? Did you actually just say, 'Dismiss me?'"

William gets up and, moving around me, shuts the door and stands a few feet in front of me. "I am not letting you leave until I know why you are acting like this."

"Like what?" I snap, losing control of my emotions. "Tell me, William, how am I acting? Am I not being *helpful*? Am I not being a *nice* girl? Am I not *performing* well as your assistant?"

I see recognition flicker in his eyes.

"You heard what I said to Guy."

"I did. I'm glad to know I am a nice, helpful girl." I turn around and go to open the door, but his voice stops me.

"What would you like me to have said, Mary-Kate?"

I freeze. I turn around and see that William is now leaning against the edge of his desk, watching me with those intense eyes.

"What?" I ask, my heart pounding against my ribs.

"Please expand. You're the writer. How would you have scripted my response about you to Guy?"

Damn it. What do I say? I've opened my big mouth and let my emotions get out of control. And nobody has ever done that to me before, until now.

"I don't know," I snap, losing it. "I don't know anything anymore except that I feel like we're playing a game." Tears prick my eyes, but I blink them back rapidly in an effort to hide them.

"Is that what this is to you? A game?" William asks.

"What would you call it, Mr. Cumberland?" I reply defiantly. "If this isn't a game, what is it? Please, define it for me."

William stares at me with a creased brow but says nothing.

For once, I have rendered him speechless. "Exactly. Good night, Mr. Cumberland." I go to the door, open it, and walk out, shutting it behind me.

And as I do, I close the door on any notions of a romantic involvement with William Cumberland as well.

Chapter Eleven

I should be elated right now.

Jennifer Lewis loved my article for the Beautiful Homes Network and is going to put it on their site. In fact, she loved it so much that she scheduled a meeting to discuss future articles. I picked up ten new readers to my blog, too. So I should be happy. Happy that what I have wanted for so long—a successful career—is starting to happen.

But all of that fades into the background compared to my current state of misery.

It has been two weeks since that awful day in William's office, and we're right back to square one. We call each other by our last names, all of our interactions are business, and the days are horrifically long.

William has been irritable and short with people on the phone, while I have been fluctuating between being pissed off at myself, pissed off at him, then back to me for allowing myself to get into this mess in the first place.

And when I'm not pissed, I'm flat out miserable.

I haven't even blogged since our fight, as I can't think about anything else but him. My heart aches. I miss his texts, I miss his smile, I miss the sexy, witty way we bantered back and forth.

I just miss *him*. Everything about him. Which scares me to death. I mean, how did this happen to me? How did I let flirting escalate to ... to ... feeling like this?

Of course, I have kept my misery to myself. I didn't want to see the knowing look in Renee and Emily's eyes. And I can't talk to Michelle because she doesn't participate in any conversation that doesn't involve the wedding of the century.

All I want to do is run to an airline ticket counter, throw down my MasterCard, and purchase a one-way ticket to the south of France as an escape.

But since I'm about to board a flight to London, that isn't an option.

I draw a deep breath of air as I wait in the lounge at the gate at O'Hare. Now I get to sit next to William in luxury class, and what seemed like an awesome trip a few weeks ago seems like the voyage of the damned.

There is no sign of him anywhere. Of course, I know he is probably in the Premier Airlines Executive Club, as he is a member at the highest level. But I am so anxious about this trip and upset that I'm relieved I don't have to see him right now.

"Welcome to Premier Airlines Flight 1697 to London Heathrow," the gate agent announces, interrupting my thoughts. "We would like to extend an invitation for luxury class passengers to board at this time."

My stomach tightens as I have my ticket scanned. I board the aircraft and prepare to take my seat next to the window. The flight attendant takes my coat and offers me a glass of champagne, which I gladly accept. I sink down into the oversized seat and exhale.

I stare out the window at the workers below and feel like I want to throw up. How am I going to sit next to William for a whole transatlantic flight? *How?*

His deep baritone voice interrupts my thoughts. "I assume I can sit here," he says. "Unless you have managed to reseat me in cargo."

I turn my head the second I hear his voice. Oh mother of God, he's wearing the jeans and leather jacket. *The jeans!* He hands his leather jacket to the flight attendant, and now he's standing there in a pale blue dress shirt, one that makes his eyes look *so* blue. Oh, he looks devastatingly handsome.

I don't say anything. I turn. Looking at him for extended periods of time hurts too much.

William sits down and clears his throat. "Mary-Kate," he says slowly, deliberately, "you have to know you are more than an assistant to me."

My heart stops, and I turn to face him. His intense eyes burn into mine. I can't breathe.

"You have to know that," William repeats.

I notice he is flexing his right hand restlessly on his thigh, stretching his long fingers out and in. Then he lifts his hand, hesitates for a moment, and gently reaches for my hand. He entwines his fingers around mine and places our hands onto the table between us.

The second he touches me, the very instant his hand is wrapped over mine, I know everything is going to be okay. He hasn't explained anything to me, but the fact that William did this—that he is *holding my hand*—tells me everything I need to know.

"Mary-Kate, I had to throw Guy off," he says quietly. "I had to respond to gossip, which I *loathe*, in the way he's accustomed to. Which I did. Rather successfully, based upon your reaction."

William begins stroking the top of my hand with his finger-tips, and heat sears through me from the sensation of feeling his skin brush against mine.

"Why didn't you tell me that?" I ask in confusion.

William exhales. "I guess I was surprised you didn't see through me. You always do, Mary-Kate. And I wanted to hear how you thought I should have handled it."

"I'm sorry," I say, swallowing hard. "I'm really sorry."

William shakes his head. "I'm sorry, too. I should have said something to you before now. But after our row, after you asked me how I'd define us—I was confused. I had to sort things out."

"Have you sorted this out, William?" I ask softly, my stomach knotting up, as I'm almost afraid to hear what he has to say. What if he is holding my hand to soften the blow? Oh no, I hadn't thought of that.

"Mary-Kate, I know you want to know what this is between us," William continues. "I know you don't want a serious relationship, as you told me yourself. Am I wrong about that?"

Panic fills me. A full-fledged panic attack. I feel sweat on the back of my neck. My chest draws tight. *A serious relationship.* William wants to make sure that isn't what I want.

I can't breathe. I swallow hard, trying to calm the feeling that is threatening to take over me. Of course I don't want a serious relationship. I want my career. I don't need romantic complications.

Or do I?

The panic increases because my brain can't make sense of what is happening. Can someone change their mind after one weekend? Is that why I have been so upset?

Because I want something more, my heart whispers. *I'm upset because I want more from you, William.*

Crap, I have lost my freaking mind. Of course I don't want that.

"You're not wrong," I force myself to say with conviction. "And you don't want a relationship because of the demands of your empire, right?"

I watch as his eyes flicker, as he assesses my words. He looks away briefly and then back at me.

"Correct. So while I cannot define what we have," William says softly, his fingertips continuing to dance across the top of my hand, "I do know I want what we had back. Can we go back to being just William and Mary-Kate? Please?"

My panic evaporates. My heart feels joyful at his words. As I see the sincerity in his eyes, I know it is going to be okay. We can go back to having fun and being ourselves but knowing there is a line: the line where we become something serious, which we will never cross.

"Yes," I say, smiling at him as relief fills me. "Yes, we can."

William grins back at me. He moves his fingers so they are entwined with mine again. "I'm glad you are agreeable to this, Mary-Kate."

Just like that, sexy, flirty William is back. God, how I missed him. "I'm very agreeable, William," I reply smartly. He laughs and so do I.

"Hold on for a moment," he says as he picks up his iPhone and shuts it off. Then his hand is immediately back over mine, which sends shivers down my spine. "So what have you been up to since we had our falling out?"

I burst out laughing and then snort, which makes him laugh

loudly.

"Well, I haven't done a thing with your penthouse décor because I was so irritated with you," I tell him honestly.

I watch as his expressive blue eyes completely light up. Once again, I know William is not used to my honesty. And, once again, I instinctively know he likes it.

A smile plays at the corners of his full lips. "Is that so?"

"Very much so," I flirt back. "But since we have come to a mutually agreeable situation, I shall get on it."

"Speaking of getting on it, you haven't written on your blog."

"I'm flattered you were still checking it," I say, lifting an eyebrow at him.

"Well, as you would say, just trying to keep my finger on the pulse of American decorating and baking trends," he quips.

I laugh again, and he does as well.

"Speaking of trends," he continues, "once we are airborne, I want you to look at a marketing proposal for Connectivity and TATS. I want your thoughts on it."

I furrow my brow. "But I don't know anything about marketing."

"Irrelevant. You're brilliant. That's all I need."

My heart does an excited flip. William wants me to review a marketing plan. *He really does think I'm brilliant*, I think with a sense of amazement.

"What, did you think I exaggerated your brilliance to Guy?" he asks, stroking his fingertips over my hand again as he reads my mind in that uncanny way he has.

"Maybe."

"I didn't," he declares.

"Thank you," I say quietly.

85

"You're welcome," he whispers, his eyes locked on mine.

Here we are, mere inches apart. The world around me disappears, and I'm only aware of William. I can smell the pine scent on his skin. I drink in the glorious wavy hair, the way his cheekbones are so sculpted. I think of how he flirts with me, the way he makes me feel so beautiful and sexy and desired. The way he thinks I'm brilliant enough to review his marketing plans. My eyes shift back to his full lips.

I want him to kiss me. I want to know what that is like, to have William's mouth on mine, right here, right now.

I lift my eyes to meet his again, and he's staring back at me. I draw an eager breath. My heart is pounding. He has this look in his eye, and I know he is thinking what I'm thinking.

He leans a bit closer, dipping his head toward mine. I move toward him as well, desperate for this to happen. I *need* to kiss him. The desire is so intense and urgent and one I have never felt before. I need this like I need air. I need to kiss William like I need water or anything else to survive.

My pulse is racing as I tilt my face up. Our eyes are still locked. *Now. Kiss me now.*

"Welcome aboard Premier Airlines Flight 1679 to London. We are continuing to board …"

William jumps back the second the flight attendant's voice comes over the PA, as if he'd been in another world and was reminded he was in public. I hear him exhale, and he rakes a hand through his sexy dark waves, pushing them back into place, and then he directs his attention to the front of the cabin.

My heart is beating so fast I think it very well might explode. *Oh my God. Did we almost kiss?*

As I try to regain control of myself, William picks up my champagne glass and hands it to me.

"Since we are in public, perhaps a toast would be more appropriate," he says softly, acknowledging what almost happened. "This is a toast to you, Mary-Kate. And to all the adventures you may have in London. Cheers."

My heart is still pounding as I clink my glass against his. "Cheers," I say. I take a sip of the bubbly and swallow it down. I can't help but think my adventure has already begun.

And kissing William Cumberland is now at the top of my adventures list.

Chapter Twelve

I practically press my face against the glass of William's Bentley as the city of London rolls by on Tuesday afternoon. I'm in *London*. William has asked his driver to take us all over so I can see the landmarks before going to work. I see Big Ben ... The Tower of London ... Buckingham Palace ... It is amazing to be here!

"I'm *so* moving here one day," I cry in utter delight. "This is more fantastic that I even dreamed it could be."

I glance at William, who is scrolling through his iPhone.

"Well, I suppose if I need your assistance today, I should look for you outside of Buckingham Palace," he quips.

I laugh. "Or The Tower of London."

William gives me a sideways glance. "Or Harrods."

We both laugh. I grow serious for a moment as we drive through London, headed for The Shard, the modern office tower that is home to Connectivity. Today is my first day meeting everyone at headquarters, and I know it isn't going to be easy.

"What are you worried about, Mary-Kate?" William asks, giving me his full attention. "I can see it in your face."

"The people in the office," I admit. "I know they already

have an impression of me, and it's not favorable. They think ..." My face grows hot, as it is rather embarrassing to say what they think of me.

"They think what? That we are having an illicit affair? It is none of their business what we have, and if anyone says anything to you, I'll sack them."

William's light blue eyes blaze as he gets all badass mogul. Lord, could he be any hotter?

"I know, but—"

"No. You know I *loathe* that word," William says firmly. "You will take advantage of this opportunity to meet people and impress them with your intellect. *Full stop.*"

"You're right. But can I please tell Arabella to go screw herself? She is the one who started all this gossip in the first place. And I *loathe* her."

William roars with laughter, and I laugh, too. I realize he is right. To hell with what anyone thinks about me. I'm here to learn and experience new things for my career.

And as I watch him go back to his cell, my heart whispers that it wants to experience new things as well.

Before I know it, we're dropped by his driver at a glittery, modern high-rise. My pulse zips with excitement as I stare up at the glass building. The world headquarters for William's ever-growing media empire. Who would have thought I would be here just a few months ago?

"Ready to face your fans?" he quips.

I turn my gaze to him and note how gorgeous he looks on this cold London day. He's wearing his black cashmere trench coat and has the scarf wrapped just so around his neck.

And, good Lord, whoever would have thought I'd be here with William. William, who held my hand on the airplane yesterday. William who almost kissed me …

As I look at him, my doubts about gossips slip away. Screw them. Let them say what they want. Gossips and jealous people are in every workplace. I know what is important. This career experience is important.

And so is William.

"I'm more than ready," I say to him, tilting my chin up with confidence. "They can bring it."

He flashes me a brilliant smile. "Ah, very American of you. I rather like that."

Flanked again by his security team, we head into the building. Everyone stops when he appears, and you can tell his presence changes everything. People stare at him, quickly address him in greeting, and press elevator buttons for him. Holy crap, no wonder he didn't know how to pick out a chair at Pottery Barn.

We get into the elevator and ascend to the floor where his office is. His team goes to follow him, but William thrusts his hand out.

"You may take the next one," William says.

"But Mr. Cumberland—" one of them protests.

"No buts, I loathe that word. And I'll be fine," William assures them, punching the button to close the door.

As soon as it closes, I smile at him. "You know they hate when you go all independent on them."

"It's good to challenge them," he quips. "Anyway, I told Arabella to find a suitable place for you on this floor," William tells me as he yanks off his leather gloves.

"So I'm based out of a broom closet this week?" I ask, arching an eyebrow at him.

"Well, it will be handy if you spill anything. Which I will say is a strong possibility with your track record."

Instinct takes over, and I slug him on the arm. "Shut up."

I watch as his eyes completely light up. First, in surprise—I'm pretty damn sure nobody has ever slugged him in the office—and then, in delight. He roars with laughter and his eyes ... oh, they are so expressive. I can see he loves that I did that. And that I told him to shut up.

"Careful, Mary-Kate. I have not conducted your first employee review yet," William teases. "Telling your boss to shut up is not considered proper behavior, I believe."

"So, William, does that mean you want me to be a very good, proper girl?" I say, feeling flirty.

Oh dear God, did I just say that?

He hesitates for a moment. Then he rakes his hand through his glorious waves.

"You may be a very good girl, Mary-Kate, only if the situation deems it appropriate," he responds sexily, raising an eyebrow right back at me.

Now I am roasting in this elevator. I loosen my layers and try to act like this sexual banter is doing nothing to me at all.

Which is becoming very challenging.

The doors open, and we step out. I instantly stop. This office is *magnificent.* Everything is glass and modern and sleek. It screams future and technology, and it is so ... chic. Very, very chic.

"Mr. Cumberland, welcome back," a woman behind a black and glass reception desk says.

"Thank you, Ms. Reid," William says. "Ms. Bridget Reid, I'd like for you to meet Ms. Mary-Kate Grant, my assistant in the United States."

I watch Bridget's face. Her eyes flicker knowingly.

Yep. It's official. I'm William's whore.

91

But as I stand here right now, I shockingly realize I don't give a damn what she or anyone else thinks about me. I'm here for my career. I'm here for William. End of story.

"Hello," I say, extending my hand. "It's a pleasure to meet you."

"Likewise," she replies, shaking my hand. "I've heard a lot about you, Ms. Grant."

Ha, I bet you have, I think, smiling at her.

William leads me through the floor, introducing me to all the different people. Everyone is very pleasant and nice, but I can see in their eyes, in the female eyes in particular, the look of "Oh, *this* is the infamous MK."

Finally, we come to William's office. Which means we have now come to Arabella.

"Ms. Dalton, how are you?" William asks, sweeping past her and into his office. "Ms. Grant, you may drop your things in here until you have a chance to get situated."

Arabella swivels in her chair, and her green eyes narrow for a split second. She stands up and follows us into William's office.

"Mr. Cumberland, it's good to have you back," she says, smiling brightly at him. "I will have your afternoon tea brought in at once."

"Thank you," he says, taking off his scarf and coat.

Arabella turns to me and flashes me a smile that I know she does not want to give. "MK, I hope your journey was favorable."

Right. If she had an ejector button, I would have been dumped out over the Atlantic in flight.

"Very much so, thank you," I say as I put my Modalu tote bag down on one of William's guest chairs.

"Mr. Cumberland, please remember your one o'clock meeting with advertising," Arabella says. "I will have lunch brought in for that."

"Fine," William says, going around to his desk and sinking down into his chair. "Ms. Grant, I would like for you attend that meeting please."

Arabella's nose wrinkles. "But, Mr. Cumberland, I will take the notes for the meeting as I always do. Ms. Grant can be freed to do something else."

William quickly swivels around in his chair. Oh God. I see it in his eyes. He hasn't been here fifteen minutes, and he's already majorly annoyed with Arabella.

"Ms. Dalton, I believe as owner and chief executive officer of this company, I do not need to run a list of meeting attendees past you for personal approval," he says bluntly. "Furthermore, I still need you to take notes and distribute the action plan. Ms. Grant will attend the meeting in a different capacity. One that I do not need to explain to you. Am I clear?"

Bah ha! I do my best to keep a neutral face, but I really want to laugh.

"Of course, Mr. Cumberland." Arabella nods gravely.

"Now please show Ms. Grant where she will be working during her stay here," William says. Then he looks at me. "Come back here a little before one, Ms. Grant, so I can go over some things with you."

"Yes, Mr. Cumberland," I say, grabbing my tote and purse.

"Follow me," Arabella says with a pinched smile.

I follow her out of William's office. She is striding angrily before me, slamming her stilettos down on the hardwood floor, and I'm practically running trying to keep up with her.

We twist and turn through the building, and I know she

found the cubicle farthest away from William that she could to stick me in.

"Here," she snaps, stopping in front of a vacant cubicle area.

I catch my breath and look around. It is obvious this area is designed for future expansion, as it consists of half-constructed cubicles and boxes of office supplies. In fact, my cubicle has two walls, one open side where a wall should be, and boxes and boxes of crap shoved off to one corner of the desk.

Wow. The broom closet might have been nicer.

"Thank you," I say, putting my tote bag down.

"Are you going to run to Mr. Cumberland and tell him you don't like it?" Arabella says with a fake sweetness in her voice. "I mean, everyone here knows you have him eating out of your hand."

I turn around as I shimmy out of my coat. She wants to go there with me? Okay, fine. I'll go.

"First of all, nobody controls anything Mr. Cumberland does," I say firmly, draping my coat across the back of my desk chair. "And, no, I would never bother him with something as trivial as a cubicle. I don't believe in wasting his time with matters like this, do you?"

Arabella cocks her head to one side. "Oh, you are so full of it, MK. We all know you've somehow cracked the code on William Cumberland. He's intrigued by you—God knows *why*, but he is. Do tell, are you shagging the hell out of him? Because I think that would be your only intriguing quality."

Rage fills me. I seriously want to slap her across the face. My temper is lit, and I say the first thing that comes to mind.

"You," I say, staring Arabella dead in the eyes, "can screw off. And I hate to disappoint you, but I don't give a shit what you say or think about me."

Arabella blinks. I don't waver. I can tell this reaction isn't what she had hoped for.

"Well, that's all fine and well that you don't care," she declares in a huff. "But let me give you some insider information. William might be fascinated with you and America now, but rest assured *London* is his home. Not Chicago. He will come back here permanently by June and, trust me, he's not coming back with *you*. You are stark raving mad if you think anything different."

Then she turns on her heel and storms off before I can go another round with her.

I'm so angry I'm shaking. How dare she say these things to me? But even though I am livid, a bigger emotion is sweeping through me.

Fear.

Yes, I know William and I will never be in a serious, long-term relationship. We both agreed that would be best in light of what we have going on with our careers right now.

But I never thought about him leaving Chicago for London on a permanent basis.

So if that is the case, if I know I will never be with William like that, why does the thought of him leaving make me feel absolutely terrified inside?

Chapter Thirteen

I sit and watch the video presentation in the large conference room. The advertising team is showing William their latest campaign idea for cross-promoting Connectivity with the networks.

I glance across the table and see that he has his head down, typing on his iPhone.

I watch him, as I have been stealing glances at him throughout this boring presentation, I let Arabella's words go right into my mental trash can. I'm living in the now. I'm not worried about the future.

And the now includes studying how William's gorgeous dark-brown waves look when his head is bent over. I bet his hair would feel like silk if I were to touch it—

My phone silently vibrates in my lap. I glance down and see I have a new text message:

I'm gone for more than two months, and this is the best campaign they can come up with? WC

I stifle a laugh and text him back:

Are you going to express your displeasure? MKG

I hit send and wait. I glance at William again, and now he's holding his phone against his chin, acting like he is very interested and deep in thought, which I know he's not.

I quickly add a second message:

Nice move with the phone on your chin. You look very intrigued by this crap advertising campaign. MKG

Then I hit send again.

William lowers his phone and glances at it as my messages come across. I know when he has read the last one, because the corners of his full lips pull up into a slight smile.

Finally, the presentation ends and Jecca Brown, the head of advertising, shuts off the TV and looks at William for feedback.

"Your thoughts, Mr. Cumberland?" she asks.

He sets his phone down. Then he puts his fingers together and rests them against his lips. He is silent for a moment and stares hard at Jecca.

"I'm rather astonished to see that in the months I have been in America, your team has only managed to put together this crap advertising campaign," William declares. "Please, Ms. Brown, expand on how on earth you thought I would be on board with a campaign with absolutely *zero* edge to intrigue the younger demographic. I'm all ears."

Ooh, William is pissed and in full-on badass mogul mode.

And I'm secretly giddy he used my saying.

The room falls deadly silent after he speaks. I think you could hear a pin drop; it is that quiet and tense.

Jecca quickly starts speaking, trying to explain the campaign to William. I watch as a lot of backpedaling and new ideas are frantically being thrown about. He's still annoyed—I see that in his eyes—and finally he ends the madness and sends them back to the drawing board.

Once everyone scurries away, it is me, Arabella, and William left in the conference room.

"Ms. Dalton, please type up the action items, recap this meeting, and distribute to the group," he says, nodding at her. Then he turns to me. "Ms. Grant, please review the creative points and note my thoughts, and then we'll meet to review that."

Arabella shoots me a look. Obviously, anything William needs is her ordained duty, and I should only be around to make copies and file.

She flounces past me, and I follow her out, even though I'd like to stay and talk to William.

I take the long walk back to banishment, and by the time I am there, my phone vibrates with a new message:

I need to get out tonight. Dinner? WC

William wants to take me to dinner! My heart jumps excitedly in response. But I decide to play this smart and type back:

I shall dine with you only if you promise to take me on the London Eye at some point during my stay. MKG

I wait to see if he will put up with my ridiculous, touristy request.

Done. I'll pick you up at 7 at your hotel. Wear something sharp. WC

Every nerve in my body explodes with his last text. I'm going out in London *with William.* Somewhere nice, where I need to dress up ... I'm so happy I could burst with joy.

Who knows what the future holds in June. I don't care about that right now.

All I care about is tonight.

* * *

I draw an excited breath and take one final check of my appearance in the hotel bathroom mirror. It is a few minutes before seven, and I want to make sure I look perfect for tonight.

I'm wearing a cocktail dress, but not your ordinary little black dress. No, I like the unexpected. So I am wearing a cream, cap-sleeved dress, one that has a folded collar neckline that plunges into a V. The dress falls right below the knee but has a sexy slit up to mid-thigh on the right side to flash a little leg. High, strappy silver heels and a silver cuff bracelet complete the look.

I pick up my skinny, black satin hairband and slide it into my hair. Then I touch up my apricot lip-gloss and spritz my neck with Versace perfume.

There, I think, staring at my reflection. *I'm ready.*

I hear a knock at my door. Butterflies take off in my stomach. *William is at my door. To take me on a dinner date.*

I want to scream it from the top of my lungs. I have never been this excited to go on a date in my entire life. I make myself walk slowly to the door—despite the fact that I want to run—and check the peephole to confirm it is him.

It is indeed William. He's wearing a gorgeous black suit and tie.

A tie!

I unlock the door and open it. All I can do is stare at him because he looks impossibly dashing tonight.

William is in a gorgeous black suit. Prada, I am sure, as he has told me that is one of his favorite lines. A crisp white dress shirt is underneath, and he is wearing a sharp black tie.

I swallow hard. He's beyond perfect. My eyes meet his, and I realize he is looking at me in the same way. His light blue eyes flicker over me in an intense gaze, one that makes my pulse jump wildly in response.

"My God, Mary-Kate," William whispers. "You look beauti-ful."

I feel my cheeks burn from the compliment. "Thank you. Please come in," I say, opening the door for him. "And you look rather handsome yourself tonight."

William steps past me, and I smell the familiar scent of him, of his soap and pine needles. Oh, how I love that smell.

"Let me get my coat," I say, walking over to the sofa in my suite. I pick my coat up, and William is right there to help me put it on. I turn to him and smile, and he is still staring at me with those intense eyes. "Thank you," I say.

"You're welcome," he replies. He rakes a hand through his hair, and my breath catches as his wavy strands get all ruffled up. "Are you ready?"

"Yes." I grab my silver clutch. He sweeps his arm out to gesture for me to go first, and I do. But I somehow manage to trip over my own feet and go flying forward, about to crash right into the coffee table until I feel William's strong hands on me, catching me as I stumble.

He turns me around so we're inches apart. His arms are now around my waist. As I look up at him, I see his mouth curved up into a smile.

"Are you all right?" he asks.

"Um, yes," I manage to say.

"Good. Because I would hate to see you fall and cut your head on the edge of the coffee table. A nasty gash here," William says, slowly rubbing his thumb across my forehead, "might have required stitches. We'd be late for dinner, and that would be tragic, wouldn't it?"

Heat sears through me the second his thumb brushes across

my forehead.

"Um, yes," I manage again. "Tragic."

"Shall we go? I have reservations at Alain Ducasse, and we don't want to be late."

"That restaurant is *famous*," I gasp.

"So does this restaurant meet with your approval?" William asks, smiling back at me.

"Yes!" I cry excitedly.

He laughs and places his hand on the small of my back. "Then let's go."

I begin walking and relish the feel of his fingertips on my back, as if guiding me in a protective way. We haven't even left the hotel, and it is already the best date I have ever had.

We take the elevator down to the lobby of the chic boutique hotel and walk out into the chilly March air, with his detail discreetly following behind us.

"I'm right there," William says, nodding in the direction of several expensive cars that are all lined up.

"Wait, you're driving?" I ask, delighted.

William grins. "Yes, I am."

I watch as he reaches into his coat pocket and takes out his keys. He hits the fob, and the lights of a sleek silver Aston Martin flicker.

I stop dead in my tracks. I literally feel my jaw drop open. "You drive an *Aston Martin*?" I exclaim.

William bursts out laughing as we walk toward his car. "Well, technically it is a One-77 Aston Martin, but, yes, I drive one."

I stand at the passenger door, still in awe. "This costs as much as a house."

"It is one of only seventy-seven made in the world," William explains.

I stare at him, then back at the car. "Holy crap," I gasp.

"It is one of my indulgences," he says. Ever the gentleman, he quickly opens my door for me.

"Thank you," I say, slipping into the seat.

"You're welcome," William says, shutting my door. He circles around to the driver's side, slips behind the wheel, and starts the car. Damn it, how can I be expected to be cool and collected when he is driving a car like this? Sexy man, sexy car... I clear my throat and refocus.

"This is a gorgeous car." Then I laugh. "Sometimes I forget you have money."

He glances at me as he pulls out into London traffic. "I like that about you," he says quietly. "More than you know."

My heart stops. I study his profile, his perfect cheekbones and glorious hair and the way he just glanced at me out of the corner of his eye.

I'm so falling for you, William. More than you know.

We reach Alain Ducasse at The Dorchester, and it is beyond posh. It is absolutely stunning inside. Contemporary and sophisticated. I cannot believe I'm here.

As we are led to our table, I eagerly drink in the experience with my eyes. I want to remember every moment of this night.

After discussing the menu, and because William wants me to have the full experience, we start with an assortment of appetizers. He is so food-savvy, so educated on wines, so different than any man I have ever known. We finally order, and I get fish. William dines on beef, and the service is impeccable all evening, as is the food. Conversation flows freely between us the entire night and, in a word, it is perfect. This is the most perfect evening I have ever had in my life.

I gaze at him in this setting, wondering how on earth I got

here, to be with this incredible man right now. *Blessed*, I think. *I am blessed.*

After our entrees are cleared from the table, William raises an eyebrow at me. "Cheese course?" he asks.

I smile at him. "You tell me, William. You are the gourmand here."

He laughs, that gorgeous laugh that makes the breath catch in my throat. "Yes, well, then we shall."

So we finish the evening with a delicious assortment of French cheeses and condiments, and it is the most amazing end to the best meal I have ever had.

"Thank you so much for this," I say after we have finished. "It was spectacular. And I know it cost a fortune."

William rubs his lower lip with his fingertips, and my pulse jumps in response. "Ah, yes, it was expensive, but I did check my bank account before leaving home. Luckily for you, I can just manage to afford it."

I laugh, and so does he. We leave the restaurant, which makes me sad. The evening has come to an end, but I'm not ready for it to be over. We're back to my hotel in no time, and William idles the car out front. I bite my lip. I'm not ready to let him go. I don't want to call it a night.

"William," I say impulsively, turning toward him, "would you like to come up for some coffee?"

He stares at me, a crease on his brow. "Come up to your hotel room?"

Oh crap. I asked him to my hotel room. I merely want to keep talking to him, but now I realize this invitation has taken on a whole new meaning.

I feel my cheeks flaming. "For conversation," I blurt out.

"Conversation," William repeats, his brow still furrowed.

Shit. Why didn't I ask him to get a coffee at the lobby bar?

"I don't think it is appropriate, Mary-Kate, that I come up to your hotel room for coffee," he says slowly.

I want to die. I want to punch him on the arm and yell, "Ha, just kidding. See you tomorrow!" But that isn't an option since William can read every thought in my head.

"Right. Of course," I say, beyond embarrassed.

"It wouldn't be appropriate because I don't drink coffee. But I will come up for tea and conversation," he declares as a huge grin passes over his face.

"William!" I yell as I realize he was teasing me the whole time. "Don't do that to me!"

He roars with laughter, and despite my efforts not to, I do, too. He whips the Aston Martin into the valet lane. We make our way back to my room. I swipe the key card and let us in, and remove our coats, with William helping me take off mine first.

I grab the room service guide and hand it to him. He places an order for tea and then hangs up the phone while I make myself comfortable on the guest couch in my living area.

William takes off his suit jacket and tosses it onto the back of the desk chair. We look at each other for a moment, and I wonder if his pulse is racing like mine is right now.

He sinks down onto the couch next to me, and I can't help but think I'm the luckiest girl in the world right at this moment.

"William, thank you so much for tonight," I say, staring at him. "I feel incredibly lucky."

"Lucky?" he asks, his eyes searching mine.

I nod. "That I got to have this amazing experience in London," I say softly. "I had the dining experience of a lifetime. I got to sit in this gorgeous restaurant and have this incredible conversation and meal. But most of all, I'm lucky because I got to share this experience with *you*. I wouldn't want this experience with anyone else."

I watch as his blue eyes take in my words. Then I see the intensity flash within them.

I know the moment has come.

William leans in closer to me. I can't breathe. My heart is racing faster than it ever has in my life.

"Mary-Kate," he whispers, "I know it is probably most inappropriate for a boss to kiss his assistant."

"Yes," I whisper back, my eyes never leaving his. "It probably is."

I watch as William lifts his hand. He hesitates for a moment, and then ever so slowly, brushes a finger against the side of my face. Every nerve I have jumps the second his warm skin makes contact with mine.

"With that being said," he whispers sexily, his eyes searching mine, "I am asking if I can kiss you."

His fingertips are dancing against my cheekbone, and I swallow hard.

"You're asking for permission, William?"

"I am," he says, tenderly stroking my skin with his fingers.

"Permission granted," I whisper to him.

And then his mouth is on mine. First, it is a brush of his lips. A simple kiss that makes my heart slam against my ribs. Heat sears through me the second our lips meet. His mouth slowly caresses mine open in a slow, sensual kiss. His tongue sweeps inside my mouth, sending heat searing through me. Oh, God. His kiss is sensual and hot, and I'm lost in his warmth, his scent, his taste. I wind my fingers through the curls at the back of his head, moaning softly as he continues to explore me with his lips and tongue. I feel the barest hint of stubble scratch deliciously against my face; I relish the way his mouth is eager to take from mine.

One of his hands slides around my back, pressing me closer to him as he deepens the kiss. The other is entwined in my hair, caressing it. I move both my hands around his neck, drawing him to me, my tongue matching his tempo as we discover each other for the first time.

He moves his lips from mine, and a whimper of protest involuntarily escapes my lips. William's mouth begins moving from my jawline down the side of my neck. I shiver in delight and tilt my head back, giving him greater access to it. I close my eyes as he continues to kiss me, and then his mouth stops on my pulse point, his tongue sweeping over the spot and causing a gasp to escape my lips.

"Your pulse," he whispers against my neck, his words coming out in a hot rush against my skin, "is as rapid as mine."

Then he kisses me again in the very same spot.

I'm still trembling as William makes his way back up my neck, to my jawline, and his lips are finally back on my mouth, where he oh-so-gently brushes his lips against mine. Then he presses his forehead to mine in the sweetest of gestures. "May I do that again?" he asks softly.

"You don't have to ask permission anymore," I whisper. "Just kiss me."

William's mouth claims mine once again, his lips demanding immediate access, his hands moving up my back and to my hair as his kisses burn against my mouth. His hands are caressing me, his mouth is devouring mine, and I grasp onto his shoulders as I lose myself in his arms. One of his hands snakes up to the back of my head, then to my hairband, and he removes it. A groan escapes his throat as my hair falls freely into his hand, and I kiss him back harder in response.

Now I know what I have been missing my entire life. William is passionately kissing me and touching me, and I match every move, drowning in this man with a desperate need I have never known before this moment.

"My God," he murmurs against my mouth, "why did I wait so long to do this?"

I respond by lifting my hands to his hair. "I don't know. But I don't want you to stop," I urge him.

William responds by kissing me harder. I tug on the hair at the back of his head; he responds by taking my lower lip between his teeth and sucking on it.

Oh. My. God.

Can this be any hotter? Can it?

William eases me back on the couch, his entire body weight resting on top of me, and his hands move up my bare arms, stroking me as his lips continue to ravish mine. I have never known a feeling as delicious as this, as having William's body pressed against mine, his mouth as desperate for me as I am for him.

Our bodies and mouths remain entwined until there is a knock on the door from room service.

"Bloody hell," William whispers, breaking our kiss. "Why did we order anything anyway?"

I laugh and give him a light kiss on the lips. "Go get it. I'm not going anywhere."

He smiles and goes to the door. Our tea is brought in, and after William tips, we are left alone. Since we are content to make out like two teenagers, the tea remains untouched for the rest of the night as we go right back to where we were before there was a knock on the door—kissing passionately. We continue to kiss even after our lips have gone numb.

Eventually, we stop, and I snuggle up against him, blissfully listening to how his heart is racing underneath his dress shirt. He plays with my hair, and I fiddle with his tie, wishing this night would never end.

"What time is it?" William finally asks.

"I don't care," I say honestly.

He chuckles, lifts my head toward him, and brushes his lips against mine. "I don't want to care, but I have a meeting early tomorrow."

He raises his arm and reaches around me to see his watch. "Damn, it's after one o'clock. I need to go, Mary-Kate. I have an eight-thirty in the morning, and I need to look at some stuff tonight."

"Okay," I say, not meaning it at all.

William gets up and slips into his suit jacket and then his coat.

I reluctantly follow him to the door.

He slides his hands up to my face and tilts it up toward him, giving me another hot, sensual kiss before he opens the door.

"I'll see you tomorrow," he whispers, pressing his forehead against mine and linking my hands with his. "Good night."

"Good night," I say, wishing he would stay. "See you tomorrow."

He goes out the door. I shut and lock it, leaning against it. Electricity flows through me, and I brush my fingers against my lips, reliving every kiss he gave me tonight.

Then I hear my cell phone ring, and I know it is him. I go over to my purse and fish it out. And there's a message from William on my iPhone:

Sweet dreams Mary-Kate. Already cannot wait to see you tomorrow. WC

"Ahh!" I squeal happily, flopping down onto the couch. I eagerly text him back:

Be careful going home. Cannot wait to see you, too. MKG

I put down my phone and grin. I know it will be impossible to sleep tonight, with thoughts of William kissing me running through my head.

And if there were any matches left in my book, I blew through the rest of them tonight.

Chapter Fourteen

I'm in a frantic rush to get ready for work. Of course, after a rather delicious night of making out with William, I couldn't sleep until like four in the morning and now I'm running late. Way late, which is not like me at all.

I quickly throw my head upside down and run my brush through it. I flip back up, grab a black quilted hairband, and shove it into place. I move as fast as I can in my gray wrap dress to my closet and remove my tall black boots. I am pulling them on when there is a surprise knock on my hotel door.

"Room service," a male voice announces.

What? I didn't order room service. Confused, I walk to the door and look through the peephole. Sure enough, there is a cart with a covered dome. And a large bouquet of flowers in a stunning vase.

My breath catches in my throat. William must have sent me flowers. I quickly open the door.

"Good morning, Ms. Grant," the man says. "Per Mr. Cumberland, we are to deliver breakfast and this to you," he says, handing me the stunning arrangement of flowers.

I take the vase, which holds white roses and hydrangeas, and inhale before putting them down. Meanwhile, the server sets up a table for me with toast, eggs, juice, coffee, fruit, yogurt ...

"All of this is for me?" I ask, eyeing the huge spread.

"Yes, Ms. Grant," he says. "This is for you, too." Then he hands me a card.

"Thank you," I say, my heart jumping as I take the envelope.

"Have a good day, Ms. Grant." The server leaves, shutting the door behind him.

I excitedly tear open the card and read:

Mary-Kate,

Good morning. I was not sure what you liked for breakfast, so I ordered a variety of items. Hopefully, you will find something that suits you. Please come to the office later if you wish. I am going to be tied up until at least 10:30. But I'm very much looking forward to seeing you today. WC

P.S. I hope the flowers smell as beautiful as the perfume you were wearing last night.

I clutch the card and read it over and over. I'm so happy and excited and just blown away by his kindness, his thoughtfulness, and the lovely comment he made about my perfume. Oh, what is this man doing to me?

Of course, I'm going to get to the Connectivity offices as soon as I can. One, to prove I am a professional, and two, to hopefully get a glimpse of William through the glass panels of his ultra-modern conference room so I can see him in mogul action, which is always a turn-on.

I nosh on a piece of toast and finish getting ready. Then I bundle up—it is cold and rainy today—grab my red umbrella, and head out to get a cab.

As I ride through London, my cell phone goes off. At least I know it is not Arabella. She is probably seated next to William in that meeting and assisting him.

I bite my lip. That annoys me. *I* should be the one helping him. I sigh as I pull out my phone. But she is the lead assistant here, and whether I like it or not, she gets to be his right-hand person.

I have a hard time with that idea, especially after last night. But I shove the thought aside. I glance down at my phone, and to my delight, I see it's a text from William:

Please tell me you are wearing one of your hairbands today. I rather like those on you. WC

My cheeks are burning from his flirty little text. I respond:

It is your lucky day. I am. Thank you for breakfast and the beautiful flowers. You are too generous to me. P.S. Aren't you supposed to be running an empire meeting right now? MKG

My spine tingles as I await his response. Which comes rapid fire:

I'm bored with this meeting and these people. I want to see you. WC

Ooh! He can't focus! Butterflies take off in my stomach knowing he is as distracted as I am. However, I decide to tell him what he needs to do. William likes that about me anyway:

You, sir, need to focus. Quit texting me. MKG

I smile to myself and wait. Again, an instant response:

Bossy American. See you later this morning. WC

I laugh out loud and drop my phone back into my bag. Soon I arrive at Connectivity World Headquarters. I make my way to William's floor and decide to take the extra-long route to banishment, which will require me to pass by the conference room. I unbutton my coat so he can see my wrap dress, black opaque tights, and tall, heeled boots.

Hmm. I feel like a bit of a seductress. Which is so funny,

because I've done anything like this in my life. I have never *wanted* to before. But I feel like I know what I'm doing, so perhaps watching all those episodes of *Is it Love?* did pay off in some form or another.

I turn the corner and spot the conference room in front of me. I see William talking at the head of the table. Then he puts his fingertips to his lips as he listens to someone respond. I watch as his eyes move, scanning the other people in the meeting to watch their facial responses and assess what they are thinking.

Then he sees me.

William immediately drops his hands away from his face and stares at me. His eyes change. They are *intense* now. I flash him a flirty smile and watch as he completely loses focus. His eyes remain on me, and only me. I turn the corner and grin to myself as a shiver of electricity shoots down my spine. Ah, yes, this seductress thing is kind of fun.

I get back to my desk, take off my coat, put down my bag, and get ready to start my day. Of course, Arabella has left me a stack of crap to do, like make thousands of copies of stuff I am not even sure she needs but provided as a means to keep me away from William's office.

About a half hour into typing labels for her new filing system—blah, like I am *her* assistant—my cell goes off with a text alert:

Meeting over. Please come to my office. Bring a stack of folders with papers. WC

Yay! I finally get to see William. I grab a bunch of folders and toss some copies in them. I carry them like I'm carrying the most important FBI files in the world, all business, all official, and head toward his office.

I'm about to enter his office when Arabella sees me coming.

"Whatever you have, MK, I will take in for you," she says stiffly from her chair. "Mr. Cumberland has an extremely tight schedule today."

Is it wrong that I really want to punch her?

"Mr. Cumberland asked me to bring these to him," I say firmly.

"I shall give them to him," Arabella says coolly, standing up.

"Ms. Grant, is there a reason why you are delaying in bringing me those files?" William snaps from his doorway, looking all CEO-like.

I turn to Arabella and lift an eyebrow. She glares at me, which makes me want to laugh. "Coming, Mr. Cumberland," I say, entering his office. He shuts the door behind me and then strides over to his desk. I glance out of his window and see Arabella craning her neck to see what we are doing.

"Okay, so I'm now acting like I am reviewing these documents for you," I say, flipping open a folder.

"Well played," William says, studying me. "But I do have a serious issue to discuss with you, Ms. Grant." His eyes are shining brightly, and I know he is about to tease me.

"Yes, Mr. Cumberland?" I ask, playing along.

"In regard to last night," he says, leaning back in his leather chair and putting his fingertips to his lips in that steeple position, "it was not exactly appropriate for me to kiss you, was it, Ms. Grant?"

I cock my head to one side. "No, it was not, Mr. Cumberland."

"It was reckless."

"Indeed. Very reckless."

I watch as he removes his hands and reveals his handsome

114

face to me. "While there is truth to that," he says, picking up a silver pen and clicking it, "I have never been so bloody glad to be reckless in all my life."

Ooh! My heart leaps with that comment.

"Me, too," I admit, smiling at him.

"I want to see you tonight," he says.

I flip a page in the folder. "Hmm. It could be possible."

William furrows his brow. "Possible?"

I give a fake sigh. "My schedule might be free for you."

"I see," he says, his mouth curving up in a sexy smile. "Well, if you are indeed free, would you like to come over to my place for dinner? We can eat and watch the telly, if you find that to be an acceptable arrangement."

My breath catches in my throat.

William is inviting me to come over to his place.

"I find that very acceptable," I reply calmly, my voice not betraying the pure elation I feel inside because of his invitation.

"Don't dress up," he says. Then he cocks an eyebrow at me. "Wear what you would for an *Is it Love?* night with the girls."

"William, come on. That is a hoodie and yoga pants," I blurt out.

"That," he says, "is who you *are*. And that is who I want to see tonight."

My heart is melting. Seriously melting. "All right," I say, shutting the folder. "I will see you tonight."

"I'll pick you up after my conference call at six."

"No," I tell him, shaking my head. "It would be more discreet if I take a cab."

William frowns. "I don't like that. I can send my driver for you."

"I know you can, but let's be smart about this. Just because we didn't get caught last night doesn't mean we will always be so lucky."

He stands up. "But we're not doing anything wrong."

"I know that, and you know that, but you know how it is."

William rakes a hand through his waves and lets out a sigh. "Right. You're right." He nods toward the window. "Is Arabella still staring?"

I casually glance out into the hallway. As soon as Arabella sees me, she snaps her head back around. "Oh, yes. She is trying to spy."

"You'd better go back," William says. Then he groans. "And send her in on your way out so I can give her some stuff to do so it looks like I am being a bloody boar to both of you."

"Okay," I say, laughing. "You can yell at me for good measure on the way out."

William grins at me. "Fine. If you insist, I'll yell." I'm about to go out the door when he stops me. "And, Ms. Grant?"

"Yes?" I say, stopping and facing him.

"You look beautiful," he tells me softly. "Rather distracting, actually. I thought you should know that before I yell at you."

Happiness sweeps through me from the compliment. "Thank you," I reply, smiling softly at him.

William gets up and moves behind me. "Okay, ready?" I nod and open the door.

"And, Ms. Grant, I anticipate you will be able to have those reports to me by the close of business today," he says in his badass mogul tone as we exit. "I realize London might seem like a holiday, but it is *not*. It is imperative that you focus."

Bah ha ha! Focus. William is the one who can't focus today.

"Yes, Mr. Cumberland, understood," I reply seriously.

I briskly walk over to Arabella. "Mr. Cumberland would like

to see you now," I say, dropping my voice. "And, good luck; he's in quite a mood."

She blinks. I shake my head gravely and resist the urge to skip past her right down the hall. I have a date with William tonight. In the intimate setting of his home.

And something tells me I'd better get a new matchbook for this evening.

Chapter Fifteen

I step out of the cab after it stops at William's apartment building in Mayfair. I take a deep breath and gather myself on the sidewalk, gazing up at the ten-story building, and, in particular, the top floor, where I know he is waiting for me.

William Cumberland, founder and owner of Connectivity. William Cumberland, one of the most powerful players in the media industry. William Cumberland, one of the wealthiest men in the world. William Cumberland, my boss.

But that isn't who William Cumberland is to me. At all.

To me, he's just *William*. William, the amazing man I find myself falling harder and faster for every second I'm with him.

I know this is so, so dangerous.

I know it is probably wrong.

I know I could end up getting hurt if I'm not careful.

And I know I absolutely don't care.

The one thing I am certain of is that for the first time in my life, my heart is alive. My heart is telling me what it wants, what it *needs*, to be happy.

And what my heart needs is waiting for me in the 10th floor penthouse right now.

Butterflies shift in my stomach in anticipation. I dash up

118

the steps and am greeted by a doorman as I step into the chic lobby of the building.

"Good evening. I am here to see William Cumberland," I say, smiling at him. "He's expecting me. I am Mary-Kate Grant."

"Let me check," the doorman says, going over to the desk and picking up a phone. He hits a button. "Mr. Cumberland? I have a Ms. Grant here to see you ... All right, thank you." He turns to me and smiles. "Please come with me, Ms. Grant."

I follow the doorman down the corridor, and he stops in front of an elevator, hitting a button. "This is Mr. Cumberland's lift. It will take you directly to his residence."

I furrow my brow. "He ... has his own elevator?"

"Yes, Ms. Grant," the man answers as the doors open. "Have a good evening."

William has his own freaking elevator? I think. *Unreal.*

I glance at my reflection in the mirrored walls of the elevator. I'm going to his penthouse in a white T-shirt, black hoodie, and folded-over black yoga pants. I check my teeth to make sure there is no lipstick and then adjust my hairband. Which, of course, I'm wearing specifically for him tonight.

The elevator zooms to the 10th floor, and the doors open right to William's living room.

I stand still, in shock. It is beyond breathtaking. Everything is white and modern: from the floors and walls to the low-backed sofas and glass tables. There is a wall of windows providing a spectacular view of London at night, just as amazing as the view he has in his Chicago penthouse.

But by far the most fabulous view is that of William, who is walking toward me. He's wearing a chocolate brown V-necked sweater—one that matches his hair—jeans, and rugged lug-soled brown boots.

"Mary-Kate," he says, stopping in front of me and cupping my face in his hands, "I know that saying 'welcome' is a most appropriate greeting for your arrival. However, I prefer another form of greeting. Do you care to know what that is?"

I can barely think as William is stroking my face and sending goosebumps sweeping over my skin. "What would be an appropriate welcome?" I manage to ask.

He answers by pressing his lips slowly and sweetly against mine, easing my mouth open in a romantic kiss as he continues to caress my face with his hands.

Oh, my. Nothing compares to kissing William. *Nothing.*

He breaks the kiss and begins running his hand through my hair. "I've wanted to do that all day."

I laugh and wrap my hands around his waist, feeling the fine cashmere sweater against my fingers. "I've wanted you to do that all day."

He presses his lips against mine once more. I melt into him and think that I would be very happy to simply kiss him all evening, just like I did last night.

William gives me another quick kiss and smiles at me. "Okay, now I will officially welcome you to my home."

My heart catches for a moment. *His home.* His real home, the one he will return to in June once the Chicago networks are running to his liking. As I remind myself of that fact, my stomach drops. I shake the thought from my head. I can't let myself go there. I can't. I step away from him and take in my surroundings as a distraction from my thoughts. "This is incredible," I say. I turn to face him. "But it doesn't seem like you. It's so *modern.* This seems more like your Connectivity offices at The Shard."

William rubs his hand over his chin. "Agreed. I bought this

place last year and had the decorator we used for The Shard do this. I didn't care about the décor, to be honest. But maybe you could redo it for me."

My heart leaps. "I would love to."

He gives me the grand tour, from the all-white kitchen with the restaurant-grade built-ins and spectacular view of Mayfair to the multiple bedrooms and the bathrooms with the ultra-modern fixtures all in white.

"William, I have a question. I know your security detail is always with you in public and when you go to work, why do you not have one at your residences?"

"Because I can't bloody stand it," he admits. "I loathe having a security detail, but it's necessary. But not at my home. I have places where you can only access through a secure lift, and I have top of the line security systems, but I have to have my private space. This is it."

My breath catches in my throat. William is allowing me into his private space. I know this is another big thing for him, to invite me into this world, and this comment reminds me of how zealously he guards it.

"Now I will show you why I bought this place," he says as we head back to the living room. "The balcony."

He opens the door for me, and I step outside. Oh, it's absolutely breathtaking. The deck wraps around his penthouse on one side, and you can see the most gorgeous view of London from here. The city glows in the distance, and I see the London Eye all lit up. I walk over to the railing and lean out over it, letting the cold March air lift my hair back from my face. William joins me, and we take in the view.

"This is fantastic!" I cry, delighted with what I can see.

"I know," he agrees. "It is a good place for me to think. I can stare out over London and sort things out in my mind here."

I steal a glance at his profile. God, he's so beautiful. I can see him out here, weighing the problems of running his empire, working systematically through issues in his head while he searches for answers in the city skyline.

"This would be a good place for that," I say.

I turn around and look at the patio chairs and chaise lounges, thinking how nice it would be to sit out here in the summer with a blanket and glass of wine. Then I notice an outdoor dining table with eight chairs around it.

I look back at William, curious. "Do you entertain here? That table is huge."

He eyes me as if I have lost my mind. "Do you *know* me?" he asks, laughing. "Entertain? Of course not."

We both laugh, and I shake my head. "Well, then why do you have it?" I ask.

"The decorator said it was a good way to fill space," William explains. "Besides, the only people who have been here are my brother and his family, and they have small children. I'm afraid to let them out here."

I pause. *His family*, I think. *This is the first time he has ever mentioned something so personal to me.*

"What about your parents?" I ask carefully. "Do you ever see them?"

William pauses for a moment. He stares straight ahead, into the lights of London, and then answers. "No," he says, his voice soft. "They've never been here. We aren't close." He lifts his hand to his mouth and slowly rubs it, and I know he is carefully choosing what he is about to tell me.

"My parents," he continues quietly, "didn't want to be parents. They married because of me. My mother was

122

pregnant. They thought it was the right thing to do."

I swallow. I don't know how much William is going to share with me, but the fact that he is telling me anything this personal is huge.

"And when I was three months old, my mother got pregnant with Rupert, my younger brother. She wasn't supposed to be able to get pregnant at that time but she did. We were both accidents," he admits.

"No," I say firmly, shaking my head. "Don't ever say that, William. You were not an accident. I won't let you say that."

He turns to me, surprise evident in his blue eyes. "What? I *was* an accident, Mary-Kate. My parents didn't want to have children."

"No. You might have been a surprise, but don't ever call yourself an accident. That implies something bad happened, and you being here is no accident. You are *meant* to be here, William."

I watch as his eyes take in what I said. "Thank you," he whispers.

"You don't have to thank me for telling the truth," I say softly.

William holds my gaze for a second and then turns away.

"They are not a good match," he tells me. "They both are passionate, temperamental artists. My father is a sculptor and my mother a painter. They live for their art and own interests. I ... I was an afterthought. Because they both come from old money, they could pursue their art however they wanted. Raising children didn't get in the way of that pursuit.

"I always had a nanny growing up," he continues. "As soon as I turned eight, I was sent to boarding school. If we were home for a holiday, we were with a nanny. My parents would come and go as they pleased. If they weren't pursuing their art, they were fighting—constantly fighting."

My chest aches. William is letting this pour out of him, and I know he has held this next to his heart his entire life. And he has chosen to trust me with the most painful secret of his past.

"When I was ten," he says, interrupting my thoughts, "I overheard my mother screaming at my father that she hated him for getting her pregnant, she hated her life, and that she never wanted to be tied down like this. Yet they never divorced because of the financial implications. I think they also never wanted to admit the relationship was a disaster. My mother lives primarily in Paris now, as she has since I was sixteen. My father splits his time between London and Rome."

Tears fill my eyes. I can't believe what I am hearing. That William—impossibly brilliant, kind, thoughtful William—was raised like this. That he was shoved off onto nannies, even during the holidays. That he actually heard his own mother say she never wanted him.

I link my arm around his and rest my head against his shoulder. I want to comfort him, I want to protect him, and I want to erase what happened to him as a little boy.

"Do ... do you *ever* see them?"

"We share the occasional visit or phone call," William admits. "But obviously I'm not close to them. Now Rupert, yes, we stay in touch all the time. My parents, however ... it is what it is. You can't make a parent want to be one if they don't want to."

A silence falls between us as we look out onto the city. I blink back tears. I know the last thing William wants is to see me cry.

"I'm so sorry," I say, my voice thick. "You did not deserve

that childhood."

"It's all right," he says, dropping a sweet kiss on the top of my head. "I'm fine. I really am."

"Thank you for trusting me with this," I tell him quietly. "I know that wasn't easy to share."

"Well, I do trust that you won't go running off to the rags with it," he quips.

"Never," I reply, snuggling in more to him and feeling fiercely protective of his secret.

"What about you, Mary-Kate? Tell me how you grew up."

And with that, he closes the door on talking about himself. So I follow his lead and tell him about my family.

"Well, you already know about Michelle," I say.

"You mean the Duchess of Milwaukee?" William deadpans.

I burst out laughing and snort, which makes him laugh.

"Yes," I say. "So we have the Duchess of Milwaukee planning her royal wedding, which thrills my mom to no end. You see, my mom is very worried about me. I'm twenty-four, and I don't have a husband. Or a fiancé."

"Why is that a problem?" William asks. I hear the confusion in his lovely British voice.

"My mom married my dad straight after college," I explain. "That was her goal of going to school: to find a husband. And she did. My dad is a dentist. Mom stays at home. Michelle went to college and majored in education, but not because she loved teaching or working with kids, but because she could have summers off. She met Jason, her fiancé, her freshman year and has been pretty much planning this wedding ever since. She will quit teaching as soon as they are married."

"And you are the complete opposite of them," William says. "You're passionate about your career. That is what drives you."

125

"Yes," I say. "I have always wanted a career, ever since I was a little girl. I always imagined going to work and being involved in fulfilling projects, working in network television ... that is my core, William. And they don't understand that at all."

"It frustrates you," he says.

I nod. "My mom doesn't understand me at all. She is constantly asking who I am dating, suggesting I join an online dating site, that I should go to church to meet nice men. She asks why I didn't stay with my last boyfriend." I sigh heavily as I think about all of this. "She actually emailed me an article about the dangers of putting a career ahead of your biological clock last week."

"You're joking," William says, furrowing his brow. "Your *mother* sent that to you?"

I cringe as I hear the incredulity in his voice. "My mom doesn't know any better. She is dependent on my father for everything. Michelle will be completely dependent on Jason. And I—"

"Want to be the exact opposite of them," William finishes for me.

I nod. He cradles me in his arms, and we look out at London in silence. In this moment, I see how our lives emotionally intersect. We both have very valid reasons for not wanting a serious relationship. William has grown up without any kind of healthy relationship role model, and he has been badly hurt by the people who were supposed to love him unconditionally.

Besides, he has an empire to run, one that has him working hideous hours and traveling around the world. Quite honestly, he would never have the time for a serious relationship.

Then there is me. I have my career to build, and I have seen over and over again how a man can distract a woman from the career path. I never want that to happen, nor do I ever want to be dependent on anyone but myself.

So, the way we are right now is just perfect.

But despite that, as William holds me in his arms, I wonder if it is possible to have more than we already have.

"Are you hungry?" he asks.

Rattled by my thoughts, I shove them out of my head. I wriggle around in his arms so I am facing him.

"Yes. Did you cook for me?" I ask, raising an eyebrow at him.

William laughs loudly. "No, I don't cook. I ordered sushi."

He wraps his hand over mine and leads me back into the penthouse. We go into the kitchen, and I hop up on one of the sleek chrome barstools while he opens the refrigerator. He pulls out a bottle of champagne, and as he does, I notice he has nothing in there except champagne and a pint of milk.

"William," I gasp, horrified. "Is that all you keep in your fridge?"

He furrows his brow. "I don't eat here."

"Obviously," I laugh. "Okay, when we get back to Chicago, I'm teaching you how to cook. And how to stock your pantry."

He grins at me and takes some plates out of the cabinet. I reach across and plate the sushi for us while he uncorks the champagne. I hear the pop and, oh, how I love that sound. Luxurious champagne, fine sushi, gorgeous man ... Yes, this evening is shaping up rather nicely.

"So, I decided that we don't need to see a movie tonight," William announces.

"Then what are we watching?"

"I don't see the need to stream a movie when we have a *Full*

House DVD we can watch."

I stare at him. "Surely you jest."

He cocks an eyebrow. "Do I?"

"I still can't believe you made me order that. And that you actually watched it!"

"Of course I did."

"Why?"

"Because it is part of your story," William says softly. He hands me a champagne glass and clinks his against mine. "Cheers."

Oh God. I'm falling, falling, falling for this man.

He takes the seat next to mine and gives me a pair of disposable wooden chopsticks. "Sorry, I never invested in permanent ones."

"I'm terrible with chopsticks," I admit, tearing open the paper sleeve.

"I can help you with your technique," William declares. He watches me fumble to break them apart. "Assuming you can separate them, that is. Do you need assistance?"

"No, don't be silly," I declare. But then I jerk at them hard, and one goes flying off and smacks William on the side of the head.

"Oh!" I gasp, horrified. "I'm so sorry!"

He stares at me with a teasing glimmer in his eyes. "Did you throw your chopstick at me?"

"No," I say, embarrassed. "It wouldn't budge, and I pulled too hard, and it flew off. I'm so sorry." I reach over and brush my fingertips against his temple and let them trail down to his hair, as I can never get enough of touching it.

William eyes my chopstick, which is now on his plate. Then he bursts out laughing.

"Stop it," I say, trying to be serious. But I'm laughing, too.

"Why? What are you going to do, launch your other chop-stick at me?" he teases.

"No," I laugh. "Apparently you can't take me anywhere, though."

William's face turns serious. "There is somewhere I would like to take you."

My heart leaps. "And where might that be?"

"I'm going to Rupert's house for Sunday dinner with his family," he says slowly, his laser eyes focused on mine, "and I would like for you to go with me. Will you go, Mary-Kate?"

Chapter Sixteen

I can hardly believe it is already Sunday.

The rest of the week went by in an incredible blur. I sat in on high-level meetings at Connectivity during the day, learning so much about all the different departments and how they ran. Every night was spent at William's place, making dinner and watching TV. Sometimes, he would work while I took out my iPad and drafted articles for my blog. It was so funny, both of us working side-by-side on his sofa—it felt like we had been doing this routine our entire lives rather than just a week.

Yesterday, I spent the whole day sightseeing by myself in London. William had a lot of work to catch up on, but we also both knew it would not be good for me if we were spotted together. So I did the next best thing. At every site I stopped at, I took pictures and texted them to William with the caption **"I am here. MKG"** and then he'd respond with some fact about the place or a suggestion of something else to see.

Of course, he would text me back the same picture of his office at his penthouse, papers all about, with the caption of **"Bloody hell, I am still stuck here. WC"** which I found rather funny.

William was most amused, however, that I spent a good

chunk of my day in the Harrods food department, which I found endlessly fascinating and made the subject of my next blog.

Now I am sitting next to him in his Aston Martin, heading to Berkshire to meet his brother, Rupert, sister-in-law, Claire, and their two children for Sunday dinner.

I steal a glance at him while he's driving. He's impossibly handsome today, dressed in a pale red and blue cotton plaid shirt, leather jacket, and jeans. He has his aviator sunglasses on, as it is a sunny day, and I find it hard not to stare at him as we head into the countryside.

I glance down at the bouquet of flowers I'm holding in my lap. I stopped to get them before we left today, since I always think it is important to bring a hostess gift.

Even more so when the hostess is William's sister-in-law.

"I hope Claire likes these," I say, glancing at the rustic bouquet a street vendor made. I had him put sunflowers, lavender, and other wildflowers together, and then he tied them up with some raffia.

"Are you kidding? She will love that you are so thoughtful," William says, reaching over, putting his hand over mine, and squeezing it. "It's perfect."

Warmth fills me the second his hand wraps around mine. I still can't believe I'm here, with William, headed out to meet the most important people in the world to him.

For a moment, my chest draws tight. I know in my head that he and I will never have much more than what we have now. My head tells me this is just a dinner, with people I will probably never see again, and William would merely like a date for a change. Or he doesn't want me to have to dine alone on a Sunday night. That makes sense.

But my heart … my heart tells me something completely different.

My heart is talking over my head. My heart tells me William would never bring me to Berkshire if I wasn't important to him. My heart tells me he would never involve his family with us if he didn't feel something for me as I am starting to feel for him.

"We're almost there," he says, interrupting my thoughts. "Are you ready for this?"

I draw a nervous breath and, without thinking, blurt out what is in my head. "I hope they like me."

"What?" William asks, glancing at me out of the corner of his eye. "Why wouldn't they like you? I mean, unless you break Claire's tea service, which is always a possibility, they're going to love you."

"William," I protest, "I won't break anything."

He laughs loudly. "Mary-Kate, do not make promises you know you only have a fifty percent chance of keeping."

"You take that back," I say, laughing.

"I only take back things I'm wrong about."

"I will start calling you Mr. Cumberland again," I mock threaten. "And if I do, I think it is most appropriate that you do not kiss me later this evening."

"Oh, Ms. Grant, are we resorting to blackmail now?"

"Indeed."

We drive into the most charming town I have ever seen, with quaint shops lining each side of the narrow road. William stops as an elderly woman crosses the road and rubs his hand sexily over his mouth.

"Hmmm, no kissing you or taking it back," he says slowly, as if he is gravely debating this matter. He turns toward me and brushes his thumb sensually over my lower lip. "I suppose, Ms. Grant, I shall take it back, because otherwise it will ruin my plans for you at the end of the evening. And I do have plans. Very detailed ones."

Is it wrong that I want William to pull this Aston Martin over right here so I can rip through the buttons on his plaid shirt, feel him up right now, and make out with him?

Okay, not an option. One, we'll be late for dinner, and two, I'd look like a hot mess upon arrival, so I'll have to save that thought for later.

Instead, I compose myself so I can give a smart reply, which I know is one of William's turn-ons.

"Yes, that would be a most appropriate choice, because I am very intrigued by your plans for later this evening."

Although I cannot see his eyes behind his aviators, I know the expression underneath them. The intense, sexy gaze is there. I can feel it.

"Well-played, Mary-Kate. Well-played, indeed."

Suddenly, we hear a car horn blaring. Obviously, the driver behind us isn't as interested in our flirtatious banter as we are. William waves his hand up in error, and we go, winding through a quaint village. We pass an amazing old church, one that has to be from at least the nineteenth century. Everything is green and lush and spacious ... Oh, England is beautiful. It's so different from anything I have ever known.

As is the man driving me through it.

William makes his way down a road, and before I know it, he is turning onto the drive of a glorious white, Georgian-style house. I nearly gasp out loud at the sight. The two-story home is stunningly oh-so-English and beautiful.

The house is set back from view on several lush green acres.

I see an arbor over the door, gorgeous windows, and even what appears to be a glassed-in conservatory on the right-hand side of the home.

William drives up to the house and brings the car to a stop. I unfasten my seatbelt.

Before I can even get out of the car, the front door opens, and two dark-haired children come flying out the door and down the sidewalk.

"Uncle William!" a little girl cries, running toward the car.

I hesitate. I watch as he gets out of the car and five-year-old Emma—William has told me all about her—leaps into his open arms.

"Hello, love, how are you?" he says, kissing her on the cheek as she wraps her tiny hands around his neck.

My heart pounds as I watch this scene. I slowly open the door to get out. I can't take my eyes off William and Emma.

This is the William only his family, and now me, gets to see. And watching him with Emma ... oh, it puts thoughts into my head that have never been there.

Like this man would be a wonderful father someday.

To my children.

"Uncle William!" another voice cries, interrupting my thoughts.

I watch as Charlie, his three-year-old nephew, rushes toward him and attaches himself to William's leg. William is still holding Emma, but he takes one hand down and affectionately ruffles Charlie's dark brown curls.

"Charlie! How are you?" he asks, grinning at him.

"Did you bring us anything?" Emma asks.

"Emma! You don't ask Uncle William for things, remember?" a male voice chides.

I turn and see Rupert coming down the walk. He is the physical opposite of William—average height, more athletic build—and as he walks toward me, his face broadens into a beautiful, welcoming smile.

I almost laugh. Rupert is the exact opposite of William in that way, too. Where William is careful and assessing and shows zero emotion upon first meeting, Rupert is coming toward me with a huge grin and his arms open.

"Welcome, Mary-Kate!" he says, pulling me into a hug. "It is so good to meet you. We've heard a lot about you."

Yes. Very opposite of William. I hug him back. "Likewise," I say.

"Let's see, did I bring you anything?" William says to Emma. "Well, yes. I brought Mary-Kate here from America. Can you say hello to her?"

Emma looks at me with disappointed brown eyes.

"Hello, Emma," I say softly. "It is so nice to meet you." I drop down on one knee to greet Charlie. "And, Charlie, it is nice to meet you, too."

Emma giggles. "You talk funny!"

"Emma!" Rupert scolds, sounding exasperated. "That is not a nice thing to say."

"It's all right. I think her accent is funny, too," William says, shooting me a flirty grin.

"I know I sound different," I say, smiling at her as I stand up. "But you will get used to it, just like your Uncle William did. And you know what, Emma? I think your Uncle William has something you will like in the trunk of his car."

"Boot," both William and Rupert correct at the same time.

I feel myself blush. "Right. Boot."

William takes Emma and Charlie around, and I see a woman

135

walking down the sidewalk toward me. She is in her early thirties and is stunning, with long, curly dark brown hair and ivory skin. She is wearing a pair of fitted jeans, flats, and a lovely pink cardigan and shell that play up her coloring.

"You must be Mary-Kate," she says, smiling at me as she makes her way toward me. "I'm Claire. Welcome to our home." She greets me with a hug.

I hug her back, thinking she and Rupert are so alike: so warm, so open, so welcoming.

"These are for you," I say, handing her the bouquet. "Thank you for inviting me to come here today."

"Oh, these are lovely," she replies, her eyes lighting up. "Why don't we go put these in a vase and let the boys supervise the children for a bit? They could use some outside time anyway."

I glance back at William, who is holding up a Peppa Pig doll and pretending to talk to Emma with it.

And once again, a phrase that I had never thought of until today rolls through my head.

The father of my children.

"Coming, Mary-Kate?"

I snap out of my thoughts, a sick feeling attacking my stomach. I smile and nod at Claire, walking with her up the sidewalk, trying to understand what I'm thinking. I know William and I will never be together. I know he's coming back to England in a matter of months. I know he doesn't want anything remotely like marriage and children.

Which would eliminate him as the father of my future children, wouldn't it?

"So here we are," Claire says, opening the front door and ushering me inside.

136

I'm distracted by the sight in front of me. I step inside a room with gorgeous pine floors, a big fireplace, bookcases filled with all kinds of books, and an Oriental rug on the floor.

"Oh, Claire, this is gorgeous," I tell her as I look around.

"Thank you. This is the living room," she says. "I love books and have a million more on my Kindle. Would you like something to drink, Mary-Kate?"

"Yes, please," I reply.

"Let's go on back to the kitchen," she says

I follow her down the hallway, the old wooden floor creaking under my feet. I pause and notice beautiful photographs of Emma, Charlie, and Rupert lining the hallway. Some are black and white, others are in color, all capturing the essence of love and joy.

I stop to take a closer look. "These are incredible," I say.

Claire stops, too, and looks over her shoulder. "Oh, thank you. I took those."

"Wow," I say, turning to her. "You're very good."

Claire laughs. "I hope so. I used to be a photographer before I had children." She pauses for a moment. "I admit, I do miss it sometimes, but I love being home with the children right now, you know?"

She begins walking again, and I follow her, my heart freezing in my chest. Another woman who gave up a fabulous career to stay at home and raise her children. I bite my lip. Does it always have to be that way? Granted, I want to focus on my career for a while, and then get married and have children, but will I have to make that choice to be a good mother?

God, what is wrong with me? Why am I thinking of marriage and children and William being the father of my children?

"Would you like wine?" Claire asks as we enter the kitchen.

I don't respond at first. I can't speak. Literally, I am speechless, as Claire has led me to the kitchen of my dreams. It is a farmhouse kitchen, one I have imagined in my head since I was, like, ten years old. The cabinets are pine and rustic. There is a fireplace. A beautiful English-style cupboard filled with all different kinds of patterned teacups and mugs. A table in-between the counter and the fireplace. I can just imagine serving a cozy meal here with a fire roaring. Then I see the yard through the windows over the sink and countertop. There are beautiful gardens out back, but even more beautiful is the sight of William, running around and chasing Charlie across the green lawn.

I'm drawn to the window and walk right over to the sink so I can watch him. William is laughing and running and acting so absolutely carefree. My heart melts at the scene before me.

William, I love who you really are: not the brilliant badass mogul the world knows, but the man who runs and plays with children without a care in the world, I think.

"Mary-Kate? Are you all right?"

I turn around and feel my cheeks burn slightly. "Yes."

"Would you like some wine? I have a bottle of Chardonnay open if you would like a glass."

"Perfect, thank you."

I watch as Claire goes to the refrigerator and pulls out a bottle. She opens a cabinet, grabs a wine glass, and fills it for me.

She hands me the glass and picks up hers. "Cheers, Mary-Kate. To being the first person William has ever brought here."

My pulse jumps at this bit of news. "Really?" I say casually, taking a sip of wine. I'm trying to be cool but I want to yell, "Really? I am the first one? Tell me more, Claire!"

"Yes," she says. "We were surprised when he called Rupert

and asked if he could bring a guest to dinner. But Rupert and I both knew it was going to be you, because you are the only person he talks about."

Ooh! Why do I want to jump up and down and scream in delight at this tidbit?

"Am I?" I ask carefully, trying to mask my excitement.

Claire selects a pitcher that is in her cabinet and fills it with water. "Oh, yes, all the time. He goes on to Rupert about how brilliant you are, how you are so invaluable to him, that you make him laugh, you know, that kind of thing. We both knew you were the one coming to dinner before he said your name. This is a big deal to him, Mary-Kate."

I swallow as she slides the wrapping off the flowers and puts them into the pitcher.

"It's a big deal to me, too," I admit to Claire.

She smiles. "I gathered that."

I watch as she begins pulling out bowls, recipe printouts, and things out of the fridge and begins heaping them on the countertop. I bite my lip. There appears to be no organization to this at all, not like when I cook.

She whips open a Jamie Oliver cookbook and thumbs through the pages. "Now, where is this salad recipe?" she asks, flipping back and forth. Finally, she finds the page and begins chopping things up.

"May I help you in any way?" I ask. I can't help but notice her knife skills are horrible. She is butchering a tomato, slicing it all wrong, and it is painful for me to watch.

"Oh, no, you're a guest," Claire says breezily. "I think I have everything under control. The chicken has been roasting all afternoon, so I know it will be done."

A warning flag goes up in my head. Oh, God, that chicken

will be overcooked when it comes out. I say nothing and take another sip of my wine.

"Bugger! I forgot to start potatoes!" Claire drops her knife and opens her pantry.

I hear her rummaging around and try not to laugh. Obviously, she is a creative genius, but not a culinary one. I glance back out the window and see that William and Rupert are now talking. A big chocolate brown Labrador runs up to William with a stick, and he throws it, with the dog bounding after it.

Oh, William, do I even stand a chance here today? Do I?

"Oh, bloody hell!" Claire drops the potatoes down on the counter with a thud. "These will take at least an hour to bake!"

"You could mash them," I suggest. "Peel, cube, boil, mash. You can get that done rather quickly if they are diced small."

"Brilliant!" she says, taking another sip of wine.

"I ... I could do them if you like," I offer. "I love to cook, actually. So I don't mind helping at all, if you don't mind, that is."

"I could kiss you," Claire says. "Oh, thank you, yes, that would be lovely."

"Do you have any rosemary?" I ask, thinking I will make rosemary mashed potatoes for the adults.

"Yes, out in the garden," she says as she consults her cookbook. "Damn it! I forgot chilies! Now I can't make the salad dressing."

"I can do that, too. I can do an herb one, if that's okay," I say.

"William better marry you. That is all I am going to say," Claire replies, going over to the oven and taking a peek. "Ooh! It's really crispy on top!"

I try not to laugh. I bet that chicken is more than crispy.

"There is a basket with clippers by the back door," Claire tells me. "You can take that to get whatever you need from the herb garden."

"Great, I'll be right back."

I walk outside into the crisp spring air. Rupert is now throwing the stick, and William is gone.

"Where did William go?" I ask, walking up to Rupert.

"Phone call," he says. "But first one he's taken since he's been here. Remarkable."

"Remarkable?"

Rupert raises an eyebrow at me and, holy shit, it is William's look. They might be physically different, but there is no doubt they are brothers.

"You've changed him," he declares.

"W-what?" I ask.

"Daddy! Charlie is throwing dirt at me!" Emma cries, running up to him.

"Sorry, duty calls," Rupert goes over to the swing set, and I desperately want to stop him. I want to make him tell me how William has changed. Is ... could ... could he be thinking about something more between us, too?

Rupert comes back with Charlie screaming under one arm and Emma holding his hand.

"Sorry, must go hose them down before dinner," he says, grinning at me.

They go through the back door. I hear it slam shut, and then I hear footsteps behind me. I turn around and see William approaching, and the expression on his face is serious.

"What's wrong?" I ask, putting the herb basket and clippers down.

William sighs and shoves his iPhone into his jacket pocket.

"That was a call about the Australia transaction. The negotiations have become sticky, I'm afraid, and I will need to go there straight from London next week to finalize the deal."

My stomach goes into a knot. I know since our relationship has changed it will be harder for me to see him leave for weeks at a time.

"I'll need to have an assistant with me," William says slowly. He takes my hands in his. "Because there is going to be lots of messaging, contracts, meal organization, that kind of thing."

I hold my breath. Excitement surges through me. First London, then Sydney—with *William*. Oh, I'm so lucky. I'm the luckiest girl in the world, I'm sure of it.

Then he looks at me. "And I am taking Arabella with me to Australia, Mary-Kate."

Chapter Seventeen

I stare at William, absolutely shocked by his words.

He is not going to take me to Sydney.

Because he doesn't want me there. Instead, he has made the decision to take Arabella over me.

Oh God, I feel like I've been punched in the stomach. I feel ... I feel *betrayed*. And as that thought goes through my head, I want to be sick.

"Mary-Kate," William says, gripping my hands in his, "I can see this has upset you and—"

I rip my hands away from his. "Upset? Upset? Why would I be upset about this, William? That you ... that you... want to take Arabella more than me? After you keep telling me how brilliant I am, how I am more than an assistant to you, after everything that has happened this week? For God's sake, you bring me to Berkshire and then turn around and do this? How do you *expect* me to feel, William?"

I storm off, anger and hurt swirling around in equal fury inside of me.

"Mary-Kate!" William hurries after me. He puts his hand on my shoulder to stop me, and I whirl around and push him back.

"Don't touch me!" I say in a loud whisper. "How can you take *her*? How?"

"Do you think I *want* to?"

"You are THE William Cumberland! You can do anything you want! And you choose to take that awful woman to freaking Australia?"

His eyes flash. "Yes, I am THE William Cumberland," he says, his voice deadly calm. "And I have to take Arabella to protect you. If people are talking now, Mary-Kate, what would they say when I bypass the lead assistant, who has always gone on big international trips, for you? How would that be perceived?"

I say nothing as I process his words. And the second I do, I know he's right. One hundred percent right.

"Mary-Kate," William continues, his voice thick with concern, "you know I want you there. Now more than ever I want that. However, I cannot put you in that position. It would be selfish of me to do so."

I look into his eyes and see worry in them. Worry that I'm not going to accept this answer.

But his words, and the expression on his face, tell me everything I need to know.

"Please," William says, stepping closer to me. "Please, believe me, Mary-Kate." He hesitates for a second, and then rests his hand against my cheek. "Please, believe what I am telling you."

I swallow hard. "I do believe you. I ... I'm sorry. I should have known there was more to it, but I just hate her so much. The idea that Arabella gets to be your right-hand person, that she gets to spend all that time with you, and after what she did to me this week—"

"What," William says, cutting me off, "has she done to you?"

Oh crap. I didn't want him to know about the exile situation.

"Mary-Kate," he says firmly, "answer me. What has Arabella done to you?"

"It's not that big of a deal," I reply, shaking my head. "It's not worth getting into."

William's blue eyes get extremely intense. "I will decide that. Tell me. Now."

I take a deep breath. Oh, he's going to be *furious.* But I have no choice but to tell after letting that slip.

"Do you know where she's making me sit at the office?" I ask.

William's brow creases. "No."

"You know the build-out section? Where nobody is? That's where she set me up. As far away from you as I could possibly be."

I watch as William takes in my words. His jaw goes tight. He removes his hand from my face. And I see nothing but anger flickering in his eyes.

"Why," he says, in a controlled voice, "did you not tell me about this sooner?"

"I'm a big girl, William. I can deal with it."

"This," he says, "should not have to be dealt with. And I will rectify it first thing Monday morning."

"William—"

"I should sack her!" he cuts me off.

"You and I both know you can't do that."

"Why not? I am *THE William Cumberland.* It should come in handy from time to time to sack people like Arabella."

I can't help it. I know he's furious, but what he said is so funny that I burst out laughing.

"What?" he snaps, obviously not amused.

"I am THE William Cumberland, fear my wrath!" I say, laughing.

He pauses for a moment. My God, he actually looks sheepish! He rubs his hand over his face and groans. Then he begins to laugh, too.

"You know what? Let's not talk about her anymore," I say.

"I'm still taking care of this on Monday," William replies.

"Fine. But can we keep calm and carry on now?" I ask, teasing him.

William laughs. He steps closer to me and links my hands with his, squeezing them tightly.

I gaze up at him, with the setting sun illuminating his dark waves and cheekbones, and I am lost looking at him.

"I loathe the idea of Arabella being in Sydney instead of you," he whispers sexily, brushing his soft lips against mine. "Loathe it."

I melt into his chest as his arms wind around me. "I loathe it, too."

"I'll make it up to you," William murmurs against my lips before kissing me again.

I can feel his heart beating under the fabric of his plaid shirt. I relish this moment, of being in this beautiful English garden, inhaling the scent of his pine cologne and leather jacket mixed with the country air, of being wrapped up in his arms and feeling his warm lips move against mine.

Suddenly, we hear a door slam, and we both look toward the house. Rupert is walking toward us, but William continues to hold me.

"Rupert, can't you see that I'm busy?" he yells out good-naturedly.

I blush furiously, and Rupert grins.

"Emma has requested that you read her some of her new books before dinner," Rupert says, his eyes dancing as he walks up. "I was told to come out here and help Mary-Kate get the herbs for the potatoes."

William gently kisses the top of my head, a move so sweet and gentle that my heart leaps with joy. "Do you mind?" he asks.

"Of course not. Go read," I say. "I have to get some rosemary, and I'll be right there."

William releases me and goes back inside.

Rupert waits until he is out of earshot and then flashes me a smile. "Sorry to have interrupted," he says.

I feel my cheeks burn. "No, no problem. Can you please show me where the rosemary is?"

He nods, and I walk with him to the back of the garden.

"I can't get over this," he says.

I hesitate for a moment. "Over what?"

"William. He's let you in, hasn't he?" he asks as we stop in front of the herb bushes.

I act like I'm very interested in the rosemary. I bend down and pick up the herb clippers. "Let me in?" I repeat, clipping off some branches.

"Yes. William has always kept himself isolated from everyone except me. He has since he was a child. Due to how we grew up, you know," Rupert adds.

I say nothing, as I do not want to share William's confidences with anyone, even his brother.

"Our parents," Rupert says slowly, "weren't meant to be parents. So where I vowed to create my own family to fill that void, William has created a global empire to keep himself busy and fulfilled. And I thought he would always be that way. Until today."

I drop the rosemary into the basket and stand up, despite the fact that I am trembling from Rupert's words.

Could this be the beginning of something more for us? I wonder, my heart jumping. *Could William want something more than the undefined relationship that we are currently falling into?*

"You're good for him," Rupert says as we begin to walk back.

"He's good for *me*," I say. "I'm the one who is lucky, Rupert."

For whatever way William lets me into his life, I am lucky.

We go back into the house, and Claire is flittering around the kitchen. She is whacking away at the potatoes with her knife, and I cringe when I see the pile of misshapen potato. Not cubes, exactly, but ... bits. Chunks and bits.

"The chicken is still roasting!" she says excitedly.

Oh dear God. I don't even want to look in the oven because I have a feeling there is a black bird in there.

"You know, making all these sides is exhausting," Claire declares.

I furrow my brow. "Sides?"

"William made it clear that you like sides with dinner," she explains. "I normally don't do them for our Sunday dinner."

I realize that William wanted me to feel at home.

If I even stood a chance today, it's over. I'm done. I'm so in over my head for this man, I can't see straight.

"Well, why don't you let me do the potatoes and the salad? You have done so much work, Claire."

She looks extremely grateful. "Bless you."

I pick up the knife and begin to make the potatoes similar in size so they cook evenly. As I am re-chopping, William walks into the kitchen and puts his arm affectionately around my waist.

"What are you making?" he asks, his fingertips dancing below my ribcage and making a shiver shoot down my spine.

"Rosemary mashed potatoes for the adults and plain potatoes for the kids," I say as I chop. "And you can help me."

"What?" William asks, laughing.

"You are going to be my sous chef. Now go wash your hands."

I can see Claire staring at us with a look of shock on her face.

"Bossy American," William teases as he walks over to the sink.

"My God, you are actually going to get him to do this," Claire says.

"I have no choice, Claire," William says, washing his hands. "Mary-Kate is very strict about me pulling my own weight, you know."

I laugh, and so does William. He walks back over to the counter where I am, and I slide him the rosemary and the cutting board.

"Chop it fine, please," I instruct, moving to the stove and dumping the potatoes into boiling water.

"Do you care to inspect my technique first?" he asks, arching an eyebrow at me as I walk back over to him.

I bite down hard on my lip. Odds are his technique is better than Claire's, so I wouldn't dare correct him in front of her.

"No, I trust you can chop an herb, William."

Claire picks up a stack of dishes from the countertop. "I'm going to set the dining room table."

As soon as she leaves, William bends down and whispers in

my ear, "I'm glad you are making potatoes and salad, because she is an awful cook."

I stifle a laugh. "I gathered that."

"Make sure you take big portions of whatever you make, so you don't starve."

"William. You're awful," I whisper.

"Whoever told you I was nice?" he teases back.

With William's help, I prepare the salad and potatoes. For fun, I even make him mash them with the masher; it's quite entertaining to see him work like that.

"All right, you all go sit down, and I'll bring the chicken in," Claire says excitedly.

William and I share a glance and try not to laugh. We sit around the table with the children and Rupert and wait for Claire's big reveal.

Then we hear a scream, a loud crash of a pan into the sink, and the oven door slam shut. And then we hear Claire.

"Bloody hell, it is black!!" she screams from the kitchen. "Black! How is it *black*? It is supposed to be golden brown not black. And there is smoke!"

"Mummy said a bad word!" Emma yells to Rupert.

"Mummy didn't mean it," he says quickly. "Let me go see what is going on."

I'm shaking from trying so hard not to laugh. I have tears in my eyes. I don't dare glance at William. I don't. Because if I see what I think I will see, I will lose it.

"Do we get pizza now?" Charlie asks.

"We always get pizza when Mummy yells from the kitchen," Emma says earnestly.

"So you eat a lot of pizza then, don't you, love?" William quips.

That does it. I burst out laughing, and so does he. I mean, we are dying laughing, and I have tears streaming down my face. I glance at him, and, holy crap, he has tears in his eyes, too.

We manage to stop and pull it together before Claire walks back into the dining room. She has her wine glass in her hand and takes a sip.

"I have a pizza in the oven. We'll eat in fifteen minutes."

"Sweetheart, it is fine. We still have Mary-Kate's salad and potatoes, too," Rupert says reassuringly.

Claire sighs heavily and sits down. We all reassure her it is no big deal. Being together is why we are here. Then we begin passing around sides and start eating.

Rupert takes a bite of his potatoes, and after he eats, he looks at me. "Mary-Kate, these are amazing."

"Thank you," I say quietly.

"Oh my God, they are," Claire agrees.

"Mary-Kate is an excellent cook," William declares. "She writes a blog about cooking, you know."

I feel my cheeks flame from his compliment.

"You write a blog? You must send me the link!" Claire exclaims. "I want to follow it!"

"Oh, you don't have to do that," I say, embarrassed.

"Isn't that the point of a blog? To have people follow it?" Rupert asks.

William shoots me an I-told-you-so look, and I blush again.

"I'll get your email address and send you the link," I say.

"That's progress," William declares, his beautiful eyes shining affectionately at me.

The rest of dinner goes by way too fast. We all have fun and laugh and linger at the table far too long. Finally, it is

151

time for us to head back to London, but before I leave, I make Connectivity Connects with both Rupert and Claire.

I climb back into the Aston Martin, and as William takes us back down the driveway, I feel a happiness I have never known before. I am so honored to have met his family. Thrilled they seemed to like me as much as I liked them. That they saw something different in William, something they had never seen before, because of me.

And while my head tells me I should be terrified by the fact that I feel like a part of his family with zero commitment from William when it comes to a serious relationship, zero acknowledgement about a future with him, I don't care. I really don't.

I have never been this happy in my entire life.

And I realize I have gone far beyond a match at this point. I've lit a candle.

The flame is hot, and I cannot touch it, but for now I'm content to let it burn. And I have to trust my heart that when June rolls around and William is headed back to England, that maybe, just maybe, something will be done to keep the flame alive—rather than blowing the candle out for good.

Chapter Eighteen

It is cloudy and gray on Monday morning as I step into the cab to go to work, but inside I feel joyous. That is the best way to describe it. I'm excited and happy, and I can't wait to see William at the Connectivity offices this morning.

I'm still glowing from last night and the fact that his family embraced me with such open arms. That they see a change in him because of me.

But most of all, I am so honored that William let me into that world—the world he has so fiercely and privately protected. It means more to me than he could ever know.

Beep!

I pick up my iPhone and see I have a text message from William:

Please text me as soon as you are at your desk in Siberia. Situation shall be rectified this morning. WC

I bite my lip. Oh, crap. I knew he wouldn't let this go but I have a feeling this will not be beneficial to me in the long run. Arabella could be really nasty to me for calling her out to William.

Of course, on the other hand, if he gives Arabella a final warning and goes all badass mogul on her, she might be careful to even breathe near me, let alone say another word to me about anything other than business.

Before I can answer, my phone beeps again with another text message from William:

Are you wearing a hairband? WC

I grin as I read his text. He has this thing for my hairbands. Probably because he likes to slowly pull them out and then play with my hair when we are making out, which I find damn hot. But today, he is not getting his wish.

I text him back:

No. I did something different with my hair today. It's a surprise so that is all you are getting for now. MKG

I touch my sleek ponytail. I brushed it back, then wrapped some of my own hair around it. Then I went with an edgy outfit: a black three-quarter-sleeved turtleneck sweater and a cobalt blue wool mini skirt, paired with black opaque tights and black booties.

An outfit wouldn't be me without something quirky, though. So being that I love old jewelry, I threw on a studded gold cuff bracelet I found at a vintage shop in Chicago, one that looks like it is from the seventies and very cool, as well as some chunky vintage cocktail rings.

I wanted to switch up the look to keep William on his toes, of course.

Beep!

I glance down and see a return text from him:

Intriguing text, Mary-Kate. Hint? WC

I snicker to myself.

No hints. You will have to see it firsthand. Now please go run your empire rather than trying to deduce my wardrobe styling for the day. MKG

I flip over to my emails and see about fifteen from Michelle with nasty subject lines on them. I take a deep breath and begin to skim the titles:

PLEASE RESPOND: BOBBI BROWN OR MAC LIPSTICK?

MK YOU HAVE NOT RESPONDED RE: LIPSTICKS.

ARE YOU EVEN ALIVE? LIPSTICK! HELLO? YOU ARE IN THIS WEDDING, ACT LIKE IT! MK, NOW YOU ARE UPSETTING MOM. RESPOND RE: LIPSTICK!

I throw my iPhone into my purse as my blood pressure goes up. I'm in *London.* Working in the *Connectivity World Headquarters.* I am learning from people at the top of the digital media world, absorbing their thoughts and ideas. I'm starting to realize what I want to pursue professionally. But does anyone in my freaking family even care? Do they understand how huge this is? No.

And they know nothing about William. My family has no idea that I am, without a doubt, falling in love with him, which is as big to me as everything going on at Connectivity. They don't know he is changing what I want and what I need and while sometimes it scares me, I find myself re-evaluating all my previous thoughts on love and relationships because of him. That I am risking my heart, which I have *never* wanted to do before I met him, on the chance he might stay come June.

So while I am wrestling with my future—*everything* in my future—I am being harassed over a lipstick brand? Give me a freaking break.

I'm steaming by the time I arrive at The Shard. I get out of the cab and head inside the building, thinking I need some amaretto to dump into my coffee to take this edge off, but that's not an option for me.

I greet the receptionist, who still gives me the *whore* look and a pinched smile every time I see her, and trek back to exile. I take off my coat, drape it over my chair, and turn on my computer. Then I grab my phone and text William that I am here. He replies instantly:

Will be right there. Don't move. WC

Alrighty then. I pull up my work emails, and there are like ten bossy ones from Arabella, so I start skimming through them. More copying, more label making, more filing, blah, blah, blah.

Finally, I hear footsteps. I look up and see Arabella and William heading toward me. He looks freaking furious, and she is hurrying behind him, her face ashen.

I stand up as they approach. William stops dead in his tracks. His eyes flicker over me, and I can tell my hair and outfit have completely interrupted his badass mogul train of thought. He rakes a hand through his waves, which interrupts my train of thought. Then he shifts back into mogul mode, strides up to me, and stops right at the edge of my cubicle.

"Ms. Dalton, please explain to me, after taking this walk all the way down to *exile*, why you considered this an appropriate place for Ms. Grant to work during her stay here?" William snaps, his voice like ice.

Arabella swallows and says nothing.

I can see she is trying to figure a way out of this, but nothing has come to her yet.

"Oh, and if you tell me nobody was on holiday or out of the office last week, you will be *lying*," William says, his blue eyes flashing. "I had Human Resources pull time off requests. And there were two vacant offices and one available cubicle on this floor that Ms. Grant could have been using this entire time."

Ooh! William is *so* good.

156

"Mr. Cumberland, I ... I ..." Arabella stammers. "I ... thought Ms. Grant might need room to spread out since she was doing so much paper assembly."

"Do not lie, Ms. Dalton. I will not tolerate it," William snaps.

"No, Mr. Cumberland, I'm not lying," Arabella protests.

I study her. Good Lord, she is totally freaked right now. Her eyes are darting all over the place, and she won't even *glance* at me.

"Fine. If that *is* the truth, which I sincerely *doubt*, then it will be perfect for you two to switch places this week. Obviously, you think one requires a whole build-out area to assemble packets or whatever it is you have Ms. Grant doing."

I furrow my brow. Arabella looks like she wants to throw up.

"What?" she asks.

"*Do I need to repeat myself?*" William roars. "You, *Ms. Dalton*, will work *here* this week. Ms. Grant will use your desk, and she will perform your duties this week on my behalf."

Bah ha ha! Arabella is getting a taste of her own medicine! And I get to work hand in hand with William. Oh, oh, this was so worth being banished here for a week.

"But, Mr. Cumberland—" Arabella begins to protest.

"Do not *Mr. Cumberland* me," he says, his voice low. "You will go back to your desk, get what you need, and work *here* for the week." William turns to me. "Ms. Grant, get your things and come back with me to my office, please, and we will go over my schedule."

"Yes, Mr. Cumberland," I say.

I quickly lean over and log off my computer. Then I fold my coat over my arm and grab my tote.

Arabella is standing there with a look of utter shock on her face. I think she might cry. I know I would if William

157

Cumberland had gone all badass on me like that.

I walk off with him, and we say absolutely nothing to each other as we move through the hallways. I see a few people glance up as we go by, and there is no doubt in my mind that this will be a big conversation in the break room today.

But I don't care. Let them talk. I know the truth. I know what I have in front of me—a good career and William—and nothing else matters. It just doesn't.

We reach his office, and he lets me step inside first. He shuts the door behind him, strides over to his desk, and leans against the front of it, facing me.

"I do believe," he says slowly, his eyes never leaving mine, "the situation is now officially rectified."

"William!" I cry, smiling at him, "You were freaking brilliant. And such a badass!"

He cocks an eyebrow at me. "I infer you rather like when I am a badass."

I can feel my cheeks flaming. "Uh ..."

"Careful now," he says, his mouth curving up in a slow, sexy smile, "You just saw how I react when people lie to me. Unless you are lying to me to provoke another badass response, which I find immensely flattering."

"Okay, yes, I find it insanely hot when you go all badass mogul on people."

Now he is really grinning. "Interesting. If that is the case, I could go run around and go 'badass,' as you say, to turn you on."

I'm quite sure my cheeks match my red hair right now.

"Speaking of turn-ons," William says, dropping his voice, "I rather fancy your outfit today, Mary-Kate."

"Thank you," I say happily.

"The ponytail is particularly fetching on you," he continues, raking a hand through his dark waves.

"That is immensely flattering of you to say," I reply, flirting right back with him. "Although, I suspect you will be undoing it later tonight."

I watch as his eyes go intense. Yes, I got him with that one. He stares at me for a moment, fiddles with his hair again, and then clears his throat.

"I have a conference call I have to be on around dinner time," he says. "But still come over at the usual time."

I nod. "Okay. I'll stop and get some stuff to make dinner, and I'll have it ready by the time you are off your call."

William stares at me. "I wish we could go be alone right now."

My heart melts. "I know. But at least I can see you now during the day." I clear my throat. "And I should probably go out there and see how many phone calls you've missed this morning."

"Right," he says, rather unconvincingly.

"And I assume you will need airline tickets booked to Sydney," I say, still hating the fact that he has to take Arabella there instead of me.

William rubs his hand over his mouth for a second. "Yes. Friday. First flight out, I suppose." Then he stares at me with a glimmer in his eyes. "Feel free to seat Arabella in cargo if you so desire."

I burst out laughing and then snort, which makes him laugh, too.

"I will make sure she is not seated with you," I assure him. I think about this for a second. "Although my guess is she will try to reseat herself next to you online."

"Oh, just seat me next to an already taken seat and put her as far away from me as possible."

"With pleasure, Mr. Cumberland," I reply professionally, teasing him.

He grins and laughs. "Thank you, Peppa."

"Stop it," I sat, which makes him laugh again. Then I go to walk out the door, but William stops me.

"Mary-Kate?"

I turn around. "Yes?"

"While we shall stick to our usual routine of you meeting me at my place this week, I have plans for our last night in London on Thursday," he announces. "I insist that I pick you up. I'll have the driver that night. And dress up if you like."

Ooh! My pulse surges at this tidbit.

"We're venturing out?" I ask, intrigued. We have made a point to keep a low profile so far, so I'm very curious about his idea to go out on our last night here.

"Indeed," William says, locking his gaze on mine. "I have something rather grand planned, but that is all you are going to get out of me for now."

"How can you bait me like this? I want to know!"

"Want to know and need to know are two very different things," he declares, walking around to his desk. He turns and flashes me a sexy smile. "Trust me, you will not be disappointed."

Oh dear God. As I study him in his white dress shirt and perfectly fitted gray suit pants, I think he could take me to a supermarket and I wouldn't be disappointed.

"All right, you win. *This time*," I say, smiling at him. He laughs, and I open the door to go over to Arabella's desk. She has already been here, as her computer is logged off and everything is clear on her workspace. I sit down and reboot her computer so I can log in.

And while I am sad it is my last week in London with William, and I don't want the week to go by too quickly, I already cannot wait to see what he has in store for Thursday night.

Chapter Nineteen

I pick up my bottle of Versace perfume and spray the base of my throat. Thursday night is finally here, and my last night in London is going to be spent on a mystery date with William.

I take my quilted, satin black hairband and slide it into my hair, excitement racing through me as I know he'll be here in minutes. And I'm pulling out all the stops this evening to look stunning for him.

Tonight, I decided to wear my favorite dress: a beautiful black Kate Spade piece I indulged in last fall. It is a sleeveless dress that plunges into a deep V-neck, and the hemline hits right below my knees. I have a skinny black patent belt around my waist to accentuate it, and I have decided to pair it with my strappy silver stilettos for a sexy look. Then I put on a beautiful black onyx and silver cocktail ring as my only accessory other than my hairband.

Suddenly, there is a knock at my door. I check myself one more time in the mirror, and then I walk across my suite to the door. I glance through the peephole and, oh my, William is dressed in a gorgeous coat and suit. My heart slams against my ribcage the second I see him. If he looks dashing through a peephole, holy shit, I might pass out when I open the door.

It is a chance, however, I'm more than willing to take.

I open the door, and the second I see him, my whole body goes electric. My heart is continuing to pound, and my pulse soars. And every nerve I have tingles as I drink in how sexy he looks.

Everything he is wearing is new. *Everything.* Sharp navy suit; crisp white shirt unbuttoned a few buttons underneath his jacket; perfectly polished black dress shoes. All topped off with the most sophisticated navy houndstooth coat I have ever seen a man wear, one that is modern, fitted, and has gorgeous lapels.

I look up into William's handsome face and see a lock of his wavy hair has fallen across his forehead. I swallow. Dear God, I didn't think I would ever say this, but I have never seen him look more dashing or handsome than he does at this moment.

My eyes meet his. He is appraising me in the same way I am him; I can see it in his light blue eyes.

"Mary-Kate," he says softly, taking my hand as he steps inside the suite, "you look spectacular tonight."

"Thank you," I say quietly. "And, William, you look dashing in that suit and trench coat."

I step closer to him and put my hands on his jacket lapels. "New suit?" I ask, lifting an eyebrow at him.

William's full lips curve up into a smile as his hands wind around my back. "Very astute of you to notice, Mary- Kate. Indeed, it is. I purchased everything from Burberry. Does it meet with your approval?"

Oh good Lord. Does it meet with my approval? He looks so smoking hot in it, I would command he wear it daily if I could get away with it.

"Indeed, it does," I say, smiling up at him.

"Good," William says. "I had to go up a size. Apparently since I have been around you, I have been focused on things other than work. Like eating."

I can't help it. I slide my hands underneath his trench and finely tailored navy jacket and feel his ribs through his white shirt.

"Mm, yes, I do think you have put on a little weight, which I find *very* attractive," I tell him in all honesty.

William lifts an eyebrow. "Five scones worth?"

My face instantly flames in embarrassment. "That was a long time ago," I cry, laughing at the idiotic thing I wrote in my blog.

"I think it is most appropriate that you take that back," William teases.

"I don't take back things I don't mean," I say, reusing his line and lifting an eyebrow right back at him.

He laughs loudly. "*Touché.*" He lowers his lips to mine and gives me a slow kiss. "I really do think," he whispers against my mouth, "that you look stunning tonight. Gorgeous." Then he kisses me again.

Oh my. I could stay like this all night, wrapped up inside his jacket, inhaling the cologne on his skin, feeling his mouth against mine.

As I consider this option, William breaks the kiss. "All right, we need to go. I have a schedule to keep for our last night in London."

My stomach lurches with that thought. I cannot bear the idea of it, of never coming back here with William, of this truly being our last night here. All I can do is pray his heart is growing the same way mine is and this is only the first of many trips we will have here to—

"Mary-Kate?"

I blink. "Yes, let me get my coat," I say, reluctantly letting go of him. I pick up my trench, and he helps me slip into it. I grab my clutch, and we are ready to go.

We get into the elevator, and William reaches for his iPhone. "Excuse me, just have to send a quick message on my mobile."

I laugh and punch the elevator button for the lobby. "Cell. It's called a cell, William."

He gives me a sideways glance. "Have you forgotten what country you are in?"

I laugh, and he finishes his text. Then I hear my phone going off in my purse as we reach the lobby.

I pull it out and see the text is from William. I look at him and furrow my brow.

"Um, I'm right here," I say, confused. "Why are you texting me?"

"It's more fun that way."

Puzzled, I turn and look back at my phone to see what he wrote:

Please know that while in public, I will not display any outward form of affection towards you—just in case we are seen—but I am holding your hand right now in my head. WC

I read the text and melt. I glance over at him, and he winks at me, and my heart is over the moon for this man, and this man only.

"And I'm holding yours," I whisper back to him.

We share a gaze, and right now, he is the only person in the world to me. And I can't believe I'm so lucky to be in this moment with him.

We exit the hotel, and his car is waiting for us. We slip inside, and William doesn't say a word about where we are going.

Which is making me crazy.

"You have to give me a hint about our destination," I say.

He keeps his eyes straight ahead. "Do I?"

"*William!*" I cry, exasperated, which makes him laugh. "Seriously, I must know."

"Seriously, you will know soon enough," he counters.

"Fine, you win. Be William Cumberland, International Mogul Man of Mystery tonight," I say, gazing out the window.

"The mystery," he says slowly in his sexy baritone voice, "will be revealed shortly."

We drive through London, and as we do, I realize we are getting close to the London Eye, the famous wheel on the banks of the River Thames.

"London Eye!" I say excitedly.

"I promised you I would take you," William says, "and I will always keep my word to you, Mary-Kate."

My heart leaps. Oh, how I love the sound of that sentence, that he will always keep his word to me.

"But first," he says, "we are headed to the Royal Festival Hall. I have reservations at Skylon before the Eye."

"What kind of food is it?" I ask. Then I laugh. "But you know I don't care. I'm just so excited to ride the Eye."

"Then why I am I taking you out for modern European cuisine in a posh setting overlooking the Thames? I could have gotten a pizza."

We both laugh. The driver stops at the Royal Festival Hall, where Skylon is located. We slip out of the car and his security team escorts us inside. And as we enter the restaurant, I am once again awed by how chic and beautiful the setting is. Lots of white, beautiful floor-to-ceiling windows overlooking the river, gorgeous light fixtures—everything is perfect for a chic date night.

Once we are seated next to one of the windows, we decide on some wine, and then William proposes a toast.

"To you, Mary-Kate, and your very successful tour of London," he declares.

I incline my head and clink my glass against his, savoring the taste of the fruity pinot noir as I swallow it.

"William, this whole trip has been beyond my dreams. I appreciate you letting me sit in on all those meetings, hearing everything that is going on, but most of all, asking for my input."

His brow creases. "Why wouldn't I ask for your input? I'd be an idiot not to ask for it."

My heart leaps at his words. Of course, I love the fact that William finds me beautiful and sexy, but I think he finds my brain just as sexy as well. And I love hearing him say that to me as much as when I hear him say I look gorgeous.

"Thank you," I tell him softly. I hold my eyes steady on his. "And I want to thank you for sharing your world with me. For letting me into your home every night, for letting me meet your family ..." I trail off for a moment, swallowing before I continue. "And you have been nothing but a complete gentleman to me when we are alone."

William's eyes remain fixated on mine, and I can tell he is trying to read what I am saying. But I feel like I have to address the issue of sex, because I know that is the direction we are heading, but my head is overruling my heart on this one. No matter how much I desire him, and, oh God I do, I can't go there yet. Not without knowing there could be some kind of chance at a future with him first.

"What I mean is, I know ..." I pause, looking for the right

words, "... that you might expect more as far as a physical relationship at this point. But you have not once pushed me or even acted like it was an issue, and I want you to know I deeply appreciate that. Because ..." I feel my face grow warm as I grapple with this. "... I can't rush into something like that. Even if I deeply want to, I have to make sure it is right."

I grab my glass of wine and take a big sip. I look at him, praying he understands this.

William traces his finger around the rim of his wine glass as he stares at me across the table. "Thank you," he says softly, "for being so honest with me. Because the last thing I want is for you to feel uncomfortable about anything. There is no timetable for this. When it is right, we'll both know it. I respect you too much for anything less to be acceptable."

I exhale in relief at his words.

William's eyes flicker, and then he laughs. "Were you nervous about that?" he asks, grinning.

"Very," I say, taking another sip of my wine.

"No need to be," he says, his eyes holding on mine. "And while there is no timetable for *that*, there is a timetable for tonight, so we should think about what to order."

We move on to the menu, and this time I get the fillet of beef, and William gets the rack of lamb. Dinner is exceptional. The view of the River Thames is stunning, the food spectacular, and having William as my date ... I still think I am the luckiest girl in London as I gaze at him across the table.

After dinner, we decide to walk to the Eye. William arranged for us to be on the last ride of the night. The wind is chilly tonight, and I'm glad I am bundled up in my trench. I take in the scene around me, of London lit up, of the River Thames and the Houses of Parliament, and I still can't believe I am here. The Eye is so glorious in lights, and I can hardly contain my excitement about being able to ride it tonight.

There is a line, of course, but with William having a certain kind of ticket, we are bypassing a lot of things. Finally, we board, and I notice we are the only two people in our capsule. Well, two plus two security people, but they are so good at blending in it doesn't even bother me.

"Private capsule," William explains, helping me take off my coat.

"Oh this is so cool!" I cry happily.

He grins and takes off his trench. "I'm glad you approve."

I laugh. "Oh, I definitely do."

We're greeted by a host and served champagne and pink champagne truffles. I truly can't believe this. I'm not only on the London Eye, but in a private capsule, being served champagne, and sharing it all with William. I stand at the window, completely captivated by the city lit up below us as we move.

"Show me everything," I exclaim. "Be my tour guide."

"Ah, yes, my second job as a narrator on the London Eye," William quips. But then he moves behind me and pulls me to his chest, his beautiful hands wrapping around me and holding me protectively to him.

Oh God. Suggesting he be my tour guide was the best idea ever.

William narrates to me, pointing out all the things I might not recognize on sight, and we talk about all the other amazing buildings of London. He leans down to talk into my ear softly as he does this, and it is beyond romantic.

As William is holding me in his arms, I see Big Ben, the Houses of Parliament, and St. Paul's Cathedral twinkling in the black night sky, and I'm in heaven, talking a mile a minute, listening to him point out other things to me that only a native would know.

"This is everything I dreamed it would be," I say, delighted as we near the top of the Eye. "Just breathtaking. I am so, so lucky to be here, William."

"I'm lucky, too," he murmurs in my ear. Then he brushes his lips against my temple in the sweetest of kisses, and I feel my body go weak from his touch. Then he clears his throat. "Would you like some more champagne?"

I turn around to say yes. But then I see it. Next to my champagne glass on the table is a flat, square box from Tiffany & Co. The infamous Tiffany Blue box with a white bow on it.

"William," I gasp, my heart pounding. "Is that for me?"

"Yes," he says simply. "A little gift from me to you."

I move over to the table, stunned. I pick up the blue box and stare at him. "William, you didn't have to do this. Don't you know being with you is enough for me?"

I watch as his blue eyes go soft, very soft. He approaches me, cups my face in his hands, and then brushes his lips against my forehead.

"I know you mean that," he whispers. "So that is even more of a reason why I wanted to give you something."

He steps back from me, and I stare back at him. *Oh, William Cumberland, I think this might be the night I fall in love with you.*

"Please, open it," he encourages.

With a shaking hand, I undo the ribbon. I lift up the top of the box and break the silver seal on the crisply folded tissue paper. And as soon as I see what is inside, I gasp. It is a gorgeous silver and Tiffany blue linked charm bracelet. I hold it in my palm, staring at it in shock.

"Each charm has meaning in regards to our time here," William explains quietly. "The blue Tiffany bag charm is because this is the first gift I have given you, the double-decker bus is one of the things you did on your tourist day, the London taxi is what you took all over the place because you refused to let me drive you, the Bond Street charm because it is famous, and last but not least, that is a silver Chinese zodiac rooster. Closest thing I could find to a chicken. Which we both know has significant meaning from Berkshire."

I'm stunned by this, by the thought William put into this gift, that every single charm represents our time in London together. I gaze at it, knowing full well this cost him at least a couple of thousand dollars, but I also know that the money is irrelevant to him. He wanted me to have something significant, something special, something that only we would understand and nobody else. A gift reflecting our private time in London.

William is this beautiful man with such a beautiful heart, and tears escape my eyes. "I have never received a more thoughtful and meaningful gift in my whole life," I say, my voice cracking. "This means everything to me, William."

"So it meets with your approval?" he asks as he gently brushes away my tears with his fingertips.

I nod. And then I can't help it. I squeal excitely and throw my arms around him in total joy.

"I love it!" I say joyfully. "I love it, I love it, I love it!"

I step back, use the lapels on his Burberry blazer to pull him closer, and kiss him while our capsule is at the top of the Eye. I melt into him, and William responds to my lips on his. He kisses me slowly and sweetly. I taste the champagne on his lips and let my right hand reach up to the nape of his neck, where I play with some of his silky curls as he kisses me.

He breaks the kiss and takes the bracelet from me. He puts it on my left wrist and then extends my arm out to take a look at it.

"Perfect," he says, looking at it.

"Yes, perfect," I say, staring at him.

We finish our ride of the Eye, and I almost feel teary again getting off the ride. Because now I know, with us stepping out of the capsule and back into the city, that my time in London with William is almost over.

He takes me back to the hotel and escorts me back to my room. He steps inside, but I notice he doesn't take off his coat.

"You can stay," I say hopefully, not willing to let go of this time, not yet.

William pulls me into his arms and holds me tightly. "You have an early flight back to Chicago tomorrow. You need to sleep."

It is all I can do not to laugh. *Right. Like I am going to be able to sleep after this evening?*

He steps back from me. I bite my lip. I'm going back to Chicago, and he is on his way to Sydney. I hate this. I don't want to be away from him now, not when we are starting to build something so amazing together.

"I'll be back to Chicago before you know it," William says, reading my mind. He gently cups my face in his hands and gazes into my eyes. "I'll text you the minute I get to Australia. We'll figure out a time to do a Video Connect on Connectivity."

I nod. "Okay."

"I should leave you now. You are going to have to be there early to get through customs as it is."

I bite down hard on my lip so I don't cry. "Right."

William puts his hand on the door. I wait for him to open

it, but he doesn't. Then he turns around and strides over to me, his eyes burning bright. Before I can blink, his hands are tangling in my hair and his mouth is on mine, hot and seeking and demanding entry. I match him with my own seeking kiss, one that is frantic and desperate as my tongue takes everything I can in this moment. I grasp onto his shoulders, then move my hands up to his hair, gripping it as my mouth moves against his. His hands are in my hair, then down my back, pressing me firmly into him. Oh, God. How can I let this man leave me? How?

Finally, William breaks the kiss, and we're both gasping for air. He lowers his forehead to mine again, nuzzling his nose to mine as we try to breathe. I close my eyes and feel his breath against my face, relishing every second his skin is against mine.

"I can't tear myself away from you," he whispers.

I stroke the curls at the back of his head. "I don't want you to go."

William moves his hands up my back, caressing me. He lifts his head and drops a feather-light kiss on the bridge of my nose.

"I must leave now," he whispers, kissing my forehead.

"As much as I don't want to, I must."

He rises and rakes his hand a few times through his hair. "Right," he says in a tone meant to convince both of us. "Leaving now."

I walk him to the door. He opens it and steps through, then gently touches my face one last time.

"Thank you for this evening, and all the other ones," he says, his eyes intent on mine.

"Thank you, William. For making London the best experience of my life," I say with all my heart. "And thank you for the bracelet. You have no idea what this means to me."

He smiles softly. "I do know what it means to you. And I know what it means to me to give it to you."

We stare at each other for a moment, and it is obvious neither one of us wants to say goodbye.

Finally, William sighs. "Good night."

"Good night," I say.

Then William turns and walks away.

I shut the door and lean against it. Then I take off my coat and look down at my beautiful charm bracelet, the one that is now my most treasured possession in the world, and clasp it over my heart.

My heart, which now belongs to William.

And I pray that somehow his heart can belong to me before he leaves Chicago for good in June.

Chapter Twenty

"I'll have the mascarpone and strawberry buttermilk pan-cakes," I tell the server. Then I close my menu and hand it to her.

Renee and Emily give their orders to the server, and she walks away. We're sitting in a booth at a hip Lincoln Park eatery, having a Saturday catch-up brunch.

Except from the way both of them are sitting across the table staring at me, I feel more like this is going to be a CIA interrogation about my time in London.

Or more specifically, the time I spent with *William* in London.

I pour some cream into my coffee and stir, keeping my eyes down. Then I glance out the big window that overlooks the street. It is cold and windy on this March morning. Rain is pouring down and blowing sideways, pelting the glass. I watch as people hurry down the block, desperately trying to keep umbrellas from folding inside out against the gusty wind.

I bite my lip, wishing I was elsewhere. Specifically, in Sydney. William and I have talked once already, but, oh, I miss him so much. It is still hard to believe just a day ago, I was in London. Just a day ago, I was with him—

"MK," Renee says, breaking the silence. "We're both

worried about you."

I turn and stare at my friends. "You have no reason to be worried," I say honestly. "Actually, I've never been better."

I watch as Renee and Emily share a glance. Now I feel like I have learned something from William, as I'm quickly able to deduce that they have practiced this conversation before I came home from London.

"MK, please hear what we have to say," Emily says gently. "You have to understand why we're concerned. You go to London. Someplace you've *always* wanted to go. Yet you haven't posted one thing about it on your Connectivity page. Not one picture, not one quote, nothing. And you've barely said anything at all about it since you've been back. That's weird, MK. Really weird."

"In my defense, I've only been home twenty-four hours. I spent most of yesterday getting settled, doing laundry, and sleeping. And I was there on business," I say firmly. "I wasn't there on vacation."

But I know that is complete bullshit. Because in reality, I feel like London belongs to me and William, and I don't want to share that experience with anyone but him.

Renee leans across the table. "Did you sleep with Cumberland?" she asks in a low voice.

"No!" I snap, my cheeks burning. "And his name is *William*."

Emily's eyes flash with recognition. "You kissed him."

I don't say anything.

"You did," Emily insists.

"MK, what are you *doing*? He's your boss. He's the owner of a worldwide global empire." Renee says. "This is completely out of character for you."

I stare at my best friends. I should be able to tell them

anything. I should be able to tell them about William, but I can't. Because what I have with him is so private, so undefined ... and it belongs to us. I feel protective of what we have, because it is new and just beginning. I'm not ready to share it with anyone, even Emily and Renee.

"I know William is my boss," I tell them slowly. "But trust me when I say I am happy."

Renee lets out an exasperated sigh. "MK, you aren't seeing this clearly. I mean, we both know he must have given you that Tiffany bracelet," she says, gesturing to my left wrist.

I immediately remove my hand from the table and rest it in my lap. I protectively run my fingers over each charm, as if guarding that night from Emily and Renee's eyes.

"That is not a casual gift," Renee continues.

Okay, I have been patient until now. But I'm starting to get mad.

"William," I say slowly, trying to keep my voice even, "wanted me to have something special from London."

"It looks like a mistress gift," Emily blurts out.

"Excuse me?" I ask. "Did you just call my charm bracelet a *mistress gift*?"

"That's not what I meant," Emily says, trying to back-pedal. "But William is whisking you off to London, buying you this crazy expensive gift, and it seems like he's ... keeping you."

Now I'm furious.

"You know what? This whole conversation is an insult," I snap angrily. "I would hope you would both know me well enough to know I wouldn't be with just anybody. I have never wanted *anyone* until I met William. He's different. He is sophisticated and brilliant, and he makes me laugh. He understands me like no one ever has. He makes me feel like I can do anything. He *believes* in me. William thinks I'm smart, he thinks I'm funny, and he thinks I'm beautiful. If anyone is worth taking a risk on, it is him."

"MK, do you hear yourself?" Renee asks. "This is *not* you. You're willing to risk everything you have worked so hard for your entire life for a romance with your boss? If this were to get out and the people at the Beautiful Homes Network were to find out ... MK! Think about what you are doing. Your reputation would be crap. You know it would. And your career dreams would blow up in your face."

"And he's *leaving*," Emily adds pointedly. "What are you going to do when he leaves at the end of June? He is *English*. His worldwide headquarters are in *London*. What will you do when he goes back to his life and you aren't in it?"

"Of course I've thought of all of this. You don't think those things scare me to death?" I cry. "Well, they do. The idea of him leaving is the worst of all those things you have mentioned, and for me to say that is the worst thing that can happen should tell you *exactly* what William means to me."

I see the worried look amplify in their eyes.

"And while I appreciate your concern," I continue, my voice shaking, "I will *not* discuss this any further. I know the risks. Believe me, I know them backwards and forwards. But for the first time in my life, I'm willing to gamble. I'm willing to gamble everything for this man."

Because I love him. I will gamble everything because I am madly in love with William.

"MK, please," Emily pleads, her eyes shining with sincerity. "We're saying this because we *love* you. We don't want to see you get hurt or ruin something you have wanted your whole life for a man you barely know."

"I know him," I say evenly, trying not to explode. "I know him better than anyone."

"How can you?" Renee asks. "Because you spent two weeks in a foreign country with him? Everything can seem romantic and perfect when you aren't fighting over what restaurant you want to eat at or if he forgets to put the cap back on the toothpaste. And what has he promised you, MK? Other than trips and gifts?"

I can't take it anymore. I slap my hand down on the table so hard that a spoon flies off and hits the floor and all the water glasses vibrate. People next to us are staring at me like I'm a lunatic.

"This conversation is over. Or I'm leaving. Take your pick, but I will not sit here and listen to both of you insult my intelligence. And I will be *damned* if I sit here and listen to you question William's motives when you do not know a single freaking thing about him."

I keep my eyes steady in a William-esque way. Emily and Renee fall silent, and now the catch-up brunch has become the most awkward brunch in the history of Chicago.

At that moment, our server walks up and cheerfully begins putting down our plates in front of us. Nobody is talking now, and I stare at my pancakes, my appetite completely gone.

I pick up my fork and listlessly begin to pick at the pancakes. My cell goes off, notifying me of a text message. I put down my fork and fish my phone out of my bag. My heart is overjoyed to see it is from William:

It is 2 a.m. on Sunday. Can't sleep. Negotiations begin on Monday. But I can't stop thinking. WC

I bite my lip. His brain is going three thousand miles per hour in all different places on how to get this deal done. I know he must be exhausted from traveling around the globe, thinking about this major acquisition, and completely stressed, too.

Write down your thoughts on the negotiations, all of them. Then put your notes aside, and we'll sort through them tomorrow if you want. You have to get some sleep. You must be exhausted. Worried about you. MKG

I take a sip of my coffee, and William sends his response:

Who says I am thinking about negotiations? WC

Ooh! I feel my pulse skip. Then he sends another text before I can respond:

I'm thinking about you. And that you are too far away from me right now. God, how I miss you. WC

He misses me. My heart is absolutely elated, and the anger I had a few minutes ago has completely dissolved. This is what matters. Not what other people think, even my closest friends. I have to listen to my heart.

And my heart tells me William is everything I need. I quickly text him back:

I miss you, too. So much. Can we Video Connect soon? I need to see you. MKG

I eagerly await his response. I hear Emily and Renee talking now, about some sale at Nordstrom, but I only want to talk to William at this moment.

I'll make time for it. I have to see you, too. 5 p.m. in Chicago is 10 a.m. Sunday in Sydney. Let me sleep for a few hours, and we'll Video Connect then. BTW, I am here. WC

He sends me a picture of the view from his bed at the Four Seasons Presidential Suite. I see contracts and papers and his iPad on the edge of the bed and Sydney Harbor twinkling through the windows of the luxuriously-appointed suite. I laugh softly, as "I am here" is now one of our running text jokes to each other.

I smile wickedly and type back:

Time is arranged. I'll be wearing a hairband. MKG

God, I love flirting with my man. He replies:

You are very much the seductress, aren't you? WC

I laugh and type back:

Indeed. Oh, by the way, I am here. Eating pancakes. MKG

I take a picture of my pancakes and attach it to my text. I glance up at Renee and Emily, who are staring at me like they have never seen me before.

"Just chatting with William," I say, because in my life, this is normal. *The new normal.* "I thought he'd like to see what I'm eating."

Beep!

American pancakes are not like British pancakes. Ours are more like a crepe. Your pancakes are ridiculously big. WC

I type back:

I shall make you some upon your return. I think I am going to be able to convince you the American ones are much better. MKG

Beep!

You are convincing me several things are better in America, Mary-Kate. WC

My heart jumps. I know he is talking about me.

Go to sleep, William. I'll see you in a few hours. MKG

He instantly responds:

Wish I could see you now. Will settle for the morning. WC

I stare at his message, my heart filled with joy. Then I put the phone down.

Despite this awful start to the day, I'm now in a fabulous mood. I pick up my fork, as my craving for pancakes has returned, and take a bite. It is cold and raining outside, but a perfect day to stay in my room with my iPad, cup of coffee on my nightstand, and work on some blog articles.

It is going to be, as William would say, a "brilliant" day.

Even though my closest friends do not believe this romance can work, that they think I'm making a horrible mistake, that this will come back to haunt me, that William will leave me, I know, I just *know* that can't be true. Not with William.

I know without a doubt he is holding my heart in his hands.

And I trust him not to break it come June.

Chapter Twenty-One

By five o'clock, I'm more than ready to see William. I have waited all day for this call, for this chance to see him. I grab my iPad, put it in the dock on my desk, and pull up my chair. I access Video Connect, tap his contact button, and request a video connection with him. My stomach does eager flip-flops as I wait for him to accept my call.

And he does.

My heart leaps inside my chest as I see his handsome face, and he smiles the second our connection is made. He looks tired—I can see that by the shadows under his eyes. And, oh my God, is that stubble on his face? I know he's exhausted now, as I have *never* seen him with stubble.

But damn, he looks smoking hot with it. *Really freaking hot.*

I greedily drink all of him in, as much as the iPad will let me see. He's wearing a lightweight khaki-colored sweater and has a T-shirt on underneath it. Oh, he's so handsome I can barely breathe as I gaze at him.

And right now, this handsome man is waiting for me to speak.

"William!" I cry excitedly. "Can you hear me?"

"Yes, perfectly," he says, his deep baritone coming through

loud and clear. "Can you hear me?"

"Yes," I reply, nodding happily. "How are you? How are you really? You look exhausted."

"I am," he admits, rubbing his hand along his jawline. "But I'm better now that I can see you. God, Mary-Kate, I miss you."

I put my hand toward the screen, and he does the same, both of us wishing we could somehow touch each other, but knowing this is the best we can do.

"I miss you, too," I say. "I miss you so, so much. I hate being in Chicago and knowing you aren't here."

"You're wearing your bracelet," William says, smiling at me.

"I am," I say happily, holding it up so he can get a good look at it. "Some dashing British man insisted that I have it."

He grins. "A man of exquisite taste, I can see."

"Indeed," I say, laughing. "He has very fine taste."

"Thank you for wearing a hairband," William tells me, his eyes flickering sexily at me. "You look fetching as always."

I touch the black, skinny ribbon band in my hair. "Thank you. Perhaps you can help me take it out when you come home," I reply suggestively.

"Indeed," William says, his eyes flashing. Then he rakes his hand through his wavy hair, and a dark lock falls down across his forehead. Oh, what I wouldn't give to be able to reach through that screen and push it back into place for him.

"So this is your room?" he asks, and I see his laser eyes looking around me.

I laugh. "I can give you a tour. Hang on." I remove the iPad from the dock. "Here you are, my tiny apartment bedroom in Lincoln Park. Don't get too jealous of my spacious accommodations."

He laughs, that deep rich laugh that I love so much.

"I shall take that under advisement. All right, details. Tell me how you came up with the interior design for this room. I should know, as I'm allowing you to decorate my penthouse. Consider this your portfolio review."

I laugh so loud I snort, and then he laughs again, too.

"Come on, Peppa, I'm waiting. You should never keep a client waiting, you know."

I give him a serious look. "Of course, Mr. Cumberland, how entirely rude of me to make you wait. I don't know if you care to consider extending me the contract after such rudeness," I say, flirting with him again.

William puts his fingertips in that steeple position against his lips. "I'm sure I can think of a way that can be rectified," he replies, his eyes lasering in on mine. "So we can maintain the verbal agreement, you know. So it will be most appropriate to make arrangements for rectifying such rudeness upon my arrival in Chicago."

Ooh, he is so hot when he does that. "I like your style, Mr. Cumberland," I say smartly.

William removes his fingertips from his lips. "As I do yours."

Okay, it is getting hot in here now. I decide to switch gears before I beg him to let me come to Sydney so I can make out with him like mad in his hotel room.

"Now, shall I show you my functional arrangement of practical, yet entirely decorative décor?"

William laughs. "Please."

I laugh, too, and show him my vintage blue-and-white striped wallpaper, the upholstered headboard that I made myself with thick white fabric and antique blue buttons, the chambray duvet cover and loads of white and blue floral pillows, the old white book shelves with my favorite cookbooks, and the desk I spray painted and refurbished to match my décor.

I finish the tour and grin at him. "Do you approve? Am I to proceed with the project?"

His eyes are completely lit up. "You're so talented. You have vision. It looks like something that should be on the Beautiful Homes Network."

Happiness fills me from his words. "Thank you."

"And I know you'll do a brilliant job with the penthouse. In fact, you may work on the place while I'm out. Paint, furniture, whatever you want to do, I give you complete control. Use my personal card. And if you want to stay there, you can."

"Stay in your penthouse?" I ask. Immediately I think of his bed. Of sleeping in his bed. Oh, I don't know if I can handle that.

"It might be easier. You wouldn't have to run back and forth between your apartment and Millennium Park. And you're closer to the office, too," William says.

I think of it. Of staying in his place. It would give me more privacy to talk to him when we Video Connect, and I would get a breather from this tense situation with Renee and Emily, too.

And in some small way, I would feel closer to William while he's so far away.

That thought seals the deal for me. "I will," I decide. "Thank you."

"You're welcome. I will have my security team bring you a key and access codes for the penthouse on Monday."

"Okay," I say, nodding. Then I clear my throat. "Now it's your turn. Show me your suite. I want to see what a

Presidential Suite looks like."

William grins. "All right."

I watch as he takes his iPad and shows me around. Oh, my. The suite is utterly stunning. My jaw hangs open while he gives the tour.

"This is the lounge area," he says. "You can see the Opera House from here and from the dining room."

"Wow," I gasp. I see a gorgeous sitting area with a large sofa and a round black coffee table, all with incredible panoramic views of the harbor.

William begins walking into a new room. "Here's the dining room," he says. I see a huge table with ten chairs around it. "This is where I will be beating my head in negotiations all week."

I bite my lip. He is going after Snap-shots, a rising star in the photo-sharing business. He thinks this is an essential cornerstone to the future of his empire, and I know that is why he flew all the way to Sydney to make sure the deal was done.

He shows me a few more things, and finally, he opens the door to the master bedroom.

"This is brilliant," William says. "Look at this bed."

I swallow hard. Oh God, help me, it is the sexiest bed I have ever seen. It is a black, four-poster, king-sized bed, with a sexy, modern linen canopy on top.

He's sleeping in that bed.

It is all I can do to not beg him to let me come to Sydney so I can share that bed with him.

"So that's all," William says, turning the iPad around.

I blink, jarred from my thoughts.

"Mary-Kate?" he asks, raising an eyebrow.

"It's gorgeous," I reply. "I wish I could be there with you."

"I know," he says, sinking back down in his desk chair and putting his iPad back in the dock. He rakes both his hands through his hair. "I wish I weren't even doing this damn Snap-shots takeover."

"William!" I gasp, shocked. "You wanted this. You said you needed Snap-shots to evolve."

"That was before," he interrupts.

"Before what?" I ask, confused.

"It is taking up too much of my time," he says firmly. "I have a damn empire, how much more do I need? Why I am I here? Why am I here when I could be—"

There is a loud knock on William's door, interrupting him.

No! I want whoever it is to go away! What was he about to say to me?

He furrows his brow. "Who is that? Hold on."

Damn it. I bite my lip, willing him to come back after telling the maid he doesn't need sheets or towels or something.

I can't see William now, but I can hear him. I hear the door open, and then a woman's voice.

"Mr. Cumberland, good morning. I know you never take time to eat, so I took the liberty of bringing you breakfast. I hope you don't mind."

Oh! It's Arabella!

"Ms. Dalton, thank you, but I am not hungry," I hear William say.

I hear them come closer. They are now in the living area, and I can see them, but Arabella doesn't know I am there. And I begin seething when I see what she is wearing.

Arabella is dressed in a sexy, black, bandage-type wrap dress, one that is form fitting and rather much for work. Oh yes. So freaking appropriate for making copies on a Sunday, which is what her ass should be doing right now.

"I got a protein power breakfast for you, and some tea with lemon, just the way you like it, Mr. Cumberland," she says, placing the box and to-go drink container on the coffee table.

"Again, Ms. Dalton, while I appreciate your concern, I am more than capable of getting my own breakfast," William says firmly.

Yes! He is putting her back in her place and telling her this is not appropriate.

Oh, how I love my man.

"Oh, I know, Mr. Cumberland, but really, I know what you need before these big negotiations. I know better than anybody. We have been together a long time, you and me."

I want to slap her.

I watch as William's eyes flicker angrily. I can tell he is done with her and this crap.

"No, Ms. Dalton—" he begins, but Arabella cuts him off.

"You have something on your sweater, Mr. Cumberland," she says, pointing to his left shoulder.

"What?" he snaps, looking down in distraction.

"There," Arabella says, moving closer to him.

I watch in horror. If she touches him, so help me I will be on the next flight to Sydney to kick her ass back to England. She reaches out and lightly flicks her fingertips across his shoulder, picking at a piece of so-called fluff and brushing it aside.

"All taken care of, Mr. Cumberland," she says, gazing at him with adoration in her eyes. "You know you can count on me to take care of everything. To the smallest detail."

She is so dead. Because I am going to kill her.

I watch as William takes a step back from her and folds his arms across his chest. "I am already working," he says in an icy tone. "I need to get back to *business*."

"Oh!" Arabella gasps, putting a hand to her chest. "I am so, so sorry, Mr. Cumberland. But we do need to meet sometime this morning to go over the menus and what you want brought up here for the meetings, and at what time you want food delivered."

"I don't care!" William snaps, going into full-blown irritation mode. "It is *food.* Just make sure you have the right amount and whatever you serve, we will *eat.* Now, please, go to your menu planning, and I shall consult with you later about the copies I need made. I am occupied right now with something *extremely important*, and I need for you to leave so I can get back to it *immediately*."

"Oh. Right," Arabella says, lifting her chin. "Yes, I will get right on that Mr. Cumberland."

I'm seething as I watch her stand there. Why is she not leaving? *Leave already! I want to talk to my man, and you are taking precious time away from us!*

"Mr. Cumberland, I cannot help but notice you are extremely stressed," she continues, gazing at him with concern. "I know you need to be at the top of your game tomorrow, so I took the liberty of making a massage appointment for you at the spa this afternoon as a break from your work."

She is trying to lure him into the spa!

I want to throttle her. I want to jump through this screen and tell her to stay away from my man.

"What?" William asks, creasing his brow. "Did you really make me a spa appointment?"

"Mr. Cumberland, you must take care of yourself," Arabella says. "A massage would ease all this tension out of your shoulders. You have to release all this negative energy so you can be at the top of your game for negotiations this week. I made one for myself at the same time."

She wants to do a dual massage with William. I'm so going to explode if she does not get out of his room right now.

He stares at her, his brow still creased.

"So let me understand correctly, Ms. Dalton," he says in a very low, very controlled voice. "You think you know what I need and when I need it, is that correct?"

"Well, Mr. Cumberland, you are extremely stressed. I thought, as your lead assistant, I would take steps to make you feel better and make your job easier. Isn't that what I am supposed to do?"

"I do not know," William says. Then he turns and looks right at me. "Let me ask my North American assistant. Ms. Grant, do chime in, please. What do you think about that?"

Chapter Twenty-Two

Arabella freezes the second William mentions my name. Her skin turns bright red, and her jaw drops open. "Wh-what?" she stammers.

"You heard me," he says firmly. He sweeps his arm out toward where his iPad is docked on the desk and looks straight at me. "Ms. Grant, do you care to say hello to your British counterpart?"

I smile brightly at Arabella. "Hello, Arabella." Her eyes pop wide open the second she sees me. A look of utter horror and shock are etched on her face.

"So, Ms. Grant, please elaborate, if you would be so kind," William says. "Do you feel it is Ms. Dalton's duty, as my assistant, to attend to my every personal need and want?"

Oh, I am so loving this. I stare hard at Arabella and answer his question.

"No, Mr. Cumberland, I do not. We are here to assist you on business matters," I say, lying through my teeth. "For example, I think you are perfectly capable of determining what you would like to eat for breakfast without my assistance."

Arabella looks like she wants to throw William's iPad right out into Sydney Harbor. Ha!

"Furthermore," I continue, "I do not think it is my place to suggest you get a massage or anything else of that nature. It is not professional for me to do so as your assistant."

But totally appropriate for me to suggest as your girlfriend, I add to myself.

Arabella is shooting daggers at me.

I smile and return them in kind.

"Intriguing philosophy, Ms. Grant," William says, staring at me. He puts his fingertips to his lips, as if he is deeply assessing the value of my words. I see his eyes shining, and I know he loves this just as much as I do right now.

Then he turns back to Arabella. "I concur with Ms. Grant. Please stick to the business at hand, Ms. Dalton. Plan the menus, make sure I have everything I need for the meeting tomorrow, and I will request things as needed as the negotiations continue. Is that understood?"

She swallows and looks down at the floor. "Yes, Mr. Cumberland."

"If that is all, I need to get back to discussing the week ahead in Chicago with Ms. Grant. She was kind enough to indulge me addressing work issues on her Saturday, and I do not care to delay her any longer than I have to."

Bah ha ha! It is getting hard to keep a straight face now.

"Yes, Mr. Cumberland," Arabella says. She gives me one quick glance, and I smile brightly at her. Her eyes narrow again, and then she turns and walks briskly out of the room.

I hear the door shut, and then I look at William, who is now walking toward me.

"Damn it, I do not have time to waste on her," he snaps, sitting back down in front of me. "This time belongs to you. That pisses me off."

I was set to be furious, to rant and rave about how she is trying to make moves on him, about what an epic bitch she is, but when I see how upset William is about losing time with me, I can't do it.

Studying his exhausted face, I know what he needs right now. And that is not it.

"William," I say softly, "Please don't be angry. You need to focus on Snap-shots."

He exhales loudly. "What if I throw a bunch of money at them to get this done? I just want to come home to you."

"William!" I cry, "That is *not* what a badass mogul does. You go in there and be *THE William Cumberland*. You make them sweat, and you get the best deal for Connectivity. That is what you are going to do. I will not stand for anything less from you."

Despite how exhausted he is, the intensity is back in his laser blue eyes. "You're right."

"I know I am," I say firmly, staring at him, wishing I could be there. "So I want you to prepare to be that badass. Go get Snap-shots. Then you can come home to me."

"I'm probably going to be here for another week," William says seriously, putting his hand back up to the screen. "Once I get the takeover done, I'll have to do interviews, which I despise, then reassure the people at the Sydney office that everything is going to transition well."

I put my hand up and touch his on the iPad screen. "I figured as much." I remove my hand and lift an eyebrow at him. "You aren't going to handpick a Sydney assistant, are you?"

"That move was only for a certain sexy redhead in Chicago," William says, lifting an eyebrow back at me.

I blush furiously, and he smiles.

I clear my throat. "I will try to have your penthouse done by the time you get back," I say, trying to make the best of the situation, although the idea of him being gone for fourteen days makes my heart hurt.

"Ah, yes, the project you ignored because you were mad at me," William teases.

"Oh, shut up," I say, laughing.

He laughs with me, and I bask in the richness of the sound.

"Seriously, though, I can't wait to see it," William says. "I know it is going to be brilliant."

"I hope so," I reply. "I'm going to start tomorrow. Tonight, I'm going to do some articles for the Beautiful Homes website."

"Good. Send them to me as you finish so I can read them."

"William, you don't have time for that."

"I," he says firmly, staring at me, "*always* have time for you."

I'm sorely tempted to tell him to throw his money around and get on the next flight headed back to Chicago.

I nod. Then I get serious on him. "Please take care of yourself."

"Make time to swim," I add, knowing that is how he relieves stress. Then I rethink that. "And if Arabella shows up poolside in a string bikini with a cocktail for you, I will kick her ass."

William roars with laughter. "I won't tell her my swim schedule."

I manage to laugh, but I don't trust her not to try that maneuver.

He exhales. "I need to go."

"I know you do."

"Let's try to video chat daily," he says. "I'll text you times that might work."

"Okay," I reply, feeling my throat grow a little tight.

"I miss you," William says again.

"I miss you, too," I say back to him. "I'll talk to you tomorrow."

"Good evening, Mary-Kate," he replies. "Sweet dreams."

"Bye, William."

And then he's gone. Swallowing hard, I get up out of my chair and flop down on my bed. I pick up one of my throw pillows and hold it to my chest, and as I do, I study my Tiffany bracelet.

I'm so in love with this man. It is crazy. It is absurd. We have only been together two weeks, if you start counting from the time since our first kiss.

As I brush my fingers over each charm, I know it doesn't make any sense to the outside world. Renee and Emily think I've lost my mind. I'm risking everything for a man who doesn't live here, for a man who has repeatedly said he doesn't want a serious relationship, for a man who runs a global empire and has always said it comes first.

But when I look into his soulful blue eyes, they tell me everything I need to know.

William is my future, my world, my everything.

And I know, without a doubt, gambling on him is the right thing to do.

So with that thought in my head, I get up to begin packing some of my clothes and get ready to go to Penthouse 57 in Millennium Park on Monday.

* * *

During the next two weeks, my world is crazy busy. I am managing everything for William at the office while he's out. I'm blogging all the time and redecorating his penthouse. I also wrote two articles for the Beautiful Homes Network website, which were so well-received that they put me on the calendar as a regular contributor.

It is so strange how things turn out, I think as I run some copies of talent contracts for William to sign upon his return. I have spent all my college years, my internships, the past two years in the working world with one agenda in mind: lining myself up for a career in television programming. But I had no idea I'd enjoy writing for a website so much or become so passionate about blogging.

My blog has totally taken off thanks to Rupert and Claire spreading the word among their friends. I now have more than one hundred subscribers. Totally crazy. My brain is so full of ideas for it, too. I'm always jotting down notes in a notebook and taking pictures, and I feel truly engaged and inspired by what I am doing.

Writing brings me so much joy that I'm wondering if maybe that is the direction I should pursue, despite my lifelong dream of working in television programming.

I finish the copies and gather them up into my arms. My heart jumps inside my chest. William is leaving Sydney tonight. He is coming *home.* God, it has been too long since I have touched him, too long since I've kissed that perfect mouth of his. I never thought it was possible to miss anyone as much as I have missed him these past two weeks.

I head back down the hallway, toward my cubicle. I also can't wait to show him the penthouse. I've painted. I've found accessories, like antique books about poetry and geography, which I know are some of his passions. I've had a new sofa and coffee table delivered. And I have some surprises, too—ones that I hope he loves as much as I do.

William's penthouse. I have stayed there the past two weeks, ever since that first night he said I could. I've slept in his bed—not an easy feat the first few nights—but then it became home to me. Penthouse 57 just feels like where I should be.

Where I am meant to be.

I reach his office and pause outside the door. Just knowing he's not there makes my chest tighten with sadness. Suddenly, I hear my cell phone go off. I walk over to my desk, put the copies down, and see that it is Michelle calling.

"Hello?" I answer as I go to sit in my chair. Except I miss, and I fall to the floor with a loud crash and bang my arm on the desktop on the way down. "Ouch!" I yell into the phone.

"MK? Good lord, what was *that*?" Michelle asks.

"Nothing!" I say, scrambling back into my chair. "What's up?"

"You know, MK, I know my wedding is not your highest priority," Michelle snaps, "But you can at least respond to my emails asking for your opinion. It is so rude for you to ignore me like this."

I bite my tongue. I responded to her list of emails, Connectivity notes, and Pinterest pins Monday. It is now Friday.

"Michelle," I say calmly, "I responded to many of them earlier this week, and there were a lot of them to—"

"That is because you do not answer in a timely fashion!" she roars.

Do not scream, I command myself. *Do not scream. Do not scream at her like you want to.*

"Michelle, at first I was busy in London," I say evenly. "I

was there for work."

"Oh my God, will you stop it already about work and London? I know you don't understand the concept of *love*, MK, but for some of us, that is all that matters."

I ignore that comment, thinking how ironic it is that she chooses to throw that in my face when, for the first time in my life, I am completely in love.

"Michelle, I have been in London. My boss is in Australia, and I have a lot of work to do for him here. I have articles that need to be submitted for the Beautiful Homes Network."

"And you don't have two seconds to respond to a message?"

Breathe. Don't rip her head off. Don't do it.

"Michelle—"

"I mean, it's not like you have a *boyfriend* who would take up your spare time, MK!"

Okay, rip her head off. Now.

"That," I snap, "is the dumbest thing you have ever said. Like I can only be busy if I have a boyfriend? And that my not responding to an email is only acceptable if I have one? That is so insulting, I don't even know what to say."

Michelle snorts. "Like you would ever have one. You're too busy with your so-called career to have anything else."

Ooh! I am so beyond pissed at Bridezilla right now that I can barely breathe.

But then William flashes through my head. *Act like William doing business. Go cold and icy and to the point.* "Michelle," I say, my voice low, "I have a career. You are calling me during business hours. I will respond to your pressing emails this evening when I have time to think about them. Now I am terminating this call until you can talk respectfully to me."

And then I hang up, access my inbox from my iPhone, and

find five emails from Michelle, all sent this morning.

CUSTOM "BRIDE" DRESS HANGER

ETSY BRIDE HANGER-WHICH ONE

ROBE THAT SAYS BRIDE

ARE YOU THERE??????

URGENT ROBE AND HANGERS

Oh my God. She went off on me because I didn't respond to her emails regarding a hanger and a robe for a wedding that is almost nine months away?

My phone rings, and I'm jolted out of my fury. Because I made William's ringtone "London Calling" by The Clash, and right now the song is playing from my iPhone.

Which means he is on the phone. I grab it and answer, shocked to see he is calling. "William?" I ask.

"Mary-Kate," his familiar baritone voice says, making my heart leap with joy, "I decided it would be better to leave Sydney sooner rather than later. I'm in Dallas right now, waiting to connect to get back to Chicago."

I realize what this means. He's going to be home in hours. "William!" I cry happily, getting up and going into his office, shutting the door behind me so I can talk privately. "You have no idea how happy this makes me!"

"Me, too," he says. "I'll be landing at O'Hare at six-thirty tonight. Would you care to pick me up?"

"I think it would be most appropriate for me to pick you up. However, do not expect me to carry your luggage," I say, teasing him.

William bursts out laughing. "Well, as I do not care for the contents of my luggage to be accidentally dropped all over the concourse, I will comply with that arrangement."

I laugh with him. Then I get serious. "I can't wait for your flight to get in. I have missed you *so* much."

"Not more than I have missed you," he declares.

We chat for a few more minutes and then say goodbye, with William texting me the flight details and me agreeing to meet him at baggage claim.

Just like that, everything in my world is about to be right again.

My man is on his way back to me. And I can hardly wait to see him tonight.

Chapter Twenty-Three

I pace around the baggage claim area at O'Hare International Airport for what seems like the thousandth time. I am so anxious to see William that I dashed back to his penthouse, changed clothes, re-did my makeup, and got to the airport extra early in anticipation of his arrival.

I sit back down in one of the uncomfortable plastic chairs and restlessly tap my foot against the tiled floor. I check his flight info on my phone—again—to make sure his flight is on time. It is. The baggage claim? Still the same.

I draw an eager breath. In fifteen minutes, his flight should be on the ground.

And I have never been so excited to see anyone in all my life.

I rifle through my purse and pull out my compact again. My hair is perfect—a new jade hairband is in play. Actually, a whole new outfit is in play for tonight. I am wearing a jade-colored, three-quarter-sleeved turtleneck sweater, and I paired it with a black and jade tweed mini skirt. My tall, black, heeled boots and a simple gold cuff complete my look.

I get up and begin pacing again. Then check my phone for the hundredth time. I swear time is freaking standing still. I want William home, and I want him home now.

I see his flight flash up on the baggage claim monitor. People begin streaming in, and I witness joyful reunions take place in front of me.

I crane my neck down the hallway, looking for William's familiar frame, his dark wavy hair, his leather jacket that he likes to travel in this time of year.

Nothing.

Now I'm frustrated. He sits in *first class*. He is always one of the first people off the airplane!

Beep!

I glance down at my phone. It's a text with a picture. From William:

I am here. WC

I glance at the photo. It is of a vacant baggage claim area about ten down from where I am standing. What? Why is he there?

Before I can even type back, he sends me another text.

Please meet me here, Mary-Kate. WC

Confused, I type back:

Why are you at the wrong baggage claim? MKG

After a few moments, he responds:

Because I find a public display of affection in a crowded place most inappropriate considering our situation. However, I do not think I will be able to keep my hands off you the second I see you. PLEASE HURRY. I'm getting IMPATIENT. WC

Excitement rips through me as I read his sexy text. I drop my phone into my purse and hurry through the throng of reunions, drivers holding up signs looking for people, screaming children, and people pushing luggage on metal carts.

I keep going, practically running as I get closer. He is waiting at Baggage Claim #3. I see the signs as I go past, knowing I am getting closer with each step. I reach a corridor and see a sign noting Baggage Claim #3 is around the corner. I hurry my pace and turn the corner.

And there he is.

Standing in front of a vacant baggage conveyor belt, just him and a few other random passengers walking from one point to another in the area.

I stop dead in my tracks, my heart pounding at the mere sight of him. William is wearing his black leather jacket with a black T-shirt and jeans, his leather bag slung over his shoulder.

And this gorgeous, sexy, brilliant man—*my man*—is waiting for me.

I feel this huge smile come over my face, and I run to him. I can't help it. I'm so in love with this man, and have missed him so much, that I can't take a second longer to get to him.

William's face lights up as I quickly approach. A huge grin spreads across his face, and his eyes are shining at me as he strides toward me, too.

We meet in the middle of the vacant claim area, and he immediately reaches for my hand. I feel as though everything is right in my world once again the second his fingers entwine around mine.

"This way," he says firmly, and leads me to a concrete pillar in a corner of the concourse. We slip behind it, and the second we are there, his hands cup my face, caressing my cheeks, his magnetic blue eyes riveted to mine.

"My God, I have missed you," William whispers urgently, his eyes intense with desire as I wind my hands around the back of his neck. "It has driven me mad not to be with you."

CHAPTER TWENTY-THREE

"William," I whisper back, "I—"

But before I can say another word, his lips find mine. His tongue sweeps inside my mouth in a slow kiss. His hands trail along my back and draw me into his chest as he kisses me, and I can feel the heat radiating off his body, which is sexy as hell.

I eagerly respond to his kiss, my heart racing, my pulse burning. I stroke his hair, feeling the familiar silky dark curls slide through my fingertips.

"Two weeks," William whispers against my lips, "is too long to be without you."

He kisses me again, his mouth urgently claiming mine.

I'm melting into him in this little corner of O'Hare that is like our own world right now. I move my hands from his hair to underneath his leather jacket and, oh, he is wearing a cashmere T-shirt. I feel the fine fabric underneath my fingertips, the firmness of his waist, toned by swimming, and inhale the scent of his cologne wrapping around me.

Then he breaks the kiss. I rest my head against his chest, and I can hear his heart racing underneath the expensive fabric of his T-shirt.

"I missed you so much," I murmur into his chest. "It felt like you were gone forever, William. I hated it."

He kisses the top of my head and runs his hand over my hair. "I know. I despised being away from you for that long. I will never do that again."

I turn and look up at him, my heart stopping. I know he is talking about the now, but could he be talking about the future, too? That he won't leave for London without me in June?

"Never?" I ask, my eyes desperately searching his.

William stares back at me, his hand now running over my hair in a comforting manner. "I'm supposed to go back to

London for two weeks in April. I think that will be dropped to one. I can muddle through one week without you. But two weeks is bloody unbearable."

I smile at him and tug on the lapels of his rich leather jacket. "I think that sounds like a fantastic plan. Since I do require you to be a badass international mogul, travel is sometimes required."

He grins at me. "Anything to turn my Bossy American on."

I blush furiously, and William roars with laughter. "Come on, Mary-Kate. Let's go see if the airline has retrieved my luggage. But first, do tell. Are you wearing a new outfit?"

"Yes," I say, stepping back while holding his hands so he can see my jade sweater and tweed mini skirt. "Do you find it agreeable?" I say flirtatiously.

"I find it more than agreeable," he says in a low voice, pulling me back to him and holding my hands over his heart. "I find it rather sexy on you. You know I like you in skirts."

"And hairbands," I add, flashing him a smile.

"Indeed," William says, gently pressing his lips against mine. "Now let's go retrieve my luggage. I want to go home and see my new penthouse."

"I hope you like it," I say as we start to walk.

"I'll love it," he replies simply. "If you did the décor, I know it will be brilliant."

He lets go of my hand, and we walk through the terminal side-by-side, without touching, just in case anyone from Collective Media Enterprises is in the airport. Not that I would be recognized by most people, but William definitely would.

His security detail appears out of the woodwork and walk with us. I blush thinking of the kiss they discreetly witnessed, but I also understand this is part of being with William until we are back at home.

As we near baggage claim, I stare up at his profile. My God, he is so handsome. I drink in the sight of him, the sculpted cheekbones, the delicious wavy hair, the full lips. I watch as he scrolls through his iPhone, no doubt mentally sorting through the hundreds of urgent texts and emails he has waiting for him.

You are so sexy brainy, I think, still staring at him. I can see in his eyes he is making rapid-fire decisions: delete, irrelevant, deal with, intrigued. I can see everything in those laser blue eyes of his—

Wham!

I feel a horrific pain in my hip as I clip the edge of a metal luggage cart rack. I go flying forward and end up in a heap on the tiled floor of O'Hare, my purse tumbling forward and all its contents scattering around, passengers dodging out of the way as I yell out in pain.

"Mary-Kate!" William is instantly by my side, his eyes filled with concern. "Are you all right?"

I'm so embarrassed. Why can't I be normal in front of him? *Why?*

"I'm fine," I lie, scrambling to my knees and quickly trying to pick up everything that has spilled out.

William begins to help me and pauses as he hands me my wallet.

"This feels rather familiar," he quips.

"You shut up," I cry, laughing, thinking of that horrible day when I smashed his tea set to pieces.

"I bet you wanted to tell me that when I suggested you needed a tea trolley," he says, handing me my iPhone.

"Oh, I wanted to tell you more than to shut up," I say, smiling at him.

His eyes are dancing at me, and he laughs. "Yes, I bet you did." William gazes over my shoulder at the luggage rack behind me. "And how ironic. You clipped a trolley rack while you were busy staring at me."

I blush furiously, and he laughs loudly.

"I can't help it that I find your handsome profile incredibly distracting," I say, being one hundred percent honest.

"Yes, I am rather dashing for a mogul," William teases. I laugh so hard I snort, which makes him laugh, too. "Come on, Peppa, off the floor now," he says, helping me up.

We get to the baggage claim, and his bags are already there. William grabs them, and then I lead him to where I have parked.

The air is crisp on this late March evening, but not unbearable. I watch as William draws a breath of air, and I cannot help but notice how tired he looks. I know this trip was exhausting, and I want nothing more than to take care of him tonight.

I lead him over to my car, a red Fiat, and hit the fob to unlock it.

William stops dead in his tracks and stares at the car, then back at me.

"How am I supposed to fit in *that*?" he asks.

"Don't be ridiculous. It is a perfectly comfortable car," I declare.

He lifts an eyebrow at me. "Are you forgetting I am six foot three?"

I think about this for a moment. "Well, this is the only car I have, William Cumberland, so you are going to have to slide the seat back and deal with it."

He grins. And I want to laugh, as I am sure nobody has ever driven William Cumberland around in a Fiat before and told him to suck it up.

"Let me open the *trunk*," I say specifically.

"Odd American term," William says, lifting his bags inside. Then he slams the hatch shut.

"You are with a Bossy American in America. It's a trunk."

"Oh, yes, then it is a trunk," he quips. Then he turns to his security team. "We are good from here. We are headed straight home, you may go now."

One of the security agents—Paul—furrows his brow in concern. "We should drive behind you, Mr. Cumberland, at the very least."

"It's not needed tonight," William says.

"William," I interject, "it's for your protection. You should do what they say."

"It's for Ms. Grant's protection as well," Paul presses.

I glance at William. His eyes widen. I can tell this is the first time he has thought of me needing protection because I'm with him.

"Right," he says, raking a hand through his hair. "Do what you need to do."

Soon one security agent is off to retrieve their car while Paul waits with us. Once it is all sorted, we are finally in my car and the security team will follow us back to his penthouse.

Eventually, the city of Chicago, sprawling and majestic, appears in front of us, the skyscraper lights illuminating the sky as the sun begins to fade on this spring evening.

I valet the car at his building, and we head inside after his detail leads the way. Now we are both greeted by name, and the doorman gets the elevator for us, and once again, William tells the detail not to step inside. William declines help with his bags, and soon we are in the elevator, alone. He drops the bags and immediately pulls me into his arms, playing with my hair, not saying a word but saying everything with his need to hold me.

I happily snuggle against him, and my cheek brushes against his shirt. As I am reminded that it is cashmere, I step back and look up at him.

"You own cashmere *T-shirts*?" I ask, lifting an eyebrow.

William grins wickedly at me. "Would you rather I be wearing a white T-shirt that comes in a three-pack?"

I burst out laughing and snort, and that makes him roar with laughter. "God, I've missed you," he says, dropping a sweet, gentle kiss on my lips.

"I've missed you, too," I say, brushing my fingertips over his amazing cheekbones.

We begin kissing again, this time slow and sensually, and before I know it, the elevator ride is over way too soon.

But on the other hand, I'm excited to show him his new living room.

"Reveal time!" I say excitedly, stepping out of the elevator.

William gathers his bags and follows me.

I take the key I have been given out of my purse and anxiously open the door. Oh, I hope he loves it. And I hope he loves the surprise I have in there for him, too.

"Okay, here we go," I say, drawing a breath as I open the door.

William puts the bags down and goes to follow me, but I turn and stop him by putting my hand on his chest.

"No!" I cry, laughing. "I need for you to shut your eyes. I will lead you inside and tell you when to open your eyes for the big reveal."

William's lips curve up in a smile. "You sound like one of

those redecorating show hosts."

"You do remember you own a show like that, right?"

He grins at me. "Oh, right."

"Okay, enough. Shut your eyes, please."

William closes his eyes. And I notice his eyelashes look so long and beautiful when he does. Ooh, I bet he looks so gorgeous when he's sleeping. With his pale skin and the Chicago lights streaming into his bedroom window, illuminating that lovely face—

"Mary-Kate, please take me inside my home," he says, interrupting my thoughts. "And do not lead me into my entry table."

I blush—luckily, he can't see it for once—and wrap my hand around his. I usher him inside and lead him to the center of his living room. I draw another nervous, excited breath and then exhale.

"Open your eyes," I say.

I watch as he does. William's laser blue eyes widen and assess everything in his new living room. "My God," he says, looking around.

I watch as he takes everything in. I painted the walls a soft, coffee with cream color. There is a sectional sofa in dark chocolate brown leather. I added red-and-cream chevron pattern pillows to give the brown some pop, paired with woven cream ones. Two large chairs in a charcoal velvet fabric sit across the large rustic coffee table, to add another layer of texture and color to the room. The art on the wall behind the sofa is a grouping of red-and-white prints and patterns to draw the eye up.

William bends over and examines the books I have strategically placed on the wooden coffee table: poetry, geography, a picture book of Chicago, a historical book on London. He puts them down next to the tea service set—one that is modern and silver—that I arranged on a tray as a contrast to the rustic table.

Then his gaze shifts to the surprise.

On the round table next to one of the velvet chairs, right in front of a silver lamp and vase of red tulips, are two framed pictures.

I watch as his brow creases. He slowly walks over to the table, staring at the pictures. I am not sure how he will respond to this, and I hold my breath.

William reaches for one and picks it up. A family photo of Rupert, Claire, Emma, and Charlie, taken outside of their home in Berkshire. He jerks his head toward me, and I can see he is stunned.

"How ... how did you get this?" he asks, his voice a whisper.

"Claire and I have been talking," I say quietly. "And I asked her for some pictures. She emailed the files to me, and I had them printed."

William stares down at the photo in his hand. He puts it down and picks up the next one, which is of him and Rupert at a polo match.

I walk over and wrap my arms around him. We look at the picture together, one taken years ago, and I see how close the two brothers are. I know William's biggest fear is being abandoned, and that is why everyone has been kept at a protective distance.

"William, this is your family," I say softly. "They love you so much. They will never leave you, William. Never."

And I won't either, if you will let me stay.

He stares at the silver-framed picture in his hands. William turns to me, and his eyes are very soft.

"This," William says, his voice thick, "is the nicest thing anyone has ever done for me. Thank you."

He puts the picture down and takes another look around. "This has exceeded my expectations, which were high to begin with. It's brilliant. I love it."

"I'm so glad," I say. "The office is almost done. But I wanted this room to be perfect by the time you got home."

"It is perfect," he replies, kissing my lips. "Perfect."

As he lifts his head up, I see how exhausted he is and how he is fighting it to spend time with me.

"William," I say, cupping his face in my hands, "I should go. You're exhausted. I have already packed my things, so I can leave you to go to bed."

"No," he tells me firmly. "I don't want you to go."

"I know, but you need to eat and get to bed," I say, brushing a lock of his dark hair off his forehead. "I got some of your favorite green curry on my way home from work; it's in the refrigerator. I know you need your comfort food. So if you are hungry, eat, and then sleep."

"What if I told you that is not what I need?" William says.

"What?"

"Stay the night with me, Mary-Kate," he says, his eyes burning into mine. "I need you to spend the night with me."

Chapter Twenty-Four

I stare at him, stunned. William wants to sleep with me. *Tonight.*

My heart flutters inside my chest. Butterflies attack my stomach. My nerves jump in both excitement and fear. I'm utterly torn in half by his words. Part of me wants to make love to him so badly I can barely stand it. I think about it all the time. I imagine what it would be like to make love to someone you are head over heels in love with, as I have never felt this way before.

Which is exactly why I'm not ready.

I love William. Desperately, completely, madly love this man, though we have only been together four weeks, within the same city just two.

But this is too important to me to screw this up. I gaze into his eyes, which are holding steady with mine, and I swallow hard. I don't want this to become all physical right away. I need to know that there could be more, I need to continue to build this like we are, so when we do have sex, everything is right for us to have a serious, committed relationship with an eye toward the future.

"Oh, no, you misunderstood," William says, interrupting

my thoughts. He frames my face with his hands. "I didn't mean sex. I know you don't want that right now. I mean sleep here, in the exact context of the word. Sleep. In my bed. Next to me. I just want you here. I'm not ready for you to leave, if that makes sense."

I feel my face burn in complete embarrassment. Oh, God. Do I feel stupid or what?

"Oh," I say. "Right. Of course."

"I could be persuaded to sleep with you the other way," William says, arching an eyebrow in a teasing way. "If you have that desire, I think it would be most appropriate for me to accommodate it."

"William," I say, laughing, "*Of course* I have the desire."

"Really?" he replies, winding his hands around my waist. "I'm very intrigued by this development. Do go on."

"William," I say. "You know I do! That's why I'm not sure that my sleeping in the same bed as you is a good idea. It's too tempting."

I look away, embarrassed. Why can't I give in to this and have sex with him? Anyone else would have by now.

"Hey," he says, turning my face toward him, "I understand and respect what you are saying. And if you stay here, which I hope you will decide to do, I will be very good. You have my word. And you know I don't say things I don't mean."

I gaze into his beautiful blue eyes and know he is telling me the truth. William is fine with this. He really is. I matter more to him than the physical part of the relationship right now.

"I need you here, Mary-Kate," he says softly. "Please stay."

"Yes," I decide. "I'll stay."

A broad smile crosses his handsome face. "Thank you."

"Thank *you*, William," I whisper. "For understanding

everything."

He responds by kissing me very gently on the forehead. "I do understand."

I gaze up at him. "Are you hungry?"

"Yes," he says.

"Okay then," I say. "Why don't you grab your bags, go take a shower, and when you come out, I'll reheat some curry for you. How does that sound?"

"Good," William replies. "And it's rather nice having a Bossy American around the penthouse."

I slug him on the arm. "Go!"

He laughs and goes back out to retrieve his bags. Once I hear him in the shower, I retrieve my packed bag and do a quick change into my pajamas: flannel drawstring bottoms with a pink floral print and a pink, long-sleeved T-shirt. I throw a gray hoodie over it and brush my hair up into a ponytail.

I go back into his kitchen and turn on his oven so I can warm the naan bread. I take the curry and rice out of the fridge and set it on the counter. I also start some water for tea, as I know William probably wants that, too.

I'm taking the bread out of the oven when he enters the kitchen.

Oh, God. I begin to rethink my idea to hold off on sex when I see him wearing navy plaid lounge pants and a white T-shirt. The shirt shows off the sexy form William has: his long, lithe frame, the beautiful pale skin of his arms, the way the sleeves skim his biceps nicely, and the fabric fits just right across his chest. I feel my breath catch in my throat as I gaze at what a wonderful canvas this T-shirt is for showing off his swimmer's body.

He rakes a hand through his damp waves, and I about drop

the sheet pan I am holding on the floor. I smell the clean scent of soap on his skin, and it's driving me mad. Why am I not having sex with him right here, right now? Why? Why?

"Smells good," William says.

I jerk out of my sexual fantasy and put the pan on the range, turning my back to him. I clear my throat and do a mental reset.

"Yes, I have naan," I say.

He moves behind me, sliding one arm around my waist and pulling me to him. He kisses my neck, which practically makes my legs go out from underneath me.

"I wasn't," he says between kisses, "talking about bread."

Crap. Do I stand a chance here?

"But since you brought it up," William continues, standing upright and putting his hands on my shoulders, "I'll have some."

"Let me get you some curry, too," I say, moving over to the cabinet that holds his bowls. "I know it's not as good as that place you told me about in London, but hopefully it will do."

William leans against the countertop. "It will be brilliant," he says. He yawns and rubs his hands over his face.

"You are going to eat and then go to bed," I tell him firmly. "There is nothing on your calendar tomorrow, so you can sleep in, too."

"I'll settle for being in the office by nine," he says firmly.

I smile. I know better than to argue with him on that.

We reheat our food and sit down on the couch. I don't turn on the TV. We talk about Snap-shots, and William asks for my opinion on some things, which I always love giving him. I feel so important when he does that. I mean, I'm only twenty-four, I don't have the world experience he does, yet William picks my brain on various issues, and I feel challenged and engaged. Kind of like I do when I write. And I love that he appreciates my thoughts and values what I have to say.

I watch him as he describes his vision for Connectivity's acquisition of Snap-shots. He might be exhausted and crossing time zones, but his passion for his company still shines through.

"I know," William says, putting his empty bowl down on the coffee table, "that we have to keep adding new applications to Connectivity to stay relevant. I will not stand for status quo or stagnating."

"And mobile growth," I say, knowing that is William's big mission right now. "Connectivity will grow faster there than with desktop usage, and I know that is your other major focus right now."

His eyes completely light up when I say that. "Of course you get it. You always get me and where I'm going, don't you?"

Inside, I'm beaming from his compliment.

"Come on, let's clean up," I say, standing up with my plate. "By the way, do you have any aluminum foil? I didn't see any earlier."

"You mean aluminium?" William says.

I turn and look at him as I walk into the kitchen. "What?"

He sighs. "That drives me insane. It is al-u-MIN-i-um. Not a-LU-mi-num. And it's in the drawer next to the oven"

"Might I remind you that you are standing in Chicago, Illinois, at this very second. Which happens to be located in the United States of America. And we say *aluminum*."

He laughs loudly. "How is it that I knew you would say that, my Bossy American?"

I laugh as I put my bowl into the sink, and then take William's from his hand. "Well, your Bossy American will finish this up while you get ready for bed. *Now.*"

"You really are a Bossy American," he says, but then immediately yawns afterward.

"Go," I give him a slight nudge. "I'm following you in a bit."

I tidy up the kitchen and put everything away, including the al-u-MIN-i-um foil or whatever the hell William called it.

Afterward, I hesitate in the guest bathroom. I'm actually going to bed with this man.

I look at my hoodie. If I take it off, he can see through my sleep shirt. But I can't leave it on. Or wear a bra to bed—that's just stupid.

I close my eyes and shake my head. *Am I seriously having this conversation in my head? What am I, a virgin?* But in a way, I am. It's as if I have never experienced any of this before. William means that much to me. And my feelings are brand new in this regard. Because everything with William is different. Everything.

I take a deep breath and remove the hoodie. My heart is thumping so loudly that I can practically see my T-shirt move against my chest. I hang the hoodie up on the hook on the back door and nervously head toward his bedroom.

I pause before going in, then take a deep breath and enter his bedroom. I stop in the doorway. William is taking off his T-shirt, and the room is dark except for the sliver of skyscraper lights coming through the part in the curtains.

The light illuminates his lithe frame and pale skin. My eyes move over him, and my pulse jumps. William has powerful shoulders, wonderfully sculpted from swimming. His abdominal muscles are defined—his swimmer's body tapering to his narrow waist.

I swallow hard as I stare at him, this man who has my heart in his hands. *Dear God, you're so beautiful*, I think, watching the gorgeous man standing across the room from me.

William must feel my gaze, because he looks to the doorway, where I am standing. His eyes move over my shirt, down to my breasts, and then back up to my face.

"You're beautiful," he whispers, holding his shirt in his hand.

"And so are you," I whisper back. I walk over to the side of the bed.

There is not a sound in the room. Not one. William gently drapes his shirt over the back of a chair. He comes over to me and takes my hand in his.

"I promise I will respect you," he whispers.

What if I don't want you to? I cry inside my head.

He gives me the sweetest, most gentle kiss and then presses his forehead to mine. "I do promise you that, Mary-Kate."

"I know."

We climb into bed, and William immediately puts his arm around me and pulls me to him. I rest my head against his chest and feel the warmth of his skin against mine. I listen to his heartbeat, my fingertips gently tracing circles on his ivory skin, and my eyes fill with unexpected tears.

I didn't think it was possible to love him more, yet my heart keeps finding ways to. The fact that he is so attuned to what I need, that he is so willing to put his needs second to mine, moves me beyond words.

If this isn't love, I don't know what is.

As I hear his breathing shift and I know he is falling into an exhausted asleep, I vow that soon I will show him how much I love him, in every sense of the word. I am very close to handing everything I am over to him.

Promise me forever, William, I think as I listen to his heartbeat. *Promise me your heart forever. Take me back to London with you. Make a life with me, William.*

I gently lift my head once I know he's soundly sleeping. His eyes are closed and an errant curl of dark hair sweeps down his forehead. I swallow back the tears as I look at the man I love with all my heart.

And I pray he is thinking about forever with me, too. That I am not just his now, but his now and forever.

Because anything less than forever would completely shatter me.

He has to be thinking that, I reassure myself. *William has to.*

With that thought tucked into my head, I close my eyes and drift off to sleep.

Chapter Twenty-Five

My life has never been so perfect.

I think about this as I look over William's revisions for his PowerPoint presentation and enter them into my iPad. Things feel so right now that he is back in Chicago.

I smile to myself as I hear him speaking on the phone from his office. It is Friday, and as soon as we finish this PowerPoint presentation and get it sent off, we are going back to his place for a pizza and a bottle of rosé. Storm clouds are rolling in right now, and we thought it would be a perfect way to spend a rainy evening.

And I can't wait to start the weekend with my man.

My phone rings, and from the short ring, I know it is an internal call. I glance over and see that it is William's line. The caller is Danielle, the head of community relations for the Beautiful Homes Network and the Gourmand Channel. I pick up the phone and put it to my ear.

"William Cumberland's office, MK speaking," I say as I continue to edit the presentation.

"Hi, MK, it's Danielle. Is Mr. Cumberland available?" she asks.

"Hi, Danielle. He is on the phone at the moment. May I have

him return your call?" I say, opening the document I use to log William's calls.

"Yes, that's fine. I have some exciting news about the new community service initiative he asked me to start."

I furrow my brow. That's odd. I haven't seen any emails or documents about this, and I have full access to all of William's corporate emails.

"Oh?" I ask, curious.

"Yes. Mr. Cumberland stopped by my office when he got back from Sydney on Monday, and he expressed his desire to start an outreach program to work with girls to mentor them on careers in our industry," Danielle explains. "Starting from elementary and going through college. Mr. Cumberland said more girls should be inspired to pursue their passions to the fullest potential, to be encouraged to have careers, and we were going to start a program to give them the support, resources, and opportunity to make that happen."

My heart pounds as I take in Danielle's words.

"Isn't that fabulous?" she continues. "Mr. Cumberland said he had a conversation about it in London with someone who had never truly been encouraged and supported to pursue that career dream. He said he felt it was something he was called to do for girls in every city where he has company offices."

I rapidly blink away tears as I realize what Danielle is saying. *William did this because of me. He is doing this for girls like me.*

I can't even speak. The lump in my throat is huge, and I can barely swallow.

"You know, MK, on second thought, I'll just shoot him an email. Have a good weekend!" Danielle says.

"You, too," I manage to get out before hanging up the phone.

I put down the phone and glance at William's office. *He did this for me. And he wasn't even going to say anything about it.* He wasn't going to impress me with this by drawing attention to it, or say, "Look what I am doing because of you, Mary-Kate." No. He has done this from his heart.

And just like that, I know.

William has never talked about a future beyond now. He hasn't told me he loves me. We have only been together a month, and almost half of that time, we have been on different continents.

But William—William who is so cautious, William who speaks more with actions than with words—just told me, without saying a single word, everything I need to know.

I get up and walk toward his office. I pause in the doorway. He is bent over reading a document, his crisp white dress shirt open at the neck, his dark waves even more unruly due to humidity in the air from the impending spring storm that is headed our way.

He has his silver pen to his full lips, totally engrossed in reading. He doesn't even know I'm watching him.

I step through the doorway and shut the door behind me. He looks up and furrows his brow.

"William," I say softly, "I'm ready."

He taps the pen against his lips and goes back to his contract. "Give me a few more minutes, and then I'll be ready to finalize that presentation. I want to finish this contract first."

"I'm ready to sleep with you."

William's head snaps right up. He drops the pen from his hand; his eyes widen in complete shock.

"Sorry?" he says, his beautiful blue eyes searching mine as my words sink in.

"William," I say gently, staring at this man I love with all my heart, "I want to be with you. Tonight."

He stares at me, surprise etched all over the most gorgeous face I have ever seen. He stands up and rakes both hands through his hair, causing the waves to shift sexily all over the place.

God, I cannot wait to make love to him.

"Tonight," he says slowly.

"Tonight," I repeat firmly.

Then I see it. The surprise in his stunning eyes is replaced with intense desire.

William walks over to me. He glances toward his windows, and the blinds are open, so I know he won't touch me. But I can tell he is desperate to.

"Mary-Kate," he whispers, standing in front of me, "are you sure? Really sure?"

"Yes," I whisper back to him, "I'm absolutely sure."

William simply stares at me for a moment. If those blinds were closed, I'd seriously consider having him take me on his desk. I'm that desperate to make love to this man.

"Well, Ms. Grant," he says, and I can see a gleam come into his eyes. "In light of the present situation, I believe it would be most appropriate if we finished the presentation on Monday."

"Indeed," I say, smiling at him. "In fact, Mr. Cumberland, I think you need to take me home to Penthouse 57 right *now*."

"Give me five minutes," William says.

I smile at him and leave his office. I save what I'm working on and undock my iPad, my heart slamming against my ribs the entire time. I gather up my things and wait for him.

A few minutes later, he's ready. My heart is pounding as we walk out together. Since it is already past six o'clock, most people are gone for the weekend. I keep a good distance from him, so it looks like we are walking out together to the elevator and then going our own separate ways. His security team joins us, entering the elevator first before we do.

A couple of other people are on the elevator as we step on. Of course, anytime William is around, people want to talk to him, to get face time with the most powerful man in communications. I listen as he responds, his answers short and to the point. I know it is because he is desperate to get out of here, just like I am.

Finally, we hit the lobby. His car will need to be brought around, and to draw less attention, I usually walk to his place and meet him there. But now dark storm clouds are rolling in from Lake Michigan, and as we step outside, the air smells of a spring storm that is about to hit.

And as I step onto the sidewalk, huge drops of rain begin falling from the ominous clouds.

"I'll get a cab for you," William says, walking toward the curb. The rain is now beginning to fall.

"No." I smile at him. "I'll make a run for it."

"Mary-Kate, are you *mad?* You'll get soaked!"

There is a crack of thunder, and umbrellas pop open all around us. People scurry for cover or stick hands up for cabs, and the temperature continues to drop as the storm moves over downtown Chicago.

"I don't want to waste time in a cab when it's faster to get home this way," I say smartly. And as the skies open up, and rain begins to pour, I run down Michigan Avenue, toward his street.

I turn and look over my shoulder, and William has the biggest smile on his face. And while I expect William to wait for his car, he doesn't. William Cumberland—ultra-serious to the rest of the world, badass mogul William Cumberland—is running after me in the rain, security be dammed.

He catches me, of course, and pulls me around so I can see him. I'm stunned, as his hands are now on my waist. Oh my God, we are both drenched, and never, ever, ever has he looked sexier than he does at this moment. An errant curl drops down across his forehead; his crisp white shirt is now soaked and clinging to his chest.

"I don't bloody care if anyone sees this," William says, raking his hands through my hair and pulling my mouth to his in a hungry kiss.

Oh God. His mouth is moving over mine, and here we are, in the middle of a downpour, kissing on Michigan Avenue.

He breaks the kiss, and I'm breathing hard. William wraps his hand over mine, and we run down the street, anxious to get back to Penthouse 57.

Finally, we make it. We dash up the building steps, greet the doorman who holds open the door for us, and both try to catch our breath as the elevator attendant provides us access to William's level. He wishes us a good evening as the doors open, and we step inside.

The doors close. We're alone. I stare at William, and I'm still breathing hard. So is he. As the elevator begins to ascend to the 57th floor, my heart rate does, too.

"I want you," he gasps, taking me in his arms and pressing me up against the elevator wall. "I want you desperately."

He is kissing me again, his mouth urgently seeking mine. My senses are in frantic overload. I feel his wet body pressed against me. The scent of him is intoxicating—a combination of rain-soaked skin and pine cologne. His hands are on my face, then down my neck, then to my waist, then back up to my hair.

"I want you so much," I murmur against his mouth.

A moan escapes his lips in response, and he kisses me harder.

The doors open, and we are stumbling out, kissing and grabbing at each other until we get to the door. William thrusts the key into the lock and opens the door, and we drop our bags in the foyer as we continue to kiss and touch and make our way into the living room.

Suddenly, he abruptly stops kissing me and puts his hands on my arms, holding me still.

"Are you *sure*, Mary-Kate?" William asks, breathing hard. "I want you to be sure. We can't go back if we do this."

I fight for breath, and I see nothing but concern in his blue eyes. Once again, he is putting me first. Wanting to make sure I'm absolutely certain in the decision to have sex tonight.

I work to fight back tears. "I have never been more sure of anything, William. Please make love to me."

He responds by kissing me. Frantic, desperate, pent-up-desire-for-months kisses. I begin to unbutton his shirt, my hands trembling as I do so.

We're kissing as we move down the hallway, and I have his shirt unbuttoned. I yank it off him as we make it into his bedroom. I run my hands over his sculpted shoulders, down to his glorious chest, hardly believing he is mine to touch tonight.

William reaches for my cardigan. He begins tugging it off, and I help him as we walk farther into his room. We're still kissing passionately, and I slide my sweater shell over my head as he moves me toward the bed.

I watch as his chest rises and falls the second he sees me in my black lace bra. I swallow nervously as he reaches around and slowly unhooks the clasp.

William raises his hands to my shoulders and gently takes my bra off, sensually easing the straps down my arms, his fingertips grazing my skin. He lets my bra fall to the floor.

I watch as he draws a breath when he sees my bare breasts for the first time.

"My God," he whispers, his eyes growing soft, "you are so beautiful."

His hands skim over me in a reverent manner, and I tremble from his touch. He turns me around so my back is pressed into his chest, his hands caressing my breasts, and I'm writhing against him as his tongue flickers down the side of my neck to my collarbones with deliberation. I can feel his heat, his hardness, and everything is making me spiral further in need for him.

"Oh, God," I gasp as his hands continue to stroke my breasts. "William."

One of his hands stays in place, but the other slips between us, finding the back button and zip on my skirt. William undoes the button and yanks on the zipper, and my skirt falls to the floor, pooling at my ankles. I step out of it. Now his hands move further, to my hips, his fingertips exploring the black lace of my panties. I arch against him, and a gasp escapes his lips.

That gasp sparks something within me. I turn around and move my hands over his muscled chest, down his abdominals, to his belt buckle. I need to see him and feel him, too.

William lowers his mouth to mine again, his tongue hot and seeking now. I kiss him back, my hands fumbling with his belt buckle as I do. After I undo it, I undo the button on his pants and then lower the zipper.

"God, oh, God," William murmurs against my mouth.

Now he's shaking, which makes me grow hotter.

I jerk his pants down past his hips. I break the kiss, and as William goes to remove his pants, I stop him. I want to undress him as he did me. I want him to writhe for me the way I did for him.

I stop his hands. "I want to discover you."

A deep groan escapes his throat. I remove his pants, kneeling down to slide the fabric over his hips. My hands caress his thighs and legs, and finally I have his pants on the floor. He steps out of them. I rise back up, taking a step back so I can see him.

I gasp. William stands before me in his boxer-briefs, completely magnificent and ready for me.

Within a second, he's on me, our wet bodies tangling together as our tongues meet again in desperation. We fall back onto the bed, with William pinning me to the mattress. God, I've never known anything like this. The heat I feel, the urgent need to make love to William, is consuming me. I feel like I will die if we don't come together now. I'm trembling and desperate and spiraling for this man in a way I didn't know could exist.

His hands are everywhere, touching me, driving me crazy. I'm starting to sweat, and so is he. I grab his hair, and a low groan escapes his throat.

"Do I need something?" he asks urgently, his breath hot against my skin.

"No," I gasp, "I'm on the pill."

His mouth reclaims mine and his body, oh, his entire body is deliciously rigid with need.

A need that matches my own.

"I can't wait, I can't," William cries out desperately. "I need you now."

I burn in response to his words. "You don't have to wait," I beg him. "Make love to me. Now. Please."

And as the rain pounds against his bedroom window on this April evening, I give everything I am to William Cumberland.

Chapter Twenty-Six

"Did you notice," William says slowly, linking his fingers through mine as we lay facing each other in bed, "that it has stopped raining?"

My heart flutters as I gaze into his beautiful blue eyes. The eyes of the man whom I've just made love to for the first time.

"No, I did not," I say. I smile happily at him. "But I have been too preoccupied with a certain gorgeous, insanely sexy British man to have noticed the rain has stopped."

And that is a complete understatement.

What we shared—oh, my God—it was passionate and hot, yet very emotional, too. Because when we made love, I felt this utter sense of connection—both emotional *and* physical—to William that I have never felt in my entire life.

"I've lived like a bloody monk forever," he whispers, his eyes burning into mine, "and I would do it all over again to be with you like this, Mary-Kate."

I love you. My eyes fill with tears as I stare at the man I have given everything to. *I love you so much, William.*

"William," I say, my voice shaky, "I ... I have never experienced anything like this before."

"Me, neither," he says, caressing the side of my face with

his hand.

He leans forward and brushes his lips against mine. "Stay with me," he murmurs against my lips. "Stay the weekend here with me."

We kiss again. I slide my hand to the back of his neck, caressing his damp, wavy hair with my fingers as we kiss slowly and sweetly.

Then I tilt his head back so I can look into his eyes. "I find it most appropriate that I stay here with you this weekend."

I smile at him, and he bursts out laughing.

"Well, I am glad you are agreeable to that suggestion."

We both laugh, and then William rolls onto his back, bringing me with him. I lay my head down on his chest, and I feel his fingers raking through my hair.

"I don't have any clothes," I say, thinking of my wet sweater and pencil skirt that are on the floor.

"Don't worry, you won't need them," William quips.

I push myself up and see that his mouth is curved up in a wicked, sexy smile.

"Oh, is that so?" I tease.

He acts like he is thinking that over. "Do you need clothing? Hmmm. No. I prefer that you wear *none*."

"William," I cry, laughing. "I have to be dressed at some point."

"Why?"

"William!"

"All right, if you *insist*, I shall get you clothing."

"What? No, we can dry mine and run over to my apartment. I can pack a bag."

"No," William says.

"No?" I ask, confused. "Why on earth not?"

"That," he says, running his fingertips suggestively up and down my arm, "requires leaving this penthouse tonight, and I am *not* interested in that. What size do you wear?"

I furrow my brow. "Size four, and how are you getting me clothes?"

William gently rolls me to the side of him and then reaches down to the floor. I prop myself up so I can see, and he's reaching in his pants pocket. He whips out his iPhone, draws me next to him, into the crook of his arm, and holds me as he goes through his phone.

"What are you doing?" I ask, watching as he swipes through his contacts.

"Hold on," he says, touching a contact and putting his phone to his ear. "Yes, this is William Cumberland, and I need some outfits delivered tonight ... No, not for me ... For a stunning redhead, size four ... Get something casual to start ... let me ask her ..." William pauses and looks at me. "What size jeans do you wear?"

"Twenty-seven," I say, staring at him in complete amazement.

"Twenty-seven ..." he continues. "I need pajamas, yoga pants, hoodie, T-shirt, athletic shoes ... Right, let me ask." William again turns to me. "Shoe size?"

This is unreal. "Uh, six and a half."

William goes back to his phone and dictates more casual outfits, shoes, one formal dress, heels, and underwear, then asks me what my bra size is and what beauty products I need, and instructs the person he is talking to that he wants it delivered by nine tonight. Then he hangs up.

"William!" I gasp. "What did you just do?"

He puts his phone onto his nightstand. "I called my personal shopper," he says simply, as if this is an ordinary thing to do. "She's going to have everything sent over once she's done."

I sit up and stare at him, stunned. "I ... my God, I really do forget you are *THE William Cumberland* and things like this ... happen. You make a phone call to one person, and you have everything delivered right when you want it." I study him, my beautiful man with his dark hair against the white pillowcase. I reach over and gently stroke his hair. "To me you are always William first. Just William."

He takes my hand and gently places it over his heart.

"I know that, darling," he whispers, his eyes never leaving mine as he squeezes my hand. "And that means everything to me, Mary-Kate. Everything."

My breath catches in my throat. He called me *darling.* I mean, I know that is a British term of endearment but to hear him call me that ... my heart is melting.

And as I look at this man, this gorgeous man who is giving me everything I have ever wanted and more, I really want to make love to him again.

But I have a question for him first. "Why did you request a dress and heels?"

William sits up and cups his hands on my face. "I want to take you out tomorrow night. For dinner. That's kind of my thing, you know."

I gasp. "But ... what if someone sees us?"

He continues stroking my face. "I don't care. I don't want to be in hiding. I want to be with you. I want to go places with you. I want ..." He pauses, a worried look crossing his gorgeous face. "Unless ... unless you don't want that."

I immediately wrap my hands over his. "No, I don't care. People are already talking, William. I might as well enjoy dinner with my badass mogul if they are going to talk anyway."

He smiles and presses his forehead against mine. "I'm glad you feel that way. Let's go to the restaurant at the Peninsula Hotel. We can have drinks in the bar afterward. Like we did before. When I wanted to kiss you, but I didn't dare."

"You ... wanted me then?"

William cocks an eyebrow. "My darling, I have always wanted you. I just wasn't sure you wanted me in the same way."

Holy crap. I can't believe this, I really can't.

"I did," I say, smiling at him. "So you have most inappropriately wasted a lot of time by not kissing me sooner."

William laughs, and so do I.

"Then I think I need to rectify that immediately," he says, brushing his lips against mine.

Okay, now I want to have sex with him again.

"Are you hungry?" he asks after breaking the kiss.

I think about it. "Yes," I say, omitting the fact that I would rather have him again than dinner.

"I have the wine you like," he says. "I only need to order a pizza."

He gets up out of bed, and I get a complete view of him: the way his dark waves cascade to the back of his head, the gorgeous back muscles, how his body narrows to his waist, the nice butt he has ... Oh, did I really *sleep* with him, this insanely gorgeous English man?

William goes into his vast closet and disappears, and I know he is getting dressed. He comes out with a navy blue, crew neck cashmere sweater and jeans on. He tosses me one of his shirts—a white Prada dress shirt—and a pair of workout shorts.

CHAPTER TWENTY-SIX

"If you fold the shorts over a few times, they should stay up," he says.

"Thank you," I reply, loving the fact that I am going to be in his clothes right now. I stand up, and I feel William's eyes move over me as I step into the shorts and roll them up.

"You are so beautiful," he says softly.

I blush as I slip into his crisp white shirt. I glance at him and know our clothes won't be staying on for very long tonight from the look in his eyes.

"Thank you," I say softly. I begin to button the shirt, but William walks over to me and takes over, his fingertips lightly grazing against me as he slowly does one button up at a time.

Heat sears through me as he does this. My God, I want this man. Again and again and again.

After he does the last button, William cups my face in his hands and kisses me. I melt into him, wrapping my arms around him, knowing this man is now mine in every sense of the word.

He breaks the kiss, and we link our hands together. Our fingers are entwined, we are looking into each other's eyes, and I know I am staring at my present and future. Where that future is, I do not know, but whether it is London or Chicago, I don't care.

My future is with William Cumberland, and William Cumberland alone.

And I refuse to imagine a future without him in it.

* * *

This has been the best weekend of my life.

I think about this as I wake up in William's bed on Sunday

237

morning. I turn over and see he is already out of bed, and I know he's probably working in his office, as it is nearly nine-thirty.

I curl up happily in the fine Italian linens that are on his bed and see the dress I wore last night draped over his chair. It was a perfect evening, with me wearing a gorgeous Alice + Olivia metallic A-line dress and black peep-toe Jimmy Choo heels. *Jimmy Choo!* William put on one of his dashing black Burberry suits, and we had the best night ever at the Peninsula. We had an amazing Cantonese dinner at the Shanghai Terrace—a gorgeous restaurant with a sexy 1930s supper club décor vibe—then drinks in the same bar where we flirted like mad with each other back on Valentine's Day.

Then we came back here and decided we should investigate if the dual-head showers really did work at the same time. I smile to myself thinking of the amazing sex we had in the steam shower and, oh, *yes,* I can officially confirm they do.

"Mary-Kate?" I hear William say softly.

I roll over and find him in the doorway, holding a Venti-sized Starbucks cup in his hand.

My heart fills with joy the second I see him. "Good morning," I say happily, sitting up.

William walks over and sits down on the edge of the bed, handing me the cup.

"For you," he says, smiling. "A proper American coffee. With cream."

I take it from him. "Thank you," I say, kissing him on the lips. I take a sip. "Have you been working?"

William nods. "I went for a swim and, yes, I've been working. I have that blasted interview with the *Chicago Tribune* tomorrow, and media relations wanted to go over some things with me to prepare."

I remember putting this on his calendar and how agitated he was because he hates, or should I say *loathes*, doing media interviews. I can already see the tension on his face from thinking about it.

"Do you want me to walk in and confirm you are not asexual?" I tease, stroking my fingers through his hair in a calming manner.

I feel him relax the second I touch him, and he flashes me a grin. "Although that would make for great copy, no. What do you have planned for today?"

"I'm going to finish that PowerPoint presentation for you," I say, taking another sip of my coffee. "Then I need to begin my next article for the Beautiful Homes Network."

William picks up my free hand and brings it to his lips, kissing my knuckles. "What are you writing about this time?"

"Sunday brunch," I say. "And as homework for the article, I'm going to run down to Whole Foods and get things to make you American pancakes to eat this morning."

His brow creases. "I'm not sure I will like those. They look very thick. Not like British pancakes."

"You will at least try them, as you have never had my American pancakes with pure maple syrup."

He flashes me a smile. "Well, I am particularly fond of a certain Bossy American, so I suppose I shall try them, darling."

I feel myself blush when he calls me "darling." Oh, I love how that sounds!

"Okay, I'm going to get ready to go to Whole Foods," I say. "You work, and when I get back, I'll cook for us."

"Don't be too long," William says, getting up. He bends down and plants a kiss on the top of my head.

"I won't," I promise.

He smiles and heads back to his office. I put the Starbucks cup on the nightstand and draw my knees up to my chest. I look around his room, which feels now like our room. Everything between us is so right. The emotional connection, the physical chemistry, the way we both want to work and be together and share this life and support each other—that is what love is about. That is what I had never realized could exist until I found William.

I flop back down on the bed, feeling nothing but pure elation and joy in my heart. My nerves tingle with excitement, and I grab his pillow, inhaling the delicious scent of him as I hold it to me.

The hard part is over now. We are together, and I know we'll be together, and, really, it is just a matter of sorting out logistics. I know William hasn't said these things, but I know his heart. He's thinking the same things I am.

Comforted that it is all sorted out and my future truly is here in my hands, I happily get up to go run errands and cook the man that I love breakfast.

It's that simple. And it always will be.

Chapter Twenty-Seven

I can hardly believe it is already the middle of May.

My life has changed so much in a few short months. I'm dating William, and the world seems to know about it. We've appeared in gossip columns in both Chicago and London. He didn't issue a denial through his publicist. Rather, each report was met with a terse 'William Cumberland does not comment on his personal life' statement.

I grin to myself as I walk down Michigan Avenue, the morning sun glinting off the skyscrapers around me. This made things at work rather interesting, to say the least. But since we are nothing but professional there, and nobody would dare say anything to my face about it, it has been survivable.

Of course, I had to bring it up to my parents, who were, at first, stunned I was dating *anyone*, let alone a British billionaire. I brought William to Easter dinner in Milwaukee, and my family just seemed to sputter and stare at him, hardly believing the most powerful man in communications was not only in their living room but dating their daughter.

And then Michelle forced me to a back bedroom and accused me of trying to upstage her wedding by dating William. Through gritted teeth, I told her I will keep dating him and

241

will not apologize for him being rich and famous, and if she wanted to kick me out of her wedding, then I'd be happy to step aside and let someone else deal with her crap, because I was done. That conversation led to us not speaking for the rest of the day, which was actually kind of nice.

But it was so painfully embarrassing, the whole damn afternoon. Yet William handled it. Just like he always does. He was pleasant and even made small talk—which I know is painful for him—and I know he did all of this because he loves me. We still haven't said those words, but there are some things I just know. That is the one thing I am more sure of than anything else in this world.

He will tell me he loves me when he is ready to, I think as I enter the Collective Media Enterprises building. I know those words—those words that have never been said to William by those closest to him—are the hardest words for him to say. Even to me. But he will. I *know* he will.

I spend a lot of time at his penthouse, more than my own apartment in Lincoln Park. Things with Renee and Emily aren't the same. I realize I'm a completely different person now, and my new life, the new *me*, doesn't fit with the old life I had there with them. Once William and I discuss the future, I plan to give up my room in July, when my lease is up. Because I will no doubt be in London with him by June anyway.

I step onto the elevator and scroll through my iPhone. I have a few texts from Kristin and Laurel, two new friends I made at the Beautiful Homes Network, and, of course, one from William. He is across town promoting his new charity initiative at a women's group breakfast meeting, and I couldn't be prouder of him for doing that. My heart flutters as I read his text:

Breakfast a smashing success. Also have good news for you. Something you have wanted for a long time now. Will tell you when I get back in. WC

Gah, what good news? *What?* I hate when he tortures me like this. I quickly text back:

TELL ME NOW! MKG

I wait and receive a rapid-fire response from William:

No, not until I get back. Then you can unseal my lips. In whatever way you deem appropriate. WC

I blush as I step off on my floor. God, he can't be any sexier, can he?

I get to my cubicle and get situated. I follow what is now my normal routine, of getting things ready for William and then the other things he has me do, like add my thoughts to proposals or initiatives, which I have come to enjoy, or assist him with research, which he is big on. I enjoy that as well, and it is something I never expected.

I get started on one of the projects he has given me, and before I know it, I hear him talking on his cell phone as he comes down the hall.

"That is fantastic news," I hear him say. "Brilliant ... yes... Very well ... right ..."

I look up, and William is striding toward me, looking oh-so-suave in his navy Burberry suit and white dress shirt.

"I need to go, but I'm very pleased. Goodbye." He grins at me as he pauses outside his doorway. "Please come in, Ms. Grant."

I smile and walk past him. William shuts the door and moves around me. "I just kissed you in my head," he says, smiling as he walks past me to his desk.

I laugh softly. "Thank you."

243

"So that was Luke from London," he says, leaning against his desk so he's facing me. "Connectivity mobile revenue is going to have a spectacular second quarter. Hell, we're shattering records. I knew the focus on mobile would pay off. I knew it!"

I see the excitement on his handsome face, and I am so proud of him, I could burst.

"You're brilliant," I say honestly. "William, you are so far ahead, and all your competitors can do is play catchup. I'm so proud of you. We'll celebrate tonight."

"We might be celebrating for another reason. Because I'm not the only one who is brilliant around here," he says, raising his eyebrow. "Care to know my news for you?"

"Of course," I reply excitedly. "What do you have to tell me?"

William rubs his hand over his jaw in a thinking way. "Perhaps it should wait. I have some phone calls I need to make and—"

"*William Cumberland!* Tell me now!" I cry, exasperated.

His blue eyes sparkle at me. "Okay, I'll share. Jennifer Lewis was raving about your articles again. And she would like to interview you for a full-time writing position on her staff. The job is virtual, of course, so you can do it anywhere, but she is very interested in you for the position."

A *writer*, I think, my heart pounding excitedly. Jennifer Lewis, editor for the Beautiful Homes Network web page, wants to interview me to be a writer. I am so excited that I can hardly think. I could do this for a living. I would still be in TV, but I would be writing. In addition to my blog, which now has more than five hundred readers. I ... my God, could I actually be a *professional writer*?

"I gave her my blessing to interview you," William says slowly. "And of course, in a few weeks, you will be free to leave me and transfer over to work under her."

My elation comes to a screeching halt. My heart stops. "Wh-what?" I whisper, stunned as I process his words. "What do you mean, 'leave you?'"

William's eyes hold steady with mine. "I know working for me is not what you went to Northwestern for, Mary-Kate," he says softly. "You're not an assistant. You're a *writer*."

I start to feel sick. Really, really sick. He ... William ... he is going to let me *go*?

I swallow hard, but my throat is dry. Words can't come out. I can't get my head around this.

William wants me to leave him.

"Mary-Kate, don't be afraid to tell me how you feel," he says quietly. "I know how important your career is to you. You deserve this chance. You deserve so much more than to be my assistant. And I promised you when you took this job that you just had to commit to me for six months. You upheld that. And now I am upholding my end of the deal."

I stand still. The room is spinning. I feel torn in half, absolutely torn. Of course I want to write. But I have been doing that while being William's right hand. I enjoy working with him, being part of his day, collaborating with him side-by-side. I can't imagine not being with him in this capacity. I can't.

Except you beat it into his head that your career was above all else. And now William is trying to hand it to you. What are you going to do, turn him down?

Then I realize what I'm thinking. I'm thinking of turning down a writing job because of *love*. I'm thinking of doing the one thing I swore I would never, ever do.

But is it wrong to keep doing something I love, like working for William? And keep writing on the side?

"Mary-Kate?" he asks. "Are you all right?"

His words slap me out of my thoughts. I can't turn this down, right?

Because if I do, I think, panicking, *I'll be like Michelle. I'll be like my mom. I'll be another woman sacrificing her career for a man.*

And just like that, my world is turned upside down.

"I'm thrilled," I spit out, forcing a smile on my face. "I could be a writer! I'm so excited to have this chance!"

The words sound fake and strangled as they escape my lips.

"You *are* a writer, Mary-Kate," William says.

I see his eyes are flickering over me, assessing me, trying to read what is in my head.

"William," I say slowly, needing to convince myself as much as I do him of my words, "I am so grateful for this chance. I know this wouldn't have happened without you."

"No," he says firmly. "It might have taken longer to get there, but you have always been destined to be a writer, Mary-Kate."

We stare at each other for a moment, realizing what this means. If I get this job, it is the end of our working relationship.

And as I look at the man I love with all my heart, the man I have worked side-by-side with for six months, the man who has given me everything I never knew I needed until I met him, I cannot imagine not being a part of his day, every day, in that capacity.

But that is exactly what is going to happen if I get this job.

Suddenly, his phone rings, and I'm jarred out of my thoughts.

CHAPTER TWENTY-SEVEN

I move around him to answer it.

"William Cumberland's office, this is MK speaking," I say, realizing that if I do get this job, someone else will be doing this for him. After listening for a moment, I put the phone on hold and fight to compose myself.

"That is Mark Riggan from Snap-shots."

"Right," William says quietly, staring at me.

I quickly dart out of his office while he picks up the phone. I hear his voice, the in-command voice of my badass mogul, and I sink down into my chair, reeling from everything that just happened.

The career I want is within my grasp.

But to grasp it, I have to walk away from working with the man I love.

And it takes everything I have not to burst into tears.

Chapter Twenty-Eight

By the end of the day, I'm utterly exhausted from thinking about the bombshell that William unknowingly dropped on me by telling me about the writing job at the Beautiful Homes Network.

I'm curled up on the couch next to him, dressed in my usual evening attire of yoga pants and a hoodie, my brain trying to sort itself out while he works on his iPad beside me. I'm still shaken by today, by my reaction to the writing job and the possibility of leaving him.

God, why is this happening? I never, ever expected to be so confused about my career. Ever.

But I never expected to be madly in love with my boss, either.

I take a sip of my amaretto-flavored coffee and stare out at the beautiful city lights of Chicago from his window, wishing that somehow I could see my future with as much clarity as I see the majestic city in front of me.

"Talk to me," William says, interrupting my thoughts.

I turn. He is not even looking up from his iPad, yet he instinctively knows I am tortured.

"What?" I ask.

He swipes a few things and puts the tablet aside. Then his

blue eyes are piercing right though me. "You aren't happy about this writing job opportunity. I want to know why."

My heart freezes. William knows. He just knows.

I can't bear to see his disappointment. I stare down at my coffee, gathering up the courage to tell him the truth.

"I ... I am not sure I want to quit working for you," I admit.

"Mary-Kate, look at me."

I swallow hard and do as he says. William is gazing at me with nothing but compassion in his beautiful eyes.

"You aren't meant to be answering my phone and typing my presentations," he says softly, caressing my hair with his hand in a comforting manner. "If you were still doing those things for Paul, you'd be jumping at this chance to have a job that suits you."

"But—"

"No buts. I loathe that word," William reminds me. Then he smiles. "Of course, I understand that working for someone as sexy and dashing as myself could cause you to be rather torn about leaving your current position. However, I assure you I shall remain sexy and dashing no matter where you are working."

I manage a small laugh. "You are impossible."

"Impossibly sexy? Yes, you have told me that. Many times over," he says, lifting an eyebrow.

I blush, and he laughs. Then I clear my throat.

"William," I say, going back to being serious, "I do like collaborating with you, though. I ... I'm not sure I want to give that up."

"Who says you have to?" he asks, furrowing his brow.

"I won't be with you anymore," I say, my voice growing thick.

William takes the mug from my hands and puts it on the coffee table tray. He wraps his hands around mine and squeezes them in his. "I'll still ask you to do those things for me, Mary-Kate. I'd be an idiot not to utilize you in that capacity."

"Why can't I be your assistant and write freelance on the side?" I blurt out, thinking that is the optimal solution to the problem.

"No. Absolutely not," William says firmly, his eyes flashing with intensity. "I will not have that. I will *not*. You need to be writing. Not making copies and tea. Your voice needs to be heard, and not on a here or there basis around doing tasks for me. I will not stifle that voice in you. I want you to write like mad, Mary-Kate. Like mad. That is what would make me happy."

I stare at him, and tears fill my eyes. I know in my heart he would love for me to stay by his side, but I also know he wants what is best for me. He knows how much I have wanted a career. He knows I fell into writing by default, but that I love it. And even if it costs him, he wants me to be the writer I am destined to be.

I feel the words "I love you" on the tip of my lips. I want to say them. I want to tell him I love him, and I have never loved anyone the way I love him.

"Mary-Kate," William says, interrupting my thoughts. "Please tell me you'll go after this. Please. I know you will get this job if you are passionate about it like you are about everything else you love."

And as I see the passion in his blue eyes, how much he knows me and, in the end, what would truly make me happy, I feel as though the weight of the world is lifting off my shoulders. I see now my future, with as much clarity as I see the twinkling lights of Chicago out the window.

"Yes," I say simply.

"Yes?"

"I'm going for it." I break out into a huge grin. "I'm going to get that job, William. And I am going to write my brains out when I do."

He flashes me a beautiful, genuine, I-am-so-happy smile, the one he saves for me and his family.

"Brilliant!" he says excitedly. "Brilliant!"

He cups my face in his hands and kisses me. I excitedly kiss him back. The original feeling I had when learning about the job is back, and I feel the world is so full of possibilities.

A writer. If I get this job, I will be a professional writer.

William begins kissing my neck and moves me backward on the leather couch. "I think it would be most appropriate," he whispers against my neck, "if I find a way to reassure you I will still pay plenty of attention to *all* your needs when you are a writer."

Oh my God. Yes, this was indeed a brilliant decision.

I slide my hands up around the base of his neck, up to his hair, caressing his silky waves in my fingertips.

"Show me," I whisper in his ear, "how you would do that."

He laughs wickedly and tugs down on the zipper on my hoodie.

"My pleasure," he says, kissing me on the mouth.

And everything is right in my world again. It doesn't matter if I am a writer. It doesn't matter if I'm not with him all the time. We are *together*, *a team*, and we have been since that Valentine's Day in the bar at the Peninsula Hotel.

As his hands move over me and we begin to make love, I

think of how I worried so much about him leaving me, about William blowing the candle out, so to speak, and heading back to London to his old life without me.

But I realize now, even with life's continued unexpected surprises and turns, our candle will burn bright. This man is my life. William is everything to me, and I know I am everything to him.

Nothing could ever extinguish what we have. I am sure of it.

Chapter Twenty-Nine

"I am on top of the world tonight!" I cry excitedly.

William laughs as the cocktail server puts down our bottle of champagne and begins to uncork it. It is a glorious summer evening in Chicago, simply stunning outside, and we're seated together on a sofa on the lush terrace bar in a high-rise hotel downtown. We have a gorgeous view of the Wrigley clock tower and the Chicago River, and the sun is still setting in the sky.

And we're celebrating my new job as a writer for the Beautiful Homes Network.

Pop! The champagne is opened, and I'm as bubbly as the luscious Dom that is about to be poured into my glass.

"You might not *literally* be on top of the world," William says, laughing, "but we are high enough here for you to be close enough."

I laugh and then snort, which makes him laugh harder. Our glasses are poured, and we thank the server for our champagne. William raises his glass to me.

"To you," he says, his eyes sparkling at me. "To your new journey as a writer. You deserve this, darling. I am so proud of you. Cheers."

I clink my glass against his. "Cheers," I say happily.

We both take a sip and then put our glasses aside. I tuck my legs up underneath me and rest my arm on the back of the couch, gazing at William with nothing but love in my heart. A breeze comes up and moves his beautiful waves, and one errant curl sweeps down on to his forehead.

I reach over and gingerly brush it back. "Thank you for everything you have done to help me get here," I say honestly, stroking his hair. "I could not have done this without you."

"That's not—"

I silence him by putting my finger over his lips. "Mr. Cumberland, I find it most inappropriate that you interrupt me right now," I tease.

William grins. Then he puts his hand over mine and brings it to his lips, kissing it gently.

"My deepest apologies for my rudeness, Ms. Grant."

I laugh and so does he.

"But in all seriousness," I say, continuing, "you made me see things I never would have seen. Thank you for that."

William's eyes stay riveted to mine. I see them soften as he takes in my words.

"You are most welcome," he says quietly. Then he takes his fingertips and draws slow circles on my kneecap, which is revealed by the denim pencil skirt I am wearing on this Friday night.

"Are you trying to tempt me, William?" I ask, flirting with him as I pick up my champagne and take a sip.

"Would I do such an inappropriate thing to my assistant?" he asks, raising his eyebrow. "Oh, wait. You are no longer my assistant now, are you?"

"No," I say, getting shivers from the sensation of his fingertips grazing my skin. "I am not. But I do not know if it is appropriate for you to touch your *consultant* like this."

He grins wickedly at me. "*Touché.*"

I laugh. "This night is beautiful," I say, gazing at the city around us.

"And so are you." I turn and see William's eyes have never left my face.

"How did I get so lucky to have found you?" I ask as I look at him.

He stares at me for a moment. He flexes his hands, stretching his long fingers in and out, and then he rakes them through his hair. I notice his eyes get very serious, and he exhales.

My God, he looks serious and ... nervous. My heart skips a beat. Why would he be anxious?

"William?" I ask, concerned. "Are you okay?"

He clears his throat. "Yes ... Mary-Kate, I want to talk to you about the f—"

"Excuse me? Mr. William Cumberland?"

We both turn our heads. A young man in business attire is standing beside us.

I force a smile on my face, but inside I want to scream. This happens to us all the time, where someone approaches William and wants to tell him how they admire his business, would love to work for him, blah, blah, blah ... but, damn it, why now? What was William going to say that had him so serious and anxious?

The young man nervously talks about being a graduate of Notre Dame blah, blah, and I half listen as William indulges him for a few minutes. Finally, the man leaves, and I am right back to where we left off.

"What were you saying?" I ask.

William shakes his head. "I have decided I do not want to

have that conversation here. I want it to be private," he says firmly, stroking the side of my face with his hand. "But it is important, and we'll talk about it first thing in the morning. Tonight is for celebrating. All night long."

My heart stops. It is about the future. It is about London. I *know* it, I just do. My entire life is falling into place, and I can't believe how incredibly happy I am about everything.

Yes, the discussion of the future—*our* future—can wait until tomorrow. Right now, I want to savor this champagne, this view, my new career, and, most of all, an evening with the man I love.

And tomorrow the final piece of the puzzle, of where we are going to live together, will be put into place.

* * *

I wake up on Saturday to find William already gone. Which is normal for him. He goes for his swim, works for a bit, and then gets me a coffee from Starbucks.

I smile to myself as I stretch in bed. *He is so sweet*, I think happily. Who knew under that formal, icy exterior of William Cumberland, international badass mogul, was William who brings his girlfriend coffee every morning?

I get up and get dressed in workout pants and a T-shirt. I plan on heading to the gym for a spin class later this morning. I go to retrieve his tea mug from his office and prepare to make fresh tea, as I usually do when he's left for a while.

I walk into his office and pick up his mug, but I accidentally drop it, sending cold tea splashing across his desk and iPad.

"Crap!" I blurt out as the tea spills everywhere.

Why am I such a klutz? Why? I run to the bathroom, grab a

towel, and instantly begin to blot the iPad screen and then his papers. And then I notice what I am blotting.

An airline itinerary.

I pause for a moment, lifting the towel up so I can see. It is a Premier Airlines ticket to London, departing on Monday.

With no return.

My heart stops beating. I didn't book this ticket, like I *always* book his tickets for work.

William did this himself, without telling me. *Yesterday afternoon.*

I look at the credit card number and the last four digits. They are not his corporate card number. This is his private American Express card. This is personal travel. Travel that he obviously didn't want me to know about.

A one-way ticket back to London, for himself. And there is no ticket for me. My heart is pounding furiously against my ribs. I frantically sift through the other papers on his desk and find two files. One labeled "Real Estate Agents—Chicago" and the other "New Assistant—Chicago."

I pick up the one for real estate, my hand shaking violently as I do. There is a printout of this penthouse, with estimated listing price.

I can't breathe. William is selling his penthouse in Chicago and keeping it secret from me. I look at the date of the printout. Yesterday.

The same day he'd purchased his one-way ticket.

The same day I got the job at the Beautiful Homes Network. *The job he insisted I apply for and pursue.*

And he did all of this without saying a word to me.

Tears fall from my eyes as I pick up the other folder and flip through it. HR has provided William with all kinds of resumes.

I see a handwritten note from the HR manager for the position and read it:

Heather is a recent USC graduate. Young, determined, background in TV and film, would be a good fit to coordinate things in your office in Chicago. Would you like to schedule a phone interview? Let me know. Josh

I slam the folder shut. I feel dizzy. Panic engulfs me. He must have had this conversation with HR via the phone, because I have not seen one email about this in his corporate account. And they obviously delivered this folder straight to him and bypassed giving it to me like they do everything else.

Nausea rises in my throat. *William didn't want me to know.* So I wouldn't know he is grooming another girl like me, another girl he can sweep off her feet as he comes and goes from Chicago as he pleases.

Oh God. Oh God, oh God, oh God.

I drop the folder as the truth of the situation hits me so hard, my knees buckle. I grab William's desk chair for support, but everything is collapsing around me.

A sob escapes my throat as I stare at all the pieces of the puzzle in front of me, and they are not making the picture I so happily envisioned on the terrace last night.

Sobs rack my body. *He is not taking me back to London. William never planned to take me home with him.* And that is why he was so nervous to talk to me last night. William, the man I love with all my heart, the man who I *thought* loved me, is leaving me here. And the job at the Beautiful Homes Network is simply a parting gift he arranged before he said goodbye.

Chapter Thirty

I'm still reeling in William's office when I hear him come through the front door. *I can't breathe. I can't.* I desperately try to take in air as I steady myself against his chair.

"Mary-Kate?" I hear his deep voice call out. "Darling? I have your coffee."

Oh God. Just hearing his baritone voice causes waves of pain to rip through me.

Finally, he appears in the doorway. "I have—"

He stops the second he sees me. Instantly, his blue eyes zero in on my face, and his expression changes to one of shock and concern. "Mary-Kate! What's wrong?"

The second I look into William's eyes, my heart is gutted. I'm torn apart by this man—this man who is tossing me aside and going home without me. This man who I stupidly believed could love me forever.

And rage takes over.

I grab the folder of resumes off his desk and hurl it at him.

William ducks, and the file sails over his head, bouncing off the door and sending resumes flying like confetti. The coffee falls to the floor, splattering everywhere.

"What the hell?" he yells, eyes wide.

"So are you going to find someone else to screw you instead of me when you periodically come back to Chicago?" I scream at him. "Heather sounds like a perfect candidate, William!"

"*What*?" he cries, staring at me like I've gone insane.

"You're going back to London without me!" Tears are spilling down my face as I grab his itinerary and wave it around. "A one-way ticket home. I'm such an idiot to think I had a future with you!"

A horrified expression passes over William's face. "My God, you were going through my papers behind my back?" His voice resonates with shock.

"No, of course not. I would never spy on you!" I shout. "I came in here to get your mug, and I spilled the tea. Then I saw this ticket when I was cleaning up the mess. And thank God I did, because now I know where I stand. You are leaving me!"

I watch as William pales.

Tell me I'm wrong, I think. *Tell me you love me. Tell me this is some sort of huge misunderstanding.*

"Mary-Kate," he says, his eyes desperately searching mine, "do you actually *believe* that?"

"Why wouldn't I?" I cry, jerking my hand across my face to wipe away the tears that cannot stop. "You haven't told me anything different. It's not like you have promised me a damn thing or even told me you love me!"

I see hurt flash in William's beautiful eyes. He looks as if I've punched him hard in the gut. He remains silent for a moment, his eyes searching mine, and I'm frozen in place. Like part of me wants to take back what I said, but part of me needs to hear him respond.

He swallows hard and, finally, after what seems like an eternity, he speaks.

"You," he says, his voice taking on an angry edge, "are *supposed* to know me better than anyone, Mary-Kate. God, can you not tell how I feel about you? Have I not *shown* you how I feel?"

My eyes well with fresh tears. As I gaze into his eyes and see the hurt and anger reflected in them, I wonder if this is some horrible misunderstanding. That the man I know—*the William I know*—could not have a life without me.

"The fact that you even think that I'm capable of this makes me question *everything* between us," William says, his voice growing stronger. "That you could even contemplate this idea in your head for more than a split second is beyond me."

Bam! I jerk my head as if he has slapped me. And I feel nothing but fury and pain.

"I'm not a freaking mind reader," I say. "I *deserve* to know where I stand. And I half wonder if you arranged the job at the Beautiful Homes Network to soften the blow of you leaving me."

"Have you gone stark-raving mad?" William cries. "That is utterly ridiculous, Mary-Kate! Are you listening to yourself?"

"That's right, William. I must be mad in the head to wonder where I stand when you have made a point to say absolutely *nothing* about a future with me. And you know what? I can't do this."

I go to move past him. I have to get out of here before I say something I cannot take back. I feel out of control, and I have to get out and think.

"No, you are not leaving," William commands, his voice cold.

"I'm not a transaction. You can't make me stay here just because you say so."

261

He reaches out to grab my arm, but I angrily slap it away.

"Don't touch me!" I storm down the hall, and William follows. I go to the bedroom and grab my purse, and then my overnight bag, angrily throwing my things into it.

"Mary-Kate, you need to stop it. Stop it right now," he commands firmly.

"Why? Are you going to tell me how you feel? That I got this all wrong?"

"I," William says, his voice shaking in anger, "will not be told when I should say what I feel. And I would never say anything under a threat like this."

"Oh my God, you think this is a *threat*?" I ask, incredulous.

"Isn't it? Tell you how I feel, or you walk out? Well, I loathe demands."

"That is insane."

"This whole argument is insane and insulting," he snaps back. He takes an aggravated-sounding breath and puts his fingertips over his lips. "Do not walk out like this."

"I can't deal with this. I have to get out of here. I have to think!" I cry, a sob escaping my throat.

I rush past him and hurry to the door. I hear him behind me, and as I open it, William speaks.

"Do not leave," he commands again.

"Or what?" I challenge, turning around.

William is silent for a moment, his eyes flickering angrily. "If you leave, I will not take you back. If you make the decision to walk away from me, I will not accept your phone calls or texts or messages. It's done if you walk out this door, Mary-Kate. I mean it. I don't tolerate people who run out."

Oh God. I'm so torn up and so angry and shattered that I can't think straight. I can't see straight. I can't breathe, and I feel dizzy.

And William still hasn't said he loves me, which tells me everything. He is watching me spiral out of control, and he knows that is what I need to hear, yet he refuses to tell me how he feels because he sees it as a threat?

"Maybe this never should have happened," I say, crying. "This ... us ... we never should have been together. Maybe this was—"

"An accident?" William finishes for me, nothing but hurt reflected in his eyes.

"I didn't say that!" I sob, knowing how badly that comment hurt him.

"You might as well have," he says.

"I can't do this," I reply, whirling around and jerking open the door.

I step through it and turn around again, staring at him. I swallow down the huge lump in my throat, praying he stops me. Praying he tells me I misunderstood, that he loves me, that there is a future.

Tell me you love me, I will him. *Tell me, William.*

But he just stares back at me, silent. And his silence tells me everything I need to know.

"Goodbye, William," I say, my voice breaking.

I run to the elevator, frantically punching the button, and leave William—and the life I dreamed of having with him— behind.

Chapter Thirty-One

I tear out of William's building in a state of shock.

I don't even know where I'm going, and everything around me is blurred through my tears. I walk briskly toward Millennium Park, needing to escape, needing to be alone, needing to think.

I hurry through the park and keep going until I find a quiet spot surrounded by blooming tulips in the Lurie Garden.

I sit down, wiping the tears from my eyes with my shaking hands, and draw a breath of air as panic consumes me.

What just happened? My God, did we *break up*?

I begin to sob. I draw my knees to my chest, tuck my head down, and cry my eyes out in the park, wondering how it all came to this.

My thoughts are all jumbled and conflicted in my head. I finally stop crying—I don't think I can cry another tear—and take a deep breath. I mentally go through the evidence. The airline ticket, the penthouse for sale—they all scream that he is leaving without me.

Don't they?

After all, William didn't mention any of these plans to me. And he went out of his way so I wouldn't know about them.

But when I confronted him, he appeared visibly wounded. He seemed absolutely shocked I could think him capable of such a thing. I saw that in his expressive eyes. Were those the eyes of a man who was caught red-handed?

Were those the eyes of a man who didn't love me? Were those the eyes of a man who is leaving me behind?

No, I think as my thoughts slow down. *Even though he refused to say it, those were the eyes of a man who loves me.*

A sharp, stabbing pain rips at my heart. I frantically unzip my overnight bag, rifling through it, and withdraw the charm bracelet he gave me from London. I study each charm that he carefully selected, each charm telling our story.

Our story.

As I see the sunlight glinting on my beautiful bracelet, I realize how badly I screwed everything up.

I *know* William loves me.

I *know* he must have some reason for the ticket and the penthouse being for sale.

I *know* he must have a reason for not telling me his plans.

Because no man would treat me the way William has if he didn't love me and plan to have a future with me.

I clutch the bracelet and begin to shake. I'd been so blindsided by what I found in his office that I couldn't see straight. All I'd felt was *fear.* Intense, crippling fear that I would lose the one thing that mattered to me above anything else in this world.

William.

For so long, I told myself I was avoiding love because it would mess up my career. I was convinced love would derail me, cause me to lose focus, and that I would sacrifice my independence for love.

But nothing could be further from the truth.

I wasn't avoiding love, I realize with a shaking breath. *I just never found it until I found William.*

And when I did find love, everything in my life blossomed. I found myself pursuing a new career path, different than what I had planned, but one that brought me joy and success. My blog flourished, I have a new job, and I'm making new friends who enrich my life for the better.

All of that happened because of *love*.

Love didn't ruin my career or distract me. To the contrary, love made me a better person, a more rounded person, a happier person.

But fear of losing that love cost me the only thing on this earth that matters to me.

I lost William.

I lift my tear-stained face and look up at the sky above. Birds are flying around me, swooping through the air and singing melodies. The late-May sun is slowly warming the earth this morning, and the skies are a gorgeous blue over Chicago.

The world is going on, but my world has stopped. My heart is shattered beyond repair.

And everything is my fault.

I stare back down at my bracelet, and a torrent of fresh tears threaten to break loose. William made it very clear—*painfully clear*—that if I left, he would never take me back. With a jolt, I know this has to be a ramification from his childhood. The people he counted on to love him and stay by him—like his parents—abandoned him.

Like I just abandoned him, I think with anguish.

Of course, his fear on this is irrational, people do fight and get mad and sometimes need space to sort things out, but that hasn't been his experience in life. When people were angry, they abandoned him emotionally.

As I grapple with this, it feels like a knife has been struck through my heart. Instead of calming down on the spot and talking to him like a normal, mature person, I ran. I ran to save myself the pain of hearing him say he would leave for London without me. Which now, with a broken heart, I realize was not the case.

I fight for air as panic hits me full force. There is nothing I can do to change his mind. William says what he means. He doesn't go back on his word. We are over, and there is nothing I can do to change that.

But ... but I can't let this go. No, I will not let this go. William is going to hear what is in my heart and how I wish I could have the chance to do this all over again. That I made a mistake, one he sees as unforgivable, and I regret what I did and what I said with every fiber of my being. That I wish I could see him again to tell him how sorry I am and how I wish I could make things right. I want to tell him that although I know he will never love me again, I will always be thankful for the time I was with him.

He deserves to know that.

Most of all, I'll tell him I love him. I love him with everything I have, and I always will, even if he will never look at me in the same way ever again.

I fight back my tears and swallow hard. I pick up my stuff and stand up, knowing what I have to do.

I have to write him a letter to let him go.

* * *

I sit with my iPad in my lap, a box of tissues next to me, and a glass of wine on my nightstand. It is Monday night, and after spending all of Sunday evening crying and not sleeping, I somehow made it through the first day back at the office with William officially gone and moved back to London, his vacant office a sight that nearly brought me to my knees when I realized he would never come back here again.

A fresh batch of tears prick my eyes.

I will never see him again. Oh, sure, when he comes to Chicago for business I might run into him, but that would be it.

A crushing pressure hits my chest. I can't fathom that. Simply bumping into him, merely saying "hello" and "how is life treating you" and then "goodbye"?

No. I can't. I can't. My heart starts pounding. How can I face this new life? How can I be Mary-Kate without William? *You're not Mary-Kate anymore*, a voice inside my head whispers. *That is who you were with William. You are MK now.*

I move the iPad and bury my head in my hands, sobs racking my body again.

Suddenly, my cell rings. I reach for it on my nightstand. I'm stunned to see the caller is Claire Cumberland.

I freeze. Claire? It is the wee hours in the morning in England. Oh God, she knows! What is she going to say?

I can barely think over the pounding of my heart. I answer the phone and hear my voice shake as I speak.

"Hello?" I croak.

"Mary-Kate," Claire's familiar voice says. "I did not wait this long to find a potential sister-in-law who could cook a smashing Christmas meal like Nigella Lawson and lose her because the two of you are having a silly row!"

268

CHAPTER THIRTY-ONE

I freeze. "You ... you've talked to William?"

"He's over here right now," she says. "William said he had something important to tell us a week ago and arranged to come over when he got in from the States, but when he came in, he said you two had a horrible row, that you were broken up, and to never mention your name ever again."

I burst into tears at that point.

"Mary-Kate, stop," Claire commands. "I had Rupert ply him full of scotch so he would talk."

"*What?*" I gasp. "William doesn't get drunk!"

"He does when his heart is broken," she says slowly. "In fact, we had a heart-to-heart before he passed out in my living room. He told me what happened, Mary-Kate."

I can't keep my voice from shaking. "It's all my fault. I ... I should have ... I should have known ..." I can't even finish the sentence without sobbing.

"Mary-Kate, yes, you should have trusted him," Claire says honestly. "But he didn't exactly help you out, did he?"

"What?"

"I asked William if he told you his reasons for his actions or how he felt about you," she continues. "And when he admitted he didn't, I told him you were both bloody fools who needed to go sit on a naughty step and then work this out, but this time as adults and not children."

For the first time in two days, I feel a brief flicker of hope in my heart.

"Claire," I whisper, "do ... do you think I still have a chance? What did he say?"

"Mary-Kate, William is my brother-in-law. Who was drunk and babbling on my living room floor. So I am not going to disclose the personal things he said. But I will say this: If you want to fight for him, then do it. Do it *now*."

And just like that, my tears stop. A fire is lit underneath me. I feel hope that maybe, just maybe, I can win back the only thing that ever mattered to me.

"Claire," I say, "I have one favor to ask you. Just one."

"What is that?"

"Have William read my blog tomorrow."

Chapter Thirty-Two

Sitting alone in my apartment, I stare at my blog responses on Friday night. I sift through the new ones, desperately searching for the one response I want more than anything on this earth.

One from William.

Yet, since I posted the blog on Monday night, I have heard nothing from him. No response. No phone call. No text. I watch as the words go blurry in front of my eyes. I squeeze them shut, feeling them well with tears, as they have every day since I stupidly walked out on the man I love.

He's not coming back. William meant what he said.

I have talked to Claire several times this week. She has been my lifeline, my one ray of hope that maybe I could make things right. She keeps telling me to let him sort it out, that William has his own way and timetable of dealing with things, but I know it is done.

I glance at the clock on my phone. I'm supposed to talk to Claire tonight, and she said she would call me, but I don't think I can talk to her or anyone else right now. I would have to tell her I know William better than anyone, and my part in his story is over. Forever. He has turned the page and moved on without me.

I swallow hard. He has blown out the candle. What slight flicker I had left after writing the blog has been completely snuffed out.

I have to accept the fact that pouring my heart out in my blog didn't have the effect that I had prayed every night for since I wrote it. I scroll past all of my readers' comments—those sending hugs, those telling me I can do better, those telling me time will heal my heart—to the actual post itself, and I re-read it for what seems like the millionth time:

A Message for Mr. X

Dear Readers, I apologize in advance. This is not going to be my usual blog about cooking and decorating and making your home a beautiful place—one that is warm and welcoming, one that renews your spirit, one that makes you feel cozy and secure and happy.

This blog is about the one person who made me feel, for the first time in my heart, the passion, the joy, the comfort, and the complete gift of true love.

I had heard of this kind of love before but never knew it. I didn't believe I needed or even wanted love in my life until I found it with Mr. X.

You all have read about him on the blog many times. Mr. X, my boss. Mr. X, who slowly became more than a boss to me, as I am sure some of you could see happening even before I did through my words on this page.

Mr. X inspired me, challenged me, and saw me in a way nobody else ever has. Mr. X is smart and dashing and sophisticated. He made me laugh. He made me the happiest I have ever been. Mr. X has seen the world, and let me see it through his eyes, too.

I fell madly in love with Mr. X. I gave him everything I am, except for one thing, one thing that led me to lose him and shattered my heart in the process.

I didn't give him the benefit of the doubt when I should have.

I have a temper. I admit that. And when I saw things that I thought meant I was about to lose the only man I have ever loved, the only man I could ever see a future with, I was devastated. And the fear of losing him caused me to react horribly and accuse Mr. X of awful things. I am sick about my behavior and so deeply sorry. If I could take back my words, if I could have stayed instead of running away in fear, if I could have just talked to him and been rational, we would still be together right now.

But instead, I am facing a future I don't want to face. I am facing a future without the one man who helped me dream, to feel true love, and know such joy and happiness that I often felt my heart would burst.

I have cried more tears this week than I dreamed possible. The world seems gray. I might have to accept the fact that Mr. X will move on without me—a thought which brings me so much anguish I can hardly breathe. My heart is broken, utterly broken. But I will never move on from him.

I love him. I wish I could have told him that as I gazed into his eyes instead of here in a blog. But I love him with every fiber of my being. I will always love him, even when he chooses to love someone else.

Always, MK

I feel my tears splashing down my cheeks. I swallow against the lump in my throat and push my iPad aside.

It really is over. I have lost William, and there is nothing I can say to get him back.

I grab one of my throw pillows and clutch it to my stomach, letting the tears fall freely. How do I go on? How can I love anybody but William? No, I can't. I can't imagine—

Suddenly, my phone beeps. I wipe my hand over my eyes and pick it up.

It is a text message. From William.

My heart explodes inside my chest. I begin to shake. I see a picture of my apartment building, taken from across the street:

I am here. WC

Chapter Thirty-Three

I am here. WC

I read the words over and over. My God, could it be true? William is here?

I throw my phone aside, bolt from my room, and run frantically into the living room. I sprint to the window, which overlooks the street below. I hold my breath as I push the curtain aside, desperate to see if my prayers have been answered.

And they have.

William is pacing back and forth on the sidewalk, the light from the street lamp illuminating his black suit in the darkness.

He stops pacing and tilts his head upward, right toward my window. Tears fall from my eyes as I see his gorgeous face, highlighted by the full moon overhead.

And then he sees me.

I race from my apartment, my heart pounding inside my chest. I run down the flights of stairs, throw open the building door, and stop on the top step.

William is halfway up my sidewalk, dashing toward me.

He instantly stops the second I appear. His eyes meet mine.

And the second they do, I fall apart.

"William!" I cry, running down the stairs toward him. I throw myself into his arms and desperately clutch on to him, silently vowing to never, ever let him go again.

I'm sobbing as I feel his arms wrap around me and hold me close. I hear his heart pounding against my ear. I inhale the pine scent of his ivory skin, and I feel his hands on my back, my hair, keeping me as close as he can to his body.

"I am ... I am ..." I try to get the words out, but I'm so overwhelmed I can't speak.

"Darling," William says, his voice very thick. "Please, Mary-Kate. Please. Everything is going to be all right now."

"No, no," I cry, tightening my grip on his arms, almost as if I'm afraid he will let me go. "It's not! I ... I was ... I was ..."

William eases me back, and I'm stunned to see his eyes are watery, too.

"We," he says, voice hoarse with emotion, "were *both* wrong. Both of us. We apparently are not very good at fighting."

His face dissolves through my tears. I squeeze my eyes shut, shaking my head, needing to pull myself together so I can speak the words he needs to hear.

"I was so scared you were going to leave me," I manage to get out, reaching for his dark waves and stroking them gently. "I always react strongly when I'm upset. And nothing on this earth upsets me more than the idea of losing you. Of a life without you. I couldn't cope. I couldn't think. I ran out to clear my head, and once I thought everything out, I knew I had made a horrible mistake."

I pause for a moment and gaze into his expressive blue eyes, which are filled with unshed tears. "I love you, William. I have never loved anyone but you. And I'm ..." I swallow hard, pushing down the lump that has formed in my throat. "I'm so sorry I hurt the only person I have ever loved."

A single tear rolls down William's face, and I brush it away with my fingertips.

"Mary-Kate," he says, his voice a whisper. "You're the only woman I have ever wanted. You're the only one I have ever loved. You made me *believe* in love, Mary-Kate. And all the things you found ... were part of my plan to build a future with you. To build a future with the only woman who has ever mattered."

He strokes his hands through my hair and stares deeply into my eyes. "Once you had your job set, I bought a ticket to go back to London. To wrap things up. Mary-Kate, I was going to move here to be with *you*. I didn't know how long it would take, so I didn't book the return, but I was ready to come back to Chicago and make a home with you."

I tremble as I realize everything he was going to give up for me.

"Wh-what?" I ask, my eyes frantically searching his. "You... you were going to leave *London?*"

William nods and slides his hands around my waist. "You're an American, Mary-Kate. You've never lived abroad. I have. I know what a challenge it can be, and I would never want you to resent me for making you move from the only home you have ever known. I put the penthouse on the market so we could find a home together and make it ours. Because you are my future, Mary-Kate. You are my *life.* I love you, and I'm willing to do anything to make us work. I do not have a life without you, Mary-Kate. I *will not* have a life without you in it."

When I realize how much I mean to him, how much William was going to sacrifice to love me, I begin out and out bawling.

"Shh," he says, drawing me against his chest. "It is all right, Mary-Kate. I should have told you all of that the second you got upset. I was wrong, so wrong, not to do so. I reacted like an idiot. I questioned your feelings and I never saw the situation through your eyes. Then I acted like an arrogant jerk and demanded that you stay when you needed space. I'm so sorry."

I step back from him. "That is from your childhood," I say, my voice trembling. William blinks as he lets my words wash over him. "People got mad and upset and abandoned you. You saw me doing the same thing. The one person you loved was going to walk away."

He swallows hard, trying to hold on to his emotions. "I never thought of it that way."

"I tend to blow up when I'm mad, and I might need space to think, but I won't ever leave you, William. I promise you that."

"Please forgive me," William says. "Please say you can."

I step back from him. "Only if you forgive me, too."

He presses his forehead to mine. Our hands entwine together. "I love you," he whispers to me.

"I love you, too," I whisper back.

And then his mouth meets mine in the most gentle, caressing, loving kiss I have ever known.

We continue to kiss on the sidewalk, the noises of the city disappearing into the night. I now know, without a doubt, the man I love is my present and future and always will be.

He breaks the kiss, and I stare up at him. "William, I can't let you move to Chicago," I say quietly.

He looks stricken. "What?"

"You are *English.* England is your home. The Shard, Connectivity Headquarters, Mayfair," I say, shaking my head. "England has your heart, William. It is your heart and soul."

"No. You have my heart and soul, Mary-Kate," he says firmly. "I don't care where I am as long as I'm with you."

"I can't take you away from London. I won't do that," I tell him firmly. "But I *will* move there to be with you."

"Mary-Kate, you don't know what it will be like. The things you'll miss. Your family is here. You've only known Milwaukee and Chicago."

I put my fingertips over his full lips to stop him from speaking. "I want to make my life in England. *With you.* The man I love. I can write from anywhere, William. And for me, home is back in Mayfair with you."

He glances away for a moment and swallows. His eyes fill with unshed tears. "I love you."

"I love you more," I say, a smile breaking through.

William smiles, too. "Claire says we need to learn how to fight like normal people."

I let out a loud laugh. "She's right. But I need to let you be quiet and speak when you are ready," I say, toying with a button on his white dress shirt.

"And I need to let you blow up and storm off," William says, sliding his arms around my waist. "I can do that now that you've promised to always come home to me."

"I promise with all my heart. I will always come home to you, William. *Always.*"

We kiss again, and I have never felt such joy and completeness in my heart as I do right now.

William breaks the kiss and then draws a breath of air. "I have a confession," he says, stroking my face. "I was planning to come back to you before I read your blog. I couldn't handle being apart from you for twenty-four hours, let alone a lifetime."

I graze my fingertips across his glorious cheekbones. "Is that why you got drunk at Rupert and Claire's house?" I ask, arching an eyebrow at him.

"Oh hell," William says, laughing. "I got *pissed*. I ended up sleeping on their living room sofa."

"Claire wouldn't tell me what you said."

"Well, from what I remember, she said I was an idiot to have let you go," William admits. "And I told her I couldn't live without you, and she agreed. So I'd have to say she was right. Rupert married himself a wise woman."

"Indeed, he did," I say, thinking of how much Claire had been my only hope this week.

William clears his throat. "Your blog," he says quietly, "was the most beautiful thing I have ever read. I don't know if I am worthy of those words."

"You, my love, are worthy of every single one," I reply, getting choked up. "I only wish you didn't have to read them first. I wish I could have told you in person."

"That doesn't matter," William says. "What matters is that you mean them."

"I do," I say strongly. "I love you."

"And I you. I had never wanted anyone until the day I met you, flailing about and stuck in that binder machine. That day, I met my destiny," William says, smiling at me.

"William, why didn't you think I was a crazy woman? I was cursing and babbling about *Full House.* I sounded like a lunatic."

"No," he replies, rubbing his hands down my back, "You were real. You were passionate and intriguing and the one person who treated me like a normal man. And, by God, you were gorgeous. You know, I was not even going to enter that workroom until I saw your red hair. I was drawn to you, my darling. And I'm so grateful that you were ensnared in that binder machine so I could come rescue you."

We both laugh. Then William clears his throat. "But even if there was not a binder machine incident, we would have met another way. I am certain of that fact, Mary-Kate. We are meant to be together."

He removes his hands from me and draws another deep breath. "You are my world, Mary-Kate. You are my life. And I cannot ask you for another thing until I ask you this."

William reaches into his jacket pocket. He brings out a velvet box in his hand, and he is getting down on one knee in front of me.

Oh my God. Oh my God. I begin to shake. Violently.

"Mary-Kate Grant, I love you. I cannot live without you. I flew to Milwaukee yesterday and talked to your father. And he gave me his blessing to ask you this."

William pauses and shows me a huge—and I mean huge—Asscher-cut diamond ring, with smaller diamonds on each side, set in a pave diamond and platinum band.

"Will you marry me? Will you be my wife, Mary-Kate Grant?"

I'm so stunned, I can't speak. William asked me to *marry* him. I begin to cry. I'm so shocked, "yes" will not get past the lump in my throat.

William waits for a moment. Then I see an anxious look in his beautiful blue eyes. "If ... if it is too soon, I understand."

"No!" I croak.

The color drains from his face. "No?"

"No, I mean, no, it is not too soon!" I finally find my voice. "I mean, yes! Yes, yes, yes, William Cumberland. I will marry you! A thousand times yes!"

And then I am so excited that I bend down to hug him, but I trip, and we both go sprawling across the sidewalk, my ring box flying into the grass.

"Oh my God, my ring!" I cry, crawling on my hands and knees into the grass.

William roars with laughter. "I know you. It is fully insured."

"William Cumberland, that is so *not* funny!"

He gets up. He calmly strolls past me and picks up the box. He then plops down onto the grass next to me, takes out the ring, and holds it in his hand.

"Let's try this again," William says, his eyes shining in delight. "Mary-Kate Grant, will you please marry me?"

"Yes," I say, smiling as I hold out my hand. "I will."

He slides the gorgeous ring onto my finger. Then we kiss in the grass in front of my apartment building in Lincoln Park.

William runs his hands through my hair, caressing it, and kissing me slowly and sweetly.

"I'm so happy," I whisper against his lips.

"Me, too," he whispers back before resuming the kiss.

I break the kiss and cup his face in my hands. Then I raise my hand to study my amazing ring—my gorgeous, huge, stunning, vintage-inspired ring. My God, it is a huge rock. I wonder—

"You want to know how many carats, don't you?" William asks, grinning at me wickedly.

I blush furiously. "Yes," I admit.

"Six. I stopped in New York first to get it," he says, leaning back on his palms in the grass. "Why do you think it took me so long to get here? I had to go to Kwiat to buy—"

"You ... you flew to *New York* for my ring?"

"They have exquisite rings," William says. "I wanted something absolutely fitting for the woman who is going to be my wife."

My eyes fill with tears again. "I love you."

He smiles. "I love you. So I was in New York getting the ring, then I flew to Milwaukee to talk to your father ... That is why I had Claire keep talking to you. I didn't want to see or text you until I was ready to propose."

I stare at my ring and then at him and think about how much thought William put into what he was going to do tonight. Not only to make things right between us, but to make me his wife. He went the traditional route, even flying to Milwaukee to get my father's permission to ask for my hand.

To make me his wife.

"I'm going to be your *wife*!" I cry excitedly, the full force of it hitting me. "I am going to be the mother of your children!"

William's entire face lights up. "Just promise me you won't crash the pushchair when you are taking them around, all right?"

"William, it is called a *stroller,* and of course I won't," I declare. Then I laugh. "Rather, I will *try* my best not to."

We both laugh.

"So when are we getting married?" William asks.

I think about that for a moment. "Well, can't upstage Michelle," I say slowly. "A year from now? June?"

"Yes," he says. "Where?"

"Mayfair, of course," I reply. "That is where we are going to build our life."

William cocks an eyebrow. "We could marry at St. George's

in Hanover Square. Is the Church of England all right with you?"

I touch his face. "You know I am all right with it."

He sits up and brings my hand to his lips, kissing it. "Reception at Claridge's?"

I feel giddy at the thought. I'm getting married in England. In a historic English Church. With a reception at one of the poshest hotels in the city.

"Yes. Absolutely yes."

"Now, children. How about five?" William asks.

I furrow my brow. "Two. I only want two."

"Bossy American," he declares, laughing.

"Two," I repeat firmly, grinning at him.

"Three."

I laugh loudly. "You are a badass negotiator, William Cumberland. Okay, I will agree to three."

"Speaking of children," he says slowly, a wicked gleam entering his eyes, "we have a whole year to practice for them."

I smile. "So do you think it is most appropriate that we go home and get started on our homework?"

William laughs, that deep-down-from-his-soul laugh that made my breath catch the first time I heard it, as it does right now.

He stands up and extends his hand to me. I take it, and he pulls me up and into his arms. "Yes, I find that most appropriate. Let's get your things and go home."

I wrap my hand around William's and walk with him up the steps to my apartment.

I never knew there could be joy like this. Love like this. I am going to have a husband who completes me, brings out the best in me, inspires me, and makes me the happiest woman on earth.

The candle we lit is burning bright and will do so for the rest of our lives.

I glance at his profile, that of my beautiful English man, and sigh happily.

Perfect Connectivity indeed.

Epilogue

I pick up my tasting spoon and test the tikka masala sauce. *Perfect.* I put the spoon into my sink and gaze out the window. It is a cloudy and cold October day, and this curry will be perfect for dinner tonight—warm and spicy and comforting.

I go to my iPad and adjust my notes on the recipe. I have finally perfected my own version of tikka masala, and for sure I want it to go into the cookbook.

Cookbook. That is just crazy, but I'm in the process of writing my first book. A publisher offered me a deal to write a cookbook with recipes and stories based off my blog, *The Bossy American—Life Across the Pond with my Dashing British Husband.*

I look up from my iPad to the digital picture frame we have on the kitchen counter and watch for a moment as the memories of our life flip by. I can't help but smile at each of them, hardly believing how my life has turned out.

I see the picture of us at our wedding reception at Claridge's. I'm wearing a form-fitting Vera Wang gown and a diamond-studded hairband that he gave me on our wedding

286

day. He looks as gorgeous as ever in his Burberry tux, and the background around us is so beautiful—all white flowers, linens, soft candlelight. But the smile on his face—the genuine, bright, "I am so in love" smile—is what still melts my heart, even though it has been six years since that day.

I see our honeymoon in The Seychelles, where William rented a private villa for us to retreat in luxury and complete privacy. Then photos of this beautiful Victorian home we bought in London. It dates back to 1851 and is four floors, made of Portland stone and brick, and has a spectacular private garden. We both knew when we walked in the front door that this home was it. This was the home we wanted to spend our lives in.

After all the pictures of our home, photos of William with our black labs, Charlotte and Churchill, when they were puppies pop up, then pictures of us skiing in Aspen, pictures of us at company functions, then—

Splat!

I look up from the picture show to the highchair, where Gemma has thrown her bowl of Cheerios upside down on her tray.

"Is Mommy not paying attention to you?" I ask, walking over to her and taking the tray off.

"Mm, mm, mm," Gemma babbles, giving me a big two-toothed smile.

I smile back at my beautiful little girl and pick her up. I kiss her chubby cheek and inhale her wonderful baby scent. She is all of eight months old, with brown eyes and curly red hair. I put her on my hip and go back to my pot, stirring it once again.

I hear the back door open. Charlotte and Churchill are barking, and I hear their paws on the hardwood floor, racing toward the kitchen.

"Mummy! We're home!" a tiny voice yells out.

"In the kitchen, Valentine," I call back.

I wait for a few minutes, and I can hear William talking about taking off their boots and coats. I watch as four-year-old Valentine comes into the kitchen, with her twin, Phillip, right behind her. Valentine was named after the holiday of our first date in Chicago, and Phillip is William's middle name.

Sometimes, I look at them and still can't believe it.

We had *twins*.

And, somehow, they managed to survive—*and thrive*—in spite of me and William being first-time, shell-shocked parents who didn't have a clue as to what to do with one baby, let alone two.

"Mummy, I'm hungry," Phillip says, climbing up onto his chair at the table.

"I want milk, Mummy," Valentine says, going to her chair.

"Is that how we ask Mummy for something, Valentine?" William asks, bringing up the rear.

I smile at him. He always takes the twins for a walk when the weather is decent, and that is their daddy time. "Is that curry I smell, darling?" he asks.

"I thought it would be most appropriate on a chilly day." I smile to myself, thinking of how we have kept that phrase our entire relationship.

William pauses by Valentine's chair. The resemblance between him and the twins is stunning. The three of them all have dark brown, wavy hair and light blue eyes. Gemma is the image of me, of course, and nobody was more thrilled than William when her hair started growing in red.

"Valentine," he says, "I believe we say 'please' when we

want something."

"Please, Daddy," she calls out cheerfully.

"Thank you," William says, opening a cabinet and getting two cartoon character plastic cups.

I sigh happily as I watch him. We don't have a full-time housekeeper or nanny. We have a housekeeper come a couple of times a week, and I have a sitter part-time so I can work on the book, but we decided we would do this on our own.

And we have.

William delegates at work more than ever, but if he does work at night, he makes sure not to schedule anything the next night. Travel is limited to not more than a few days away from home at a time if at all possible. I gave up my job at Beautiful Homes Network after the twins arrived and switched to freelancing, so I was still writing, but on a manageable scale with two babies in the house.

William pours two cups and hands one to Valentine and one to Phillip. Then he walks over to me as Gemma is about to pull my hairband out of my hair.

"No, Gemma, only Daddy is allowed to take out Mummy's hairbands," he says cheerfully, taking her from me and giving her a big kiss.

I laugh, and William kisses my cheek. "You smell good," he whispers sexily in my ear. "Have plans later this evening?"

"Hmmm... Well, I *might* be available after seven o'clock," I suggest, knowing that is when all the children are tucked into bed.

"Might?" William asks, his beautiful blue eyes shining at me.

"Well, I do need to review some recipes for the book."

"Very important," he agrees.

"However," I continue, grabbing a tasting spoon and giving William a sample, "I think I could have a glass of wine with you and keep the manuscript for tomorrow when the sitter gets here."

"Just wine?" he teases, cocking an eyebrow. He samples the curry and nods. "This sauce is perfect."

"Thank you," I say, taking his spoon and putting it into the sink. I turn and flash him a grin. "Wine and other things are on the agenda, my love."

"Mummy!" Phillip shouts. "I'm hungry!"

"Just like his mum. Bossy," William teases.

I teasingly mouth "shut up" to him and turn to Phillip. "I have some rice and chicken cooking for you, sweetheart. In the meantime, you can have some yummy veggies and dip while you wait."

I go to the fridge and get out the tray I have already made with cut up veggies and dip for the twins to eat. I put it down on the table and am greeted with "Thank you, Mummy." I can't help but notice that despite our summers in Chicago, these children are one hundred percent British, just like their father.

I turn around and see William gazing at me with nothing but love in his light blue eyes.

"You are such a good mum," he says softly.

I reach over and brush my hand against his face, my fingertips grazing his gorgeous cheekbone. "And you are a good daddy."

"I love you," he says.

I sweep an errant curl off his forehead. "I love you more."

William presses his forehead against mine. "How did I get so lucky?"

I laugh as my lips brush briefly against his. "Well, you

bought a TV network in America, and ended up with a wife in the process."

"Best purchase I ever made," William declares. Gemma squeals loudly, and we both laugh.

"See? Gemma is going to be our businesswoman," he says, grinning. "She knows when Daddy makes a brilliant deal."

I laugh and go back to the stove. William carries Gemma over to the table and sits down with her in his lap, sharing the veggies with Valentine and Phillip.

This is what I live for, I think, looking at the table. Moments like this with my children and the man who makes me the happiest woman on earth. We have a beautiful life here in London, one I never could have anticipated. I never would have dreamed as a student at Northwestern that I would be a writer. That I would be living in London. That I would have twins and then another child and be completely fulfilled as a blogger, author, wife, and mother.

And be married to William. Not William Cumberland, the badass mogul billionaire, but *William*, who still brings me coffee in the mornings, edits my writing, and tells me he loves me more times a day than I can count.

The Bossy American, I think happily, *is one very lucky lady.*

Thanks to a little thing called Connectivity.

Bonus Chapter

I gaze out of the window from my home office in London on this blustery spring day. The budding green leaves and flowers are swaying in the wind, and dark clouds are rolling in. Another rainstorm is coming our way soon.

"MK, here are the finalist files you requested," Jon says, walking into my office. "I put them in order of your interviews tomorrow."

I take the files from Jon, my part-time assistant, who helps keep me organized with my blog, cookbook project, and website.

"Thank you," I say. "Any ones that leap out at you?"

Jon blinks. I hold my gaze steady on his. Jon has no idea how bright and capable he is, and I use moments like this to not only push him out of his comfort zone, but to build his confidence, too.

"Well, MK, you are the one who will be working with this intern; you know what is best," Jon says, shrugging his slight shoulders.

"I believe I'm asking you for your opinion," I say, lifting an eyebrow at him.

Jon fiddles with his wedding ring, which is what he does when I push him for his opinion.

"Jon?" I say again. "Have a seat. I want your thoughts."

He sits down across from me. "Well, they all have their merits," he says neutrally.

"But if you had to pick one based on their resume and setting up their travel, who has the lead?" I ask, flipping open a folder.

"Gracie from Leeds? Thomas from Nottingham? Or Lauren from Raleigh, North Carolina?"

"Lauren."

Ah-ha! Jon does have an opinion. I close the folder and clasp my hands over it, leaning slightly forward. "Give me your thoughts on Lauren."

"She had so much excitement and energy about the interview," Jon says. "And she sent me a thank you note for arranging her travel as soon as she received the details."

My ears perk up. "A personal thank you note?"

Jon nods. "Yes, and that's exactly what it was. A note to me, thanking me for arranging her travel and being so helpful. I've never received one of those before."

I open the file and flick to her resume. Then I pick up a silver pen and scribble a note across the top saying "polite—thank you note" across the top.

"What else, Jon? What stood out on her resume to you?" I continue.

Jon flushes. "MK, you know what is on her resume; that is why you selected her."

"But you know what is on her resume, too," I push. "And I'm asking for your thoughts."

"She has a master's degree from the University of North Carolina," Jon repeats. "All of her activities are business-related. Lauren seems very serious and career-driven. Maybe a smidge too much so, but I can't fault her for that."

"Sounds like another American I know," a deep baritone voice says.

I glance up and see William leaning against the doorframe. He's working from home today in his office, and whenever he does that, he will often pop in to see what I'm up to or to consult with me on something he's working on.

And despite the fact that it's been many years together and three children later, my heart still flutters when he unexpectedly shows up in my doorway.

Jon turns around and smiles at William. "Lauren sounds a lot like MK."

William crosses his arms and grins at me. "I don't know if we're ready for two Bossy Americans around here."

Jon stifles a laugh. William's eyes shine brightly at me. And I pretend to be annoyed.

"I think Lauren is now in the lead for that point alone," I declare. I shift my attention back to Jon for a moment. "Thank you, Jon. I appreciate you sharing your opinion with me."

He rises and leaves. William waits for him to pass and shuts the door behind him, so we have privacy.

He moves in toward my desk and sits on the corner of it. "May I see that resume, Ms. Cumberland?"

I laugh and hand it to him. William's laser-like eyes move over it, and then a slow smile spreads across his handsome face. "Hell, she does sound like you. All school. All career-driven."

"I know, she appeals to me on paper immediately because I can see myself," I admit. "Of course, I'll interview each of them and make the determination afterward, because I have to make the right choice for a year-long internship."

William nods and sets the resume back on my desk. "How is the cookbook proposal coming along?"

I feel my face flush with excitement. My first cookbook did very well, and the publisher has asked for a second book.

"I'm working on that now," I say eagerly. "Family Meals with the Bossy American. With recipes that are kid-friendly. And under thirty minutes."

"Brilliant," William says, gazing at me. "So once that is signed, do we go into family test mode again?"

My heart flutters from the look of pride and love in his blue eyes. I smile.

"Yes, you'll be subjected to all my creative whims in the kitchen," I say.

"Any other whims you care to subject me to?" he says suggestively.

I laugh. "Don't you have a takeover to manage?"

"Funny how you say Lauren reminds you of yourself," William says, rubbing his jawline with his hand. "I'm very close to closing the deal for the messaging app owned by Oliver Pratt, and he reminds me a bit of me years ago."

I furrow my brow. "What? *How?* He's off running around with princesses and models; that is so not William Cumberlandish."

"Not that part," William says, giving me a side-eye. "But he's young. Super smart. Easily bored. He has an appetite for more, but he hasn't sorted out his personal life yet. Now that should sound William Cumberlandish, as you say."

"Is that why the takeover includes giving him a spot at Connectivity to continue oversight of the messaging app?" I ask.

"Well, partially, but also because I'm intrigued by his brain. I could use him."

I laugh. "That's so you. Well-played, my love."

William smiles the second he hears my nickname for him. He reaches across the desk and picks up my hand, running his fingertips over the top.

"You never answered me," he says, his voice low and seductive, "about me catering to any whims you might have at the moment."

My breath catches in my throat. "Do you care to take me on this desk?"

His eyes instantly flicker. "My desk is bigger. And I *would* care to take you on it."

Hello, sexy times!

"So shall I meet you in your office in five?" I ask, my pulse leaping.

"Yes," he says briskly, standing right up. "Five. Not a second longer."

I smile at him. "I will be very punctual, Mr. Cumberland."

William walks over to the door but pauses and turns back to me. "Don't keep me waiting, Ms. Cumberland. I get impatient when I have to wait for something I want."

I laugh. He smiles.

Then his expression goes soft.

"One more thing," he says.

"Yes?"

"I love you, darling."

Then he opens the door and walks out.

I sigh blissfully. I love that man.

Then Lauren's resume catches my eye again. I pick it up, seeing so much of myself in her. *I wonder if she is like me,* I muse. *If maybe she needs a new career opportunity to shake up her life, like working for William did mine.*

I have a feeling about this Lauren Charleston from Raleigh. That she will not only be a good person to help me as my brand grows but perhaps someone who could blossom with time here, in London.

I rise from my desk and put the resume down. Time for a very important appointment down the hall. One with the man

I love and one very intriguing promise involving his desk.

I smile happily. I truly hope Lauren finds a life outside of her career, as I have. If she is a good fit for me, perhaps she will find it here. And I don't know what her personal situation is, but if she wasn't attached to anyone, wouldn't it be something if she found love, too?

Okay, I know I'm getting way ahead of myself. I have no idea who Lauren is or what she wants in life, but what can I say? Falling in love with William has turned me into a romantic. And who knows? Maybe a second Connectivity love story might happen after all.

Connectivity 2.0, the second book in the British Isles Billion-aires Series, can be ordered here. To keep up with release information, please join Kate, Skates and Coffee Cakes, the Aven Ellis Reader Group; sign up for my newsletter, or follow me on BookBub.

About the Author

Aven began her publishing career in 2013 with her debut release, *Connectivity.* Her books are designed to make readers laugh out loud and fall in love. Happily-ever-after endings and good-boy heroes are guaranteed.

Aven lives in the Dallas area with her family. She is a huge fan of the Dallas Stars, Dallas Mavericks, and Texas Rangers. Aven loves shopping and fashion and can spend hours playing with fragrances in any department store. She can be found chatting it up on social media, eating M&Ms, and crushing on the latest outfit the Duchess of Cambridge is wearing in her free time.

You can connect with me on:

- http://avenellis.com
- https://twitter.com/AvenEllis
- https://www.facebook.com/groups/avenellisreadergroup
- https://www.instagram.com/avenellis

Subscribe to my newsletter:

✉ http://avenellis.com/newsletter

Also by Aven Ellis

If you enjoyed this book, you might also enjoy these other romantic comedies...

Connectivity (British Isles Billionaires #1).
A Royal Shade of Blue (Modern Royals #1)
The Princess Pose (Modern Royals #2)
Royal Icing (Modern Royals #3).
Squeeze Play (Washington DC Soaring Eagles #1)
Swing and a Miss (Washington DC Soaring Eagles #2).
A Complete Game (Washington DC Soaring Eagles #3)
Hold the Lift (Rinkside in the Rockies Novella)
Sugar and Ice (Rinkside in the Rockies #1)
Reality Blurred (Rinkside in the Rockies #2)
Outscored (Rinkside in the Rockies #3)
Home Ice (Dallas Demons #1)
The Definition of Icing (Dallas Demons #2)
Breakout (Dallas Demons #3)
On Thin Ice (Dallas Demons #4)
Playing Defense (Dallas Demons #5)
The Aubrey Rules (Chicago on Ice #1)
Trivial Pursuits (Chicago on Ice #2)
Save the Date (Chicago on Ice #3)
The Bottom Line (Chicago on Ice #4)

Printed in Great Britain
by Amazon